# DEMONS
# & RABBITS

# DEMONS
# & RABBITS

by:
**KO**

Artist:
**Avery Liell-Kok**

**author**HOUSE®

*AuthorHouse™*
*1663 Liberty Drive*
*Bloomington, IN 47403*
*www.authorhouse.com*
*Phone: 833-262-8899*

*Published by AuthorHouse 02/10/2023*

*ISBN: 978-1-4772-5750-0 (sc)*
*ISBN: 978-1-4772-5751-7 (e)*

*Library of Congress Control Number: 2012914243*

*Print information available on the last page.*

I dedicate this book to all the dear friends I've lost in life.

KO Thanks the following people:

First and foremost, I'd like to thank Lynn
Klapperich my AODA counselor.
At the darkest moments in my life, she
was the light leading me back.
She literally saved my life more than once.

My friend Phil Krause
Without Phil this book would not be possible
Phil helped edit my very rough draft.

Most of all I thank my wife, Michele.
She is my guardian angel, my strength, my reason for living.
I can never thank her enough for believing
in me when no one else did.

# CONTENTS

**Part 1: Lost Innocence**

**Part 2: The Birth of Pain**

## Part 3: Embrace Death

# INTRODUCTION

## SCRAPS OF MADNESS

Throughout my life I have found myself compelled to write things down. I am not really sure why I felt compelled to write. I never looked at the torn-out pages after I'd scribbled out my cryptic nonsense upon them. When a page had fulfilled its purpose, I threw it in a box with all the other forgotten pages. Then I buried that box beneath my other junk in the darkest corner of my closet. Looking back I realized I only felt driven or obsessed to scratch my thoughts out on paper when I needed a release from the all too true reality I suffered in. The paper was like a prison for the words and thoughts I could not escape from. I believed I could trap all of the thought's I didn't want to believe were my own in the twisted pages. Once I had them imprisoned, I hoped I could erase them from my mind with years of mundane routine.

The mundane routine created years of dust but it could never erase my dark past. Many times I wanted to burn the box and destroy the pages, but I was afraid of the ghosts trapped inside. More than twenty years would pass before I had enough courage to reopen the box. I was going through my life's possessions in an effort to try to get rid of the anchors of my past hoping it might help me find some peace in my life. Most of the things I owned really meant nothing. They were all just things any ordinary person might own. I found myself wondering time after time why do I own this or why did I keep that? I no longer felt the emotional connection to these items that I must have felt at the time I had decided to entomb them in my shrine of junk. I was about to give up any hope that I had kept anything that had any real significance in my life when I pulled the box from the dark corner. It was filled with the pages and scraps of paper that I had written my little bits of madness on; hundreds of little prisons holding my darkest thoughts.

At first, I could not decide what to do with these scraps of madness. Very few of them were complete and most were far from coherent. Many of the scraps of paper were unreadable by a sane person. On some pages the words curled and swirled into scribbles while on other pages the words merged into alien mathematical formulas. On others there were things written on top of layer after layer of words until nothing was decipherable and only small glimpses of pure paper trying to escape from the cracks in between were left. The saddest pages were the ones with the words written in lead so long ago that they had smudged and smeared and could no longer shed any light into a young mind once polluted with drugs and delusional waking dreams.

I started by sorting the pages into piles. I organized them by the length of what was translatable (if you can call it that). The scraps formed into pieces of an old forgotten puzzle. As I scrutinized the scraps it was difficult for me to strangle any sense from the rotten paper. But later while struggling to sleep the pieces of blurred memories I had once lived, began to creep into the shadows and ancient whispers spoke to me in the dark.

I abandoned any hope of sleep, compelled to find the meaning in the mess of scrap paper. I pulled random pieces from the pile and as I read them, I began to seriously wonder if all the scraps were just insane ramblings of a mentally ill person or perhaps journals of a drug induced hallucination. In a sleep deprived coma I studied the mysterious scraps until I found myself looking deep into a pool of obscurity with nothing profound beneath the surface.

Even though most of the pages read like juvenile poems, they were far from the normal teenage angst. I spent the precious early years of my life homeless on the streets, addicted to crystal-meth. Dreams of death often haunted my daily life. All the scraps reflected the depression, social decay, and the grim reality of life that went with those things, but none of the poems contained the answers I was looking for.

I was ready to give up hope and burn the lot when I came across a suicide note written in my own blood. I confess that for years I was a "cutter" and still bear the scars down both arms. The need to cut myself was at one time stronger than the need to write, at times my words and my blood cried out to be released together. I just wanted to bleed out all the guilt and bad memories of my first love, tormenting me inside! At least that was how I felt when I carved the word "insignificant" in my arm with a piece of broken mirror. A mirror once black and whole showed the face I tried so desperately to forget in the shattered pieces.

The blood from the paper splashed against my wall of denial and Anamorphosis of my story began to emerge. Anamorphosis is a process where the artist strings an image out over a long distance so when you look at it from up close or directly you only perceive nonsense, but if you look at just the right angle with the correct perspective the image becomes clear.

I quickly realized I was the only person who knew the right perspective to decipher my scraps of madness. As the image of my story once again became clear in my mind, I knew why I saved these scraps of madness; so the person I once was wouldn't be forgotten. If a rational person read these pages they would only see the monstrous nonsense that the wrong perspective provided. I needed to correct the viewpoint, not for you the reader, but for myself. The story that the pieces of my insanity held needed to be released, not buried.

In my effort to release the murdered souls of my friends from the pages I found myself a prisoner in the pages. The only way for me to escape my hell was to relive and complete my story. It's not that I don't remember the dark, chaotic times of my life. For good reason I had just chosen not to. I thought I'd killed and buried all my demons. But once I read the forgotten words, I completed an incantation of sorts. My Demons were awake and risings once more. All the ghosts I thought I could just forget were dragging me back to the grave! A shallow grave lost in the corner of my mind begged to be found and the haunted memories buried there would wait no longer for me to free them. When I opened the forgotten box I became trapped within it with only a collection of encrypted messages from the past to guide me back out.

This wasn't the first time I found myself lost deep in a hole. Most people lost in the dark ask themselves the same thing; how did I get here? Where did my life go wrong? Well years ago, I awoke from a drug addicted nightmare. To find myself locked in a cold dark cell awaiting trial for the horrific murders of my friends. Accept I did not wonder how I got there. I knew how I became another victim of the street. I knew how I got addicted to crystal meth. I knew how I became a zombie junkie. I knew why my first love died in my arms. I knew why my friends where dead.

My little paper prisons held all these truths along with a map to the drug money I stole and buried. The cryptic message once incoherent was now revealed to me. To share the scraps of madness would be a waste of time but the memories they evoked told not only my story, how I had reassembled my shattered psyche, escaped from the asylum and traveled across the country to confront my demons in a last ditch effort to save my soul. But more importantly the untold stories of my friends that died far too young could now be told. I have added actual "scraps of madness" only where I thought they might add some relevance. I certainly never meant for my life to go into a downward spiral, but it did, and it all began with the simple desire to be loved.

This is my story . . . .

# CHAPTER 1

## My story

My earliest memory as a child is when as a baby my father couldn't stand the sound of my crying and decided to place me in the refrigerator. Somehow I still remember that cold dark lonely place. Many times, later in life I would flashback to this place and the feeling of life leaving my body. I was trapped alone in the dark, fighting with death in a last minute futile attempt to live. Panic quickly changed to exhaustion and desperation. I was trying desperately to let go and welcome the soothing darkness when I was released and allowed to breathe again. I had fought with and surrendered to the empty void, but death would not take me either way. That unwanted eerie feeling followed me throughout my life.

My second earliest memory is when I was still very young. An incident when the babysitter neglected to keep an eye on me. Perhaps in an effort to taunt death, I decided to stick a bobby pin into the outlet. I'm told it threw me across the room. It's very likely I was momentarily dead while the current raced through me. I only remember a very brief encounter of being somewhere else and a strong metallic smell and matching taste in my mouth.

My parents divorced when I was very young. My mom was left with no choice but to move from Colorado back home to Wisconsin. I still remember the long car ride. I remembered seeing the mountains that I had always known disappear into the horizon. It was like watching stone giants die and fade back into the earth, trading magic for fact, and all that remained of the horizon was an endless flat line.

We arrived in Wisconsin in the middle of winter. It was cold and bitter for so many reasons. We moved in with my grandmother in her exceedingly small home. Eventually we moved into our own home. Our new home was much larger than my grandmother's house, but the size only seemed to emulate its emptiness. Beside the house itself we owned little. My ordinary cardboard life droned on for years. I was raised a Lutheran and went to church every Sunday. I also attended confirmation classes on Wednesdays and was eventually confirmed in the eyes of God.

The following scrap is the earliest and most legible page I found in the box. It was neatly typed on faded white paper.

## WHAT IT MEANS TO ME TO BE A CHRISTIAN
### (MY CONFIRMATION CLASS ESSAY)

*As a Christian I can use what I learn in worship and confirmation to make a difference in my life. As a Christian, my failures don't stop God's promise. As a Christian, Jesus gives me a straight path to god even though my life is twisted. God helps me as a Christian to get outside of myself so I can get in touch with myself. As a Christian, I will always belong to god and he will never abandon me. As a Christian, I can share every problem with God and*

2

*he will listen, He will help me when I need help. My faith in God is the greatest source of strength I have in times of trouble or sadness. I'm not worthy to receive the gift of god; the day will never come when I'm pure enough to earn the right to receive the lord's gifts. He gives me these gifts freely, not because I have earned them but because Jesus died to give us this gift of forgiveness.*

It goes on for two more pages; it's more of a copy and paste project than a strong belief in Christianity. As I look back at it now the god I believed in when I wrote this did not live up to the expectations I was taught to have faith in.

My mother worked very hard as a physical therapist for the public school system. She treated severely handicapped children most of whom had already been given a death sentence at birth. My mother took the burden of watching them die as her personal crucifix and more often than not brought a day's work home with her. She never really had a lot of time to be involved with my life except for the times she brought me along with her to the clients' homes. I understood why she'd bring me along to befriend the dying. Some of these kids were bed-ridden for life. They rarely left their homes and never had a chance to have a friend. I didn't mind, I was, after all, raised a true Christian with good-hearted values, but at the same time it was a lot to deal with at a very young age. These kids weren't like my classmates, none of my classmate had ever met any kids like this and if they knew I did they would ridicule me, I knew this and yet I never felt ashamed or weird in any way. I learned from my mother to accept all people. The only thing I regretted about the friends I made was that I had to watch them disintegrate and die.

I remember this time in life well because it affected decisions I would make later in my life. It was very hard if not impossible to compete for attention against sick dying children. In time it turned my compassion into envy and then envy into hate. I no longer wanted to join my mother on her visits and I had decided it was better to be left alone than compete for the attention I felt I'd never get. Please do not confuse this sentiment for blame. I do not blame my mother for the bad choices I made. I chose on my own to go down the wrong path time and time again. Those were my choices, good or bad I take full responsibility for them all.

Time passed by as the cold winter nights grew longer; and like the shrinking day I too deteriorated further into the darkness. My life was very empty, just waiting for anything to pacify the growing hunger in me. I was never concerned about fitting in or being popular. I was the quiet kid no one ever seemed to notice. I liked it that way. They say still waters run deep but in my case that was not true. The end of my day of school held an almost empty room and that emptiness grew inside of me and somehow at the same time I grew into it.

It is hard to describe the black void and its allure, but all the same I felt it and knew it well. I only had a few books, a handful of small toys, and an old black and white TV that received only one or two channels clearly. It wasn't like today with the almost inescapable attack of media on our senses every second of the day. It was very easy to sink into the great nothing. I was just floating in a void waiting to grasp onto that one thing that would pull me out.

Where I lived the kids cruised up and down the main street in their cars. So I decided to hang out on Main Street in the hope someone would pick me up. Looking back I see now how stupid and naïve I was to think that would happen. People didn't just stop and say "Hey you're in my art class jump in." And you were driven away to adventure. But all the same that was what I believed happened so I decided to find a spot where people would see me and I would just sit there waiting until something happened.

There was an abandoned bank on the corner where Main Street went over a bridge. It seemed like a good spot to hang out. There were stop lights at the intersection so I figured people would notice me, and the front entrance provided a little shelter from the god-awful elements of Wisconsin. I had chosen my location to sit. Now all I had to do was be patient. So, I sat, and I waited for something, anything, to happen. All I wanted was someone to stop and talk to me, but no one ever did. I sat there every day for months. I sat there in the rain, in the snow; I even sat there when the freezing wind chills were so cold, I thought I would die. No matter how bad it was I would just tell myself tomorrow will be the day I have been waiting for, the day someone notices me. Sadly, that day never came. Looking back now, I feel stupid for wasting my youth sitting there every day for four to six hours watching people go by. No one cared and no one ever stopped. The loneliness broke my heart on a daily basis.

Despite my loneliness, winter got the best of me and finally won. It was just too cold to sit on my corner any longer. The wind chill in Wisconsin can get into the negative 30's, sometimes worse. I abandon my corner but still had to walk to and from school. It was on one of those long cold walks home I made a friend of sorts.

The route I took to school crossed a river and in the winter time you could save a lot of time walking through the cold by cutting across the frozen river. The downfall of crossing the frozen river was that a moving body of water is never safe even if its' frozen over. I was crossing way too close to the bridge and where the river bottlenecked under the bridge the ice was very thin. I found out the hard way when it cracked and broke beneath me.

I instantaneously plunged into the icy depths. The icy water consumed me without mercy. I gasped out in terror releasing my last breath of precious oxygen. I felt my feet hit bottom and with all my might, pushed back up to emerge from the water. It happened so very fast and when the cold water saturated me it made everything hyper real. Though it seems strange it was in a way the first buzz I ever had. When I came back out of the water and inhaled I felt so alive, my eyes were wide and every muscle in my body had a sudden surge of warmth. In that moment of hyper-awareness the dismal grey sky turned a vibrant blue and I could hear the rivers song of death as it pulled at me trying to force me along its path. I was scrambling to escape the rivers grasp when a Hmong kid named Mola came to my rescue. We had never met before but he only lived a few blocks from me and we had walked the same way home a hundred times. On this day he was walking just behind me when he saw me fall through the ice and now reached out to help pull me from the river. As we walked towards home the "buzz" I felt right after falling through the ice quickly subsided. Like many drugs the initial high was followed by a crash. I was beyond frozen by the time we got to my house. I was more than grateful for Molas help so I invited him in. There was never anybody home this time of day so I felt a I little hurt when Mola declined my invitation and went on his way.

Once inside my home I was relieved Mola didn't come in. I was so cold that I broke down in tears when I couldn't get my shoes off. The laces were frozen solid. I had to chip away at the chunks of ice with a knife to release my feet. My pants were also frozen stiff and I couldn't get the zipper to move. It was a real challenge just to remove my suit of ice. This was the third time in my life that I felt

I had crossed over into the land of the dead and back again. The pain I felt as my hands and feet thawed felt like rigor mortis setting in. For a long time after that day freezing to death was my greatest nightmare.

I didn't forget Mola or what he had done and after that day we slowly became friends. After hanging out a few times at my house, I went to his home. I thought I had it bad but when I enter Molas' house I realized others had it worse. I didn't have much but it was still way more than Mola had and he had 7 brothers and sisters to share it with. Combine the fact that they weren't much on housekeeping and the strange foreign smells from the things they cooked gave the whole house a filthy vibe.

The empty walls I called home became suffocating so I wandered the streets with my new friend Mola just to try and get enough air to breathe. The more I hung around with Mola, the more other kids I met: Sam an older black kid, the only black person in our school, Freddie a Hispanic kid, and Kurt who was just a poor white kid. They were a fine collection of the town's misfit kids. They were all basically outcasts like me but I still never felt "at home" with them.

I didn't quite fit in with them because they were more mature than me. Some in age and others in the way they acted. They smoked cigarettes and drank alcohol (which I had never done.) Most times the booze was stolen from Sam's parents. Sam was adopted by a well off older white couple who, lucky or unlucky for us, had a full bar in their basement. Cigarettes were easy to buy back then and only cost about 75 cents.

The first time the boys convinced me to drink with them it was the dead of winter. It was so cold we huddled under the railway overpass, which actually made a pretty good shelter. It had enough room to make a small fire. The fire wasn't big enough to keep us warm but did provide the illusion of heat. We drank large gulps from a bottle of whisky. It smelled horrible and tasted like gasoline! My head would shake in convulsions after taking a drink as my body would try to convince my mind to reject the stuff. After taking a few gulps I tried to chase it down with a handful of snow. No matter how much snow I ate I could not get the awful taste out of my mouth. That's when Kurt suggested I try a smoke to get rid of the awful taste of the booze. Just like that another victim was born into the world of smoking. I probably smoked 20 packs before I was told you're supposed to inhale.

I got so drunk that first time I couldn't walk home if I had wanted to and that was beside the obvious fact my mom might just figure out I'd been drinking. The others couldn't go home either so we decided to pass out in the back of Fred's brother's truck. Sam had to help me stumble most of the way. I felt warm and happy as I stumbled through the snow with my new comrades. That feeling wore off quickly in the back of the truck. I remember the four of us huddled and shivering in the back of that terribly uncomfortable truck. It was so cold I thought if I fell asleep I may never wake up. I prayed for the sun to come back. I walked home at the first sign of light. By then the smell of alcohol must have subsided because my mother never asked any questions.

The third or fourth time I got ripped with the boys. One of the fellas got a bad idea. The boys decided going to the school dance drunk would be fun. I do not know how long they had been getting drunk, but they certainly seemed to handle it a lot better than I did, always stumbling and falling down. The "Speed guzzle" style of drinking we did was far from responsible. You felt all right at first, then a rapid descent to extremely drunk. I was pretty fucked up by the time we walked across town to the school. I did not want to go inside, instead, I wanted to sit and wait for them in the cemetery across from the school, but they dragged me in any way.

I was sitting in a dark corner trying to sober up enough to walk back out when one of the girls in my church group chose this moment to notice me. Of all the times I wished someone would notice me this wasn't one of them. But as fate would have it she did and it didn't take her long to notice I was drunk. Long story short she told the teacher and just my luck, the dance that night had an officer on duty. I'm nabbed up and my "friends" all flee. What followed sucked! My mom had to come to school and get me. I got my first underage drinking ticket. The school gave me three weeks in-school suspension and I had to go to AA counseling and some first offenders group therapy shit.

During my in school suspension I had to stay in a little room with five cubicle type of desks. I was the only student in there at the time. I was only allowed to leave the room for lunch period. While on lunch one day I was standing outside the cafeteria by a large 12 foot tall window panel. Another student passing by said something about me being trash or something. Frustrated that I was once again alone and singled out I kicked the window. I didn't think it was enough force to break it, but it was! In the silence that followed I felt like a celebrity, everyone had stopped eating, talking, and walking to all look at me. Just then I was grabbed by the staff and dragged away.

Later that day, on the way home, Mola told me that the girl who reported me at the dance was scared because she felt I might do something to her. The broken window had given me some kind of dangerous bad-boy reputation. All kinds of crazy rumors were circulating and I liked the new attention. No one ever even noticed I was there before, now they were all talking about me. I decided to cater to the people, give them what they wanted. I figured I'd be cool and popular.

The next day I stole a knife from my brother. It was a big "Rambo style" survival knife. My brother had begged for it after seeing the movie. My mom had given in justifying it as camping equipment. I stuck it in my backpack and showed it off before school, bragging "I'd get that NARC". I never meant to hurt anyone. Part of me wanted to live up to my new "bad boy" reputation but mostly I just wanted to be noticed.

Well, I was noticed all right! The police came to school and I was expelled on the spot. Not the outcome I was going for. Then the police dragged me into the police station, sat me in a small concrete room and tested out their best scare tactics. Their words didn't frighten me. They would get in my face and say things like "You're on a dangerous road straight to prison" and all that kind of stuff. I didn't pay them any mind because it just seemed fake, like a poorly planned stunt, meant to scare me straight. Sadly, I did not buy it. They did not understand me at all. With police "charges" pending and my mom's nerves now strained it was decided I would go live with my dad in California.

# CHAPTER 2

## Paradise lost

The plane ride to California was the most exciting thing I had ever done up to this point. I sat in awe at my window seat as the world became so much larger. It reminded me of the time I rode my bike to the edge of town. It felt so exhilarating to see beyond the boundaries of the world. I relived the naïve magic of a child's mind, to believe beyond the edge lay only the great nothing. For a brief moment I flew with the angels, and I now knew there were no edges. The great nothing went on into forever.

Like all things shot into the heavens my time there was brief. I descended from the clouds and landed at a terribly busy Airport. For my entire journey I was treated like precious cargo. Flight attendants never left my side. They sat with me on the plane and escorted me to a special room with other kids to hang out with in-between my connecting flights. They were all very nice and had done an excellent job of making me feel safe the whole day, but now that I had arrived my guardian angels abandoned me with no adult there to meet me. I sat there in the terminal for 30 to 40 minutes unclaimed, not knowing what to think.

All the other passengers left and the terminal was empty when I finally decided to go and collect my luggage. By the time I found my way to the baggage claim my suitcase was the only one left. Just like me, it was alone, circling around and around, lost and unclaimed. I stood there with my bags at least another half an hour before I had thought about going outside. People were starting to line up for the next set of baggage and I didn't want to stand around in the airport any more. The air inside began to feel sweaty and crowded, like I had to fight for my share of oxygen.

Once outside I sat on my suitcase worried and about to cry when I noticed, over in the distance, my father waving. I immediately ran to him. I was not thinking "Why didn't he come in? Or at least tell me when I arrived to meet outside?" I was just relieved and thankful not to be forgotten altogether. Once inside my father's car the scared and restless feelings knotting up in my guts untied and I felt safe again. I was very young when my folks split and had no knowledge of what their problems were. The only thing I knew was I missed my dad and seeing him again after so long felt good.

Driving down the highway was like being on another planet to me. Sunny skies, palm trees, fancy cars, half naked people everywhere. It was a lot to take in! I came from the land of gray skies and never ending dismal cold. After a short drive we arrived at an upscale condominium complex with a beautiful view of the ocean.

I was more in awe of the pool placed in the middle of all the units than the beautiful ocean that stretched out upon the never-ending horizon. I drooled at the thought of being able to swim without constantly bumping into someone like at the public pool back home. The apartment we lived in was a small but nice two bedroom condo. The house and room I had back home were three times it's' size but my new apartment's small comfort was very nice.

The first two weeks I lived with my dad were great. It was like finding out I was royalty after living half my life as a pauper. My dad showered me with attention and I experienced things I'd never before dreamed of. We went snorkeling in the ocean, we went sailing, we went to the Pink Floyd laser light show in Balboa Park, and we shot guns in the desert just to name a few. I had more fun in two weeks than I'd had in the previous 10 years. I came from nothing, so it didn't take much for me to feel like I now lived in the land of excess. I felt like people here had so much that they took it all for granted. I did not take it for granted. Like warm liquid sunshine on the dry sponge of my soul, I soaked it up. It felt great but all good things must come to an end.

By the third week the vacation was over. My father had to get back to work. He worked at or for the condominium complex we lived in. I was not really sure what he did but he was very busy doing it. I was left to either hang around inside or linger around the pool.

I was the new kid and faced an adjustment period. The first week I was there the other kids would just look at me and walk away. Anytime I went near the pool the local clique would grab their stuff and leave, only to return to swimming when I was not around. I didn't mind having the pool to myself, but it gets boring quickly. By the second week the locals knew I was not leaving and I was not intimidated by them. They didn't want to give up the pool so they were forced to acknowledge that I existed. They did acknowledge me, but I still was not exactly welcome in their circle.

By the third or fourth week the local clique had a sense of who I was and they now they had to either welcome me or reject me. I was quite relieved when they did not reject me. While lounging by the pool one of the kids from the complex asked me if I wanted to hang out and listen to some tapes. I agreed and thought it was finally the end of me being an outcast. We did not do anything sneaky or bad. We just sat and listened to some crappy cassette tapes they had and talked. They were nice normal kids though I can't recall any of their names because after that day I never saw them again.

Later that same day my dad gave me the fourth degree about why I went missing from the pool area and when I told him he got really mad. I didn't understand why my actions had upset him but they had. He continued to fiercely grill me "What did you say to them?", "What did they say?"

The only answer I could think of was "I don't know? Stuff?"

This did not seem to be the answer he wanted and at that point his agitation boiled over. He slapped me in the face and I was forbidden to ever go back to the pool. This was the first of many times I would see my father's rage manifest itself. At the time I did not think much of it. I was just a dumb kid and figured I was punished for not giving a valid reason for leaving an area I was supposed to stay in. What I didn't know at the time was: my dad Co-managed the condos with another couple whose children I met earlier that day. Long before I moved here my dad started some kind of feud with the other couple. Whatever trouble my dad had with the other managers only got worse and finally he lost or quit this job. I don't know which; I only knew it meant we had to move because the condo we lived in went with the job.

We moved to a small dump of an apartment in the city. No more pool. No more view of the ocean. My dad's girlfriend apparently did not care for our new surroundings, and she too became a thing of the past. I am not sure why but my father seemed to be convinced all the bad things happening to him were somehow my fault. My days were no longer spent lounging poolside; they were now filled with chores.

Our new apartment was very small and to make things worse my dad had a lot of stuff. My room was more like a storage unit than a bedroom. The room was full of boxes except for one clear area in the corner big enough for my chair type thing that flopped out into a bed of sorts and a small end table. I remember that room very well and how it made me feel like an unwanted possession, tucked away. The small, crowded room held nothing for me.

Laundry was one of the chores I had to take on. I was just told to go and do it. My dad never even attempted to explain how it was done. He must have either figured it was so simple he didn't have to or he just didn't know. I was just a kid I didn't know how to do the laundry. I was attempting to do my first load when I met Lisa. Her mom made her do the laundry as well.

The first time I saw Lisa I was taken aback by her beauty. Lisa was a skinny blonde with the most innocent blue eyes. She laughed at me fumbling to operate the simple machine. Lisa, being a compassionate angel, showed me what to do. Something inside me changed that day. As I fell into a dream within her eyes I no longer wanted "popularity." The happiness I'd been looking for was somehow obtainable in her smile. I saw something in her that she also saw in me that day. Maybe it was the intoxication of her presence or just my ignorance that led to my next "mistake".

At drying time she told me she dries her laundry on a setting called "fluff". She tells me on this setting the laundry comes out super soft. I thought "that sounds great" so I set the machine to "fluff". While the laundry was drying, Lisa asked me if I wanted to smoke some pot with her, and I quickly agreed. She led me to a stone slab in the abandoned lot right behind the complex we lived in. You could get to the empty lot through a hole in the fence that ran across the length of the rear of the complex. Strange I had looked at the fence a dozen times and never would have thought on the other side the block was half empty. The view from my room faced the parking lot and the other windows in my apartment faced the street. The hole in the fence was really just two boards with the bottoms broke off and just happened to be only a few yards away from Lisa's apartment which was in the back of the complex.

When we returned to the laundry room the clothes were at the end of the cycle and stopped. Lisa's three shirts are dry on the "fluff" cycle but the dryer full of clothes I had were not dry and I had to ask for more quarters to finish the job. It was getting dark and my dad was getting more intoxicated by the minute. He assaults me with verbal abuse before throwing the change at me. I returned to the laundry room and put more quarters in the machine that was still set to "fluff." It runs the allotted time and the clothes are still wet. Not knowing what to do, I returned to my apartment with the wet laundry. My father showed his displeasure by throwing a hammer at me. I slept in fear and pain for the first time in my life that night. I was hoping being down on his luck had brought this foul mood and I prayed it would pass. It didn't and I was grounded for weeks over the laundry episode. I spent the hours of day alone in my room thinking about Lisa, questioning god why was I isolated and alone yet again.

Once my sentence expired the first place I went was to the stone slab to smoke a big joint. Lisa and some friends were already there when I arrived. Lisa introduced me to her friends Marlene and Chris. While Chris rolled out a joint he said

"I just got a new Slayer tape it kicks total ass."

Marlene interjects "You shouldn't listen to that devil worship music" as she poked Chris in the ribs.

Laughing I said "I don't worship the devil, but I love Slayer. 'Hell Awaits' it's my favorite cassette."

Lisa speaks up "I play that tape over and over; "Chemical warfare" is my favorite song". I agree with her. She is so pretty I would agree with anything she said.

Over the next couple of weeks Chris and I became particularly good friends. My new friend showed me around the city or at least the places a kid would go, the local arcade, the park, Main Street, Marlene's apartment complex and my favorite place, a place we called the circle church. The circle church was a church on a circle lot. The street wrapped around it in a perfect circle. Streets broke away from the circle in six different directions. Two of the streets that ran from it went in straight lines, one of which you could see a long way down, the other ended abruptly. The remaining 4 streets went away in angles then straighten out. From the air it must appear out of place among the perfect squares and rectangles. It was a big stone church with these large hedges planted along the corners of the building. In one of those corners there was a small opening in one of the hedges. We would crawl through the opening to a clearing behind them big enough for four or five kids to sit comfortably out of the view of any passersby. Sometimes you could hear organ music or choir singing coming from inside. We liked to go there and sit because it was a perfect place to get high away from the public eye. It was quiet and not many kids knew it was here, so no one bothered us. It was also Lisa's favorite spot because she often insisted we go there. In the short time I knew Lisa I had developed a massive crush on her. She was always nice to me but never showed a hint of liking me. I treasured my new friends and the times I was able to sneak away with them.

My father did not like my new friends or my freedom. He had grown meaner by the day and didn't like me not being around to do my chores. My father decided to set some new rules. He made up this ridiculous wheel of punishment to go along with his new set of rules. It was a sadistic little craft project. My father had drawn a circle on a large piece of paper, divided the circle into various punishment pies, and attached a crude spinner. The wheel literally had a spot that read "punch in the face". Some of the other punishment pies had things like: 10 licks (a southern word for spanking), scrub the bathroom, wash the truck, and other random stupid things. I guess he felt it was balanced. I thought it was a joke. Until the night I missed curfew by two minutes. I arrived at home to find the door locked. I knocked on the door wondering why it was locked and as it opened, I was punched in the face. I did not even get to spin the ridiculous wheel. I would refuse to spin or take part in this madness. "Fuck you!" I snarled back and torn the wheel in half before throwing it down. My dad took this as a challenge and beat me till I lay crying on the floor, promising not to disobey him again.

Summer was fading and all I had left to look forward to was a new school year and a chance to get out of my home. My life just got worse and worse. I was no longer allowed to go anywhere or see anybody. Sometimes Lisa would visit me in the laundry room while I was doing the laundry. A girl I barely knew became the only light in my dark world. Lisa never spoke much about the everyday. She lingered somewhere in-between spaces. She was never grounded enough to be here on earth and yet she could never quite grasp that ever elusive star to ascend above this world. I loved her for that because when I was with her I never had to be solid or real which I really wasn't anymore. My dad let all his anger in life bottle up inside and the only release was his favorite punching bag, me. It was better not to be here or there. It was as if Lisa and I were only given a dreadfully small amount of happiness, not enough to make us smile individually but when the tiny bits combined together, it made up just enough happy to feel content.

The first week of school brought with it the tastes of freedom and I wanted more! Escape was the only pathetic dream I had left. I had nothing left to give or lose. Sleeping with one eye open became a habit, I didn't eat in fear I might eat something my father might want later, and I never knew what horror might await me next. Like a lamb waiting to be led to slaughter. I only knew that I could not survive much longer living like this. I had to escape. I decided to pretend to go to school and never ever return. I could have called my mom, but I was already convinced I was a problem she couldn't deal with. I hadn't made it easy for her and she had already sent me away, cast me out. I was young innocent and naive. I thought I could just hang out on the warm beach all day and eat out of the garbage or something. Anything had to be better than the way I was living. I truly believed I had no other choice. Maybe if I had someone in my life that really cared I would have made different choices. But at that time in my life, I didn't believe anyone loved me. I was just another stranger in a strange land.

I made myself believe running away would be some kind of romantic adventure. Monday would be the best day for me to disappear, figuring my dad would have to go to work Monday- Friday so he'd be too busy to look for me until the following weekend. By then I would hopefully be long gone. All the time I spent in church led me to believe God would look over me while I was on the streets. He would not let any harm come to me. I was after all confirmed in his light. The romantic thoughts of my escape filled my daydreams with a false hope that gave me the confidence to go through with my plan.

Early Monday morning while my dad was in the shower I prepared for my new life. It did not take long. I grabbed a handful of weed from my dad's stash and a lighter. I did not have a backpack and it was still too warm outside for me to take a jacket without raising suspicion. I left that morning with the clothes on my back, two schoolbooks, and the weed I took from the fridge, a lighter and some money my mom sent me. I never really had anything so it wasn't hard to face a new life without any possessions. I was so naïve I did not know of all the horror this world hides. I just put on a brave face and walked into it.

# CHAPTER 3

## Danny's story

The morning I ran away I did not feel free; I felt like a hunted animal! My only instinct was to find a place to hide. I went to the circle church since it was the best place, I knew of to not be seen. I laid low in my hideout and smoked a little bit of my weed. The drugs took enough of the anxiety away for me to venture back into the open streets. I went to Marlene's apartment complex hoping the girls were ditching class. I was such a fool I did not think about the fact I had no way of telling if they were home unless I knocked on the door. I didn't want to be seen by adults now that I was on the run so I couldn't knock on the door, especially not at this time of the day. I had no clock and no sense of time so what I thought was late afternoon was really only about 11:30 AM. I was already out in the open and the arcade wasn't far from Marlene's, so I went there. By the time I walked to the arcade it was just past noon.

The great thing about arcades back then was that they were often dark and crowded with a maze of machines. They also rarely had any visible personnel "working" there. It was a beautiful place to hide. I had maybe $35.00 in my pocket, and I told myself this money would keep me alive for at least a month. I had no worries and thought I could afford to spend a little. I was deep in a neon battle when Danny appeared next to the machine I was playing on.

I met Danny in the park one day when Chris and I were looking for someone with a pipe. When you're underage and wanted to get stoned and couldn't roll a joint you either had to steal a pipe, make one or use someone else's. Danny was a real dirt ball. He never brushed his green teeth or combed his greasy hair. He also always walked a little funny, sort of hunched back or something. It fit him because he was a rotten person inside and out. He had this pipe with two chambers, and he would only put one screen at the mouthpiece end. So whenever you would pack one in his pipe most of the weed would get sucked through the bowl and wind up inside a chamber where he could smoke it later. I fell for this trick only once.

Danny was over eighteen and a drop out so he didn't go to school, but he knew I did so he asked what I was doing at the arcade during school hours.

Trying to sound bad-ass I told him "I do whatever I fuckin want to and today I don't feel like going to class."

I put some quarters in the machine so Danny could join me playing the game. I didn't want Danny to know I had cash dollars, so I told him the handful of quarters was all I had. After I ran out of quarters, I asked him if he wanted to get high. He invited me back to his house to get some lunch and said it was a safe place to smoke some weed. I had nothing better to do and since I didn't want to spend all my money on games I agreed.

I followed Danny into a part of town I'd never been to before. On the walk over to his house he told me his mother was at work and there would be no problems. I figured that meant no adults would hassle us for not being in school and smoking pot. I was so naive. When we got there the doors and all the windows all had bars on them. The bars were not odd or out of place in anyway. Most of the homes in this neighborhood had bars on the doors and windows. The bars on Danny's house however weren't there to keep out random burglars. They were there to keep Danny out.

Danny led me around to the back of the house where he had managed to loosen one of the bars covering a small window to the basement. Danny was not strong enough to pry it off by himself and wasn't smart enough to use a simple lever. He asked me to help him pry the bar up so he could crawl in.

I asked him "Why can't we use the door? Did you lose your key or something?"

He told me his mother kicked him out with his stuff still in the house. I was half serious and half joking when I asked him if this really was his house?

He replied "Yeah it's my fuckin house!"

That was good enough for me because honestly, I did not really care if was his house. With two of us pulling and prying at the bar it easily broke free from the rotted stucco leaving just enough room for Danny to crawl inside and let me in through the back door

Besides the drinking and drugs I never broke the law before. So, it felt a little exciting breaking in. In my mind there was no danger. I had no idea how much a parent can grow to loathe their own child so much that they would bar up the windows to keep them out. Once inside I quickly realized why Danny's' mother had gone to great lengths to keep him out.

I thought we would hang out, get stoned, maybe grab some food and split. Danny however had very different ideas and he immediately went for the medicine cabinet. He came out of the bathroom with a bottle of pills, grabbed two beers from the fridge and we sat down on the couch. He handed me one of the beers and began to crush and cut up the mystery pill. He was mashing it into the expensive coffee table with no regard for the damage he was inflicting on the table. In between snorting whatever these pills were he told me how on his 18th birthday his mother threw him out. Six months and three break-ins later she installed the bars, right before Christmas. Danny said he'd been working at the bars on that little window a little bit at a time during the day when no one was around.

I thought to myself "Christmas that was six or seven months ago I could of broke that off in a week or less."

After 10 minutes of crushing and snorting Danny said he needed to piss. He went into his mother's bedroom stood on the bed and began to piss all over everything. Afterwards he began ransacking her things until he found some cash, 20 bucks I believe it was. Then he began randomly breaking and spitting on everything in sight. As if that weren't enough he then took things from the refrigerator and rubbed them on and possibly in his ass. All the while he was sharing random bad memories of all the family disputes, or curse's as he called "them".

He listed them aloud, by number in no particular order. "Number 73 put me in jail on my birthday! Number 15 always made crappy ham on Thanksgiving! Number 137 the green underwear incident!"

I started feeling bad about helping him with the bars. I just wanted a sandwich and to smoke a bowl. It was clear Danny had no belongings here and did not belong here. This was way beyond any behavior I had ever seen or wanted to be part of. I did not want to be a party to burglary, vandalism, and food molestation. While finishing my second beer the guilt about what he was doing and the thought of someone finding us here had set in.

Danny was still ranting "Number 36 made me eat peppers! Number 85",

I interrupted and suggested we should leave. "Hey bud I think we should go now dude"

"I think we should shit on the furniture before we go." Danny replied with a sadistic smile and madness twitching in his eyes.

I certainly was not doing that! I just shock my head in disbelief and exited. After a few minutes of God doesn't want to know what, Danny joined me outside. That was just one of the moments in my life when I lost a part of my trusting nature. One can only see so much until eventually all the Smiling faces become masks people wear to hide their true evil nature.

I remember thinking about how someone would react when they returned home to the mess Danny left. However, I didn't feel sorry for whoever lived there; I felt, sorry for Danny even after witnessing the depraved things he did. For all I knew all the things he said were true. To me Danny's parents were faceless monsters hurting a child with hate, neglect and abuse just like they did to me. I don't justify Danny's behavior now or then, I was just disconnected from it. Under my mask there was nothing. I felt no guilt or remorse. After all, I did not break or violate their stuff. Danny did that! They were not my demons to fight or forgive.

Whenever bad things happened, I was reminded of how I blindly obeyed and worshiped God. In church I was often told that

God had a plan and that plan was almost always questioned or misunderstood. I felt extremely disconnected from the world as if perhaps I had a very small, insignificant part to play in some greater plan but decided not to show up to work that day. I surely couldn't stop the world and I didn't believe I could affect it. I was numb with indifference. If I believed my life was a series of bad dreams, I would not have to deal with the emotional weight that went along with reality. I used this twisted technique to block out morality for years of my life. As long as the dream I lived in never collapsed there would never be consequences from straying from the path of righteousness.

After leaving Danny's house he said he needed to find something "to step on" his stolen pills. I was so dumb I thought he wanted someone to step on the bottle and smash the evidence. It must have been the two beers I drank back at his mother's house. I felt dazed and a little confused. So, I just followed along like a lost dog with nowhere to be. I was content not being alone and seeing new sights. We walked to the downtown area. Everything here seemed extra dirty and run down.

We arrived at a small crap-cluttered apartment. When we went inside, I was surprised at the door by a forty-something woman in lingerie they called mom. Jim a clearly gay man dressed in makeup, a frilly boa, leather pants and no shirt sat on the couch. Sitting next to him was Pee wee, a very fat two hundred plus pound girl about 16 or 17 years of age. They were all watching gay porn together, which to me was very unnerving.

Danny and I took chairs in the kitchen. I sat with my back towards the television trying to act like sex was something I was used to. In truth I'd never seen anything more than a few magazine photos in grade school. The pungent smell of sweat and sex filled the air. I could hear the porn playing behind me and I felt like I should leave. I must have blushed when mom, as she was called, came over to the table. This was the first time I had seen a woman in lingerie. She wasn't all that hot but she wasn't disgusting.

On her way to joining us at the table. She brushed against me, played with my hair, shakes her tits, and said "Does that make you horny honey?"

Not thinking. I said "Maybe?"

"Maybe? I'd love to pop your cherry" She replied.

Then I really blushed "pop my cherry?" Before I figured out what she meant. They all burst out laughing.

After five minutes of teasing and laughing at me mom offered us a beer. The laugh they all shared was enough to welcome me into the circle.

While I was fumbling to open the beer, mom says "I knows you aint of age, but I'll let you have a beer because you're cute."

Danny wastes no time and asks about something to step on his bottle which he produced from his pocket and handed to mom. Looking at the label she laughed and retrieves what appears to be a large diaper bag full of pills. Digging through the bag she selected one of the pill bottles and said "Baby laxatives should do the trick".

Jim joins us at the table and the three of them began to crush and snort the powder. They offer me a line of whatever mixture they've cut up and I don't want to look awkward so I do it. It burns like hell as it goes up my nose. My face goes stone cold and I feel a massive head rush. I feel it sink into my throat and I gag a little while the thought of vomiting enters my mind. I quickly drink some beer and fight back the sickness. Right after I did the line mom wants to know how it was. I had never done any lines so I didn't know if what I'd just done was good or bad. I thought it was horrible but didn't want to come off as a square so I just held my thumb up while I drank my beer still trying to get rid of the awful taste stuck in the back of my mouth.

"See, its fine, he likes it" mom says to Danny and they continued to cut lines out and mix their crushed powders together.

We sat, drank beer, and smoked joints until the time blurred into night. Shortly after dark I was fighting to keep my eyes open. When mom and Jim started fucking around on the couch with Peewee watching. Danny and I decided it was a good time to leave. The drugs and beers made me completely forget I had run away and had nowhere to sleep. I ask Danny if he had a place to crash.

"You can crash at my place it's not far from here." He said with a smile. I didn't trust his smiley mask, but I now felt very sick and just wanted to lie down or puke.

We stumbled across town to an abandoned car that lay somewhat hidden and dormant in the back of an overgrown lot.

"Here it is!" Danny announced proudly.

"Here what is?" I replied, thinking we stopped walking to lite a smoke.

"My place dumbass, this is it. You can have the backseat."

I had no energy left to care so a sarcastic "Awesome" is all I could muster.

Danny's place was a real beauty. The cars yellow paint was covered with graffiti. The tires were flat or missing and the rusted body was full of bullet holes. My head was spinning as I climbed into the back. The inside was even worse. The windows were all smashed out with broken bits of glass filling most of the floor and seat. The seats had been slashed, here and there the springs poked through. After a short struggle I found the most comfortable position and looked up at the stars through the broken out back window. The car smells and is the most uncomfortable place I'd ever been but somehow I feel safe and alive. I could feel the planet spinning through space as I passed out.

The next day the sun came up vicious and mean. I was drowning in my own sweat and my head was pounding. I had terrible kinks in my neck and back. My mouth was so dry I feared my tongue might crack or fall off. My stomach was filled with razor blades and knotted up tight. My mind felt broken as I tried to recall the day before. The whole day before was now only a blur of memories: half naked women, snorting the mystery powder, Danny ransacking the house and pissing on the bed. My head hurt too much to try to reconstruct the past as the brutal reality of a new day set in. I was Homeless with very little money, no ideas, and no purpose. This pain must be my toll for doing evil I thought as I pulled myself from the car.

The sun was so bright it hurt my eyes. Once my eyes came into focus I looked around for signs of life. There were a few people milling around in the distance but none of them seemed to notice me. I don't like going to the bathroom outside but I had to get used to that now that I lived outside. I made dew in Mother Nature's facilities. Then I lit a smoke and contemplated going home.

When I finished smoking, I figured I would wake Danny to see if he had any useful ideas? Danny was still passed out in the front seat of the pile of shit car he called home. When I got close I noticed he was soaked in his own urine. I nudged the seat in an effort to wake him. He did not budge at first. "Hey Danny" I persisted, not really sure if I still wanted to wake him.

"Fuck off! Don't touch me! I'll kill you!" he shouts back and swings hitting the glove box.

"Danny it's me, your friend. Just relax. I think you had a bad night buddy."

"Buddy?" He replies, the tone of his voiced changed and a smile came over his dirty face. I don't think Danny ever had a friend. Danny had screwed over everyone he ever knew in his life and he reaped the rewards that went with those choices. I do not think he knew what it was like to do honest good things. Danny crawled from the car, puked in the grass, wiped his face on his shirt and threw it aside.

"Now what?" I asked standing six feet away.

"Now we go shopping" he said.

I didn't bother asking anymore questions I was now very curious to see what his idea of shopping was so once again I followed him. We went to a Laundromat parking lot where we sat on a bus stop bench. This particular bench had a perfect view of the large glass windows that lined the front of the Laundromat. At the time I had no idea why the clear view of people doing their laundry that our location provided was of any importance. Sitting there reminded me of all the time I wasted sitting at my corner in Wisconsin and I didn't want to sit on display downtown anymore, I had grown more than impatient when I asked "What the hell are we doing out among the general public Mr. No shirt piss pants?"

Danny insisted we just sit and wait. He informs me that people are stupid. They often throw their laundry in the washer or dryer and leave the building. After waiting for what seemed like half the day some guy shows up, throws his clothes in the wash machine, and drives off. Right after the man was out of sight Danny headed into the Laundromat and I went to the edge of the parking lot. Within seconds Danny was running back out with his arms full of wet soapy clothes. Someone was yelling "stop thief" in a thick foreign accent in the background. As he ran past me, I joined him. We ran until we found ourselves in the safety of the drainage canal about four or five blocks from the crime scene. Under the shelter of a bridge Danny changed into his new stolen clothes. Its apparent He cares only about the right now as he leaves anything he can't wear discarded under the bridge. With his new clothes on he looks ridiculous. He's a dirty bum in wet businessman's clothes. Wearing suit pants, a dress shirt and no socks he looked like GQ meets hobo town. At least the smell of laundry soap covered the vomit and piss smells a little.

I asked Danny where he'd been living since his mother threw him out? He proceeded to take me on the homeless tour of our fair city. All the places people normally do not go or drive by and never wonder what's back there. Under the overpass, down by the train tracks, some back alleys in junkie town and the park. The park is where all the kids and drug dealers went. There were some buried tube things, a picnic area, vending machines if you had money, a water bubbler, and public bathrooms.

It was late afternoon when we reached the park. I hadn't had anything to drink all day. I was so thirsty the water from the bubbler tasted like it was handed down by god! I didn't even recall telling Danny the day before I ran out of money when I used some of my money to buy some snacks from the machine and shared them with him. The park was way better than Danny's crap mobile way on the other side of town so I asked him why he didn't stay here. He told me the biggest problem with hanging out in the park was the police. They patrolled by every once in a while and you had to run or hide if you looked like a drug dealer or a homeless person. In the eyes of the law neither one was welcome in the park. Danny preferred living in the abandoned car because he could pass out without being bothered.

Danny still had some pills left and some small bags of the mixture he and mom mixed together the night before. We spent the remainder of the day in the park. Danny sold his mix of whatever to whomever. When the cops drove by we hide out of site. While Danny sold his drugs I had the pleasure to meet some other local kids that day: a pair of twin girls that were hotter than the sun and always dressed to kill and a Philippine kid that everyone called Phillip. I'm not sure if that was his name or they just called him that because he was Philippine. Phillip and the girls were hoping Danny was selling weed and when they found out he wasn't the girls were very disappointed so I offered to smoke my last joint with them. I always was a sucker for a pretty face and this time it was times two. I don't know if it was the serenity of the park, the cool night air, the pretty girls or the drugs but for some reason I felt at-ease again and my hangover was finally gone. The girls were hinting around at going somewhere else when a fun day at the park was interrupted.

More often than not in my life, just when things are going good, they end up crashing into the dirt and this time was no exception. The cops drove by and this time they went around the block. When the officers parked and exited their patrol car the crimes of yesterday slammed into my consciousness. Without further thought instinct took over and I acted like the others and scattered from the park. I had no idea which way to go. The city was completely foreign to me. I didn't even try to follow anyone I just ran as fast as I could away from the danger.

After a short run the panic of not knowing where I was slowed me down enough to look around. I noticed Danny was about a block behind me. I think he was trying to follow me so I stopped. Danny was apparently very happy to have a new friend. He now chased me like a pup. After he caught up to me and his breath; he suggests we get some food and go back to moms' apartment. Danny was grateful for the snacks I bought earlier and repays me with some fast food. Sitting in the dining room I might have felt normal again if not for Danny sitting across from me with a big smile and crazed look as he ate his food. He did not eat very often but when he did, he became overexcited and took great pleasure in consuming a simple meal.

When we left the restaurant and headed towards mom's I felt fully alive. I had no fear or regrets about running away. I was ready to take on any adventure the night might bring. This time when we arrive at mom's apartment Peewee is the only one there. She asked us in right away and it is more than obvious Peewee has taken a shine to me from the night before. She wants me to sit by her and she now wants to know all about me. I played along to be nice. Why not be nice? She was supplying us with beer, weed and a place to hang out.

We had been partying for a few hours when mom returned with a new guy. Mom and the new guy sat down in the kitchen. Danny joined them in the kitchen. I could tell the stranger seemed to know Danny but did not look happy to see him. When Mom got out her bag full of pills the stranger said something into mom's ear and Pee wee and I were asked to leave. Since Peewee's bedroom was the living room we had to go outside to mom's car. Pee-wee did not want to leave but her protests were silenced with a six pack of beer and a joint.

Pee Wee and I sat in the car and talked. Mostly we talked about how we wanted to be normal, loved, and needed. When she asked if I'd even been in a relationship, I told her I'd all ways wished I had a girlfriend but never had one. The closest I came was when a girl in my church group wanted to be my girlfriend. When rumor that we were a couple began to arise, I denied any relationship per her wishes; she broke it off with me. In fact, she never spoke to me again which hurt the most because I never had a chance to explain how I really felt. Like a drunken fool I let most of the vulnerable details of my life leak out. Pee-wee now knew I was a virgin and a runaway. Predators love innocence and desperation. They can smell it a mile away. Pee-wee could smell it on me as she constantly pawed at me like a cat playing with its prey.

I felt no attraction towards Pee-wee because I was in love with Lisa. Pee wee was a sweet girl and it felt nice to have someone paying attention to me, but she did not hold the same magic in her eyes. When I looked at her smiling face, I only saw a mask with a devious grin underneath. All the same she was my host and as long she kept her bad intentions hidden, I didn't mind being a gracious guest.

We smoked the last of my pot and I wished aloud "I wish I had more drugs."

Pee-wee was looking for any reason to oblige me "No problem, when we go back inside I can get some more for you?"

I forgot all about my unintentional wish and drank the rest of my beer. I was more than a little drunk when mom came out and said she needed the car. Pee-wee and I went back inside to find that the stranger and Danny are now best buddies, cutting and snorting away at the table. I was wasted so I melted into a chair and dozed off.

# CHAPTER 4

## Alive undead

God only knew how many hours or perhaps only minutes passed by while I was passed out in the chair. I was rudely awakened by Pee-wee who told me it was time to leave and now insisted on the money for the drugs I wanted. I was still deep in a daze and thinking I was buying more pot, so I handed her most of my precious money. My life direction was about to change from a rough road to straight down. I was given a small bag of powder similar to ones Danny sold in the park. Being drunk and naive I did not argue so I said thanks and put it in my pocket.

It was long since dark now. Danny got us a ride with Ken, the stranger that asked me to leave but partied all night inside with Danny. Ken's old 1970 something rusted out pile of a truck only had room in the cab for two. I certainly was not riding on anybody's lap and didn't mind riding in the back of the truck, so I just got in the back without being asked. The cool night breeze was sobering. I only had seven dollars left, a bag of who knows what and a whole lot of nothing. I had no plans, nowhere to be, nothing to eat and no idea how I might survive. I was so fucked up I didn't even know where we were going. The saddest part was the fact that I didn't care. It wasn't immature ignorance that made me indifferent, it was the fact that I no longer felt my life had any "worth". I'd love to describe myself as some tough street savvy kid, but I wasn't, my fearless demeanor was only a result of a personal belief that I had no value. Ken drove us back to the wrecked car that I now had no choice but to call home.

I awoke just like the day before. Day Ja fucking Vu. The burning bright sun, the terrible smell, and the awful pain of being broken were all the same! The one immediate noticeable difference was the intense heat of the day boiling up in the car as the sun blasted away at it. Now I knew why vampires hated the sun. My skin stuck to what was left of the vinyl seats as I pulled myself up. The smell of the piss and vomit was still there but Danny was not. My eyes strained against the bright sun as I tried to spot Danny outside the car. I could not see him anywhere. The heat and smell were overpowering so I got out of the car. There I was pissing outside, hungry, homeless, and lonely. I didn't mind being homeless or hungry, but loneliness is the one feeling I can't deal with. At that moment I missed Danny, even though he was the kind of scum ball we all picked on and hated in life. I felt like he was my big brother guide through the underworld. Whatever evils he had done to others he spared me from. Maybe he went to find breakfast or maybe he went to sell more drugs? I did not really know what Danny's motives in life were; I only knew that he was gone.

I sat in the shade of one of the nearby trees and waited. I only had one cigarette left. Like me it too was all crushed and bent. I could not help but feel a burning uncertainty as I lit my last smoke. Was this my destiny? To be burned out, discarded, and forgotten? I could not and would not wait any longer for Danny to return. I had taken on the weight of my own choices when I ran away and now, I had to bear that weight. Not knowing what else to do I thought of the park and that water that tasted so good.

I was extremely paranoid as I walked to the park. The whole universe seemed to look down upon me. I noticed people looking at me with the expression that something horrible just happened; like I was an enemy wounded soldier emerging from the smoke of battle. They were horrified by my condition but still completely detached and unwilling to help. I was somewhat confused why strangers looked at me this way but at the same time I couldn't help but notice some of the horrible smell from the car was now following me.

When I saw myself in the mirror in the bathroom at the park, I didn't want to recognize the face. I did not want to face what I was becoming so I tried to wash it away. I tried my best to clean up by rinsing my shirt out in the sink and sticking my head up under the water. It was impossible to get my head under the tap in such a shallow sink and even more impossible to get clean this way. I tore large chunks of my tangled hair out with my cheap pocket comb as I tried to fight off the image in the mirror. After half an hour of wrestling with my self-image I gave up. The image I was left with was not great but at least I didn't look so destitute. I looked down into the sink at my hair ripped out and back at my face in the mirror. I could see myself again but some of my life had been sucked away. Science tells us that time is solid and cannot be manipulated but any drug addict will tell you that is false. When stoned days and weeks can be reduced to minutes and sobriety turned seconds into days waiting for your next fix. While time still passed in the usual manner for the rest of the world the toll it now took on me was somehow different. Time was never my friend. I withered years of my life away in its name only to become a slave to a cruel and relentless master.

I was truly becoming something different. I did not feel like an innocent child anymore. I no longer felt being homeless was some kind of fun adventure. I used some of my money for a soda and a snack, but my stomach now felt sick and would have none of it. I threw up the little bit of life my body had left, and I sat alone in the park. I waited there most of the day but no one I knew came around and no one else seemed to notice me. Not wanting to be alone was the only thread holding me to life. When the world abandoned me once again, I died, right in the middle of the park, with a dozen strangers watching. I am not sure who I expected to care? After all, one more death made no difference to the streets. Perhaps I had to die so what was left of my soul could survive. The world of the living had already forgotten me. My spirit was crushed by the thought that no one cared or even noticed me. The only thing that did notice me that day was the weather. The heavens above noticed my passing and marked the occasion by crying gentle teardrops of rain.

As the day grew old, I realized the park was not for the dead. It only held magic for the living. The dead are never welcomed in the light. The tender teardrops of rain turned into icy daggers driving me out of the park. I returned to the only place I had left to find shelter from the rain, my rusted-out casket. I felt so alone, cold, and wet as I climbed inside and curled into a ball trying to keep warm. My metal tomb offered very little comfort as I screamed out cursing a God that had forsaken me. The rain was now pounding the drums of doom on the roof as I felt my eyes crystallize and freeze over. My body felt like it was entombed in ice. I remembered the time I fell through the ice into the river. How the river consumed me in its cold embrace and then spit me out. I felt more frozen now than I did that cold day in February back in Wisconsin.

As I lay cold and shivering, I thought "The true pain in death is felt after you die when you first realize you're dead." Nothing compared to the feeling of my own life just out of grasp. I was scared, alone and did not know what to do. The loneliness and uncertain future became a stone in my mind that grew and grew until the stone weighed so heavy on my mind it crushed me into the earth and held me there. I felt weak and powerless against the denial burying me.

It rained for days until the only light left in me was finally snuffed out. I was just decomposing in my coffin listening to rain mix with the great nothing when in the darkness hours of the night I began to hear a new voice. A voice sometimes muffled and obscured would become clear. It said "You have to become nothing. Let go of everything. Everything has already let go of you. Just let go." I believed that I had to become a "ghost" before emptiness would become one with me. Even after everything is gone and you have embraced nothingness there's always one thing left that you can't get rid of: Hunger. It is this terrible hunger that eats at you constantly, that drove me to wander.

Just another dirty homeless person I now wandered the streets as a ghost. I went to parts of the city I had never been. I walked round and round in pointless circles. The living looked through me and the other dead looked upon me with only bad intentions in mind. There was no doubt in my mind that I had crossed over to the land of the dead. Heaven and hell were both held by rules and technicalities in those rules left way too many dead walking among the living. I just had not notice any of them until I was one of them. Now that life had left me behind, I believed I knew why the dead were stranded among the living. Heaven wouldn't have us, and hell was embarrassed to take us. Just like we were rejected in life the outcasts were now rejected in death. With no choice, the living dead were left here to rot among the other forgotten leftovers.

I found myself hiding in the shadows looking for someplace dark to hide my face. I hated God and his light. The sunshine was God's love and it burned me with its indifference. I preferred the comfort of the dark. The cold darkness offered a diluted reflection of the life

I once led. Alive or dead, what did it matter? I was not noticed in life and now in death I preferred not to be noticed. The great meaning of life was all just pointless circles. Round and round only to find yourself back at the beginning. Forever going nowhere and still compelled to complete the circle.

I plotted down my circle to all the places I thought I might find life again. The path I trod grew only deeper and the puppet master just kept me going round and round. I was so lost and so hungry for life that one morning I found myself walking my old route to school. The dead are still slaves to fate and perhaps I was drawn here for reasons I didn't yet understand.

# CHAPTER 5

## Chris's story: the storm unleashed

This truly was a strange place. It was so hot during the day and so bitter cold at night. The morning I was drawn back to my old school there was a faint mist lingering in the crisp morning air. Just when I was starting to get lost in the cloudy haze of another pointless circle, I noticed familiar faces. It was Chris, Marlene, and Lisa, walking toward me. Our bodies and our mother earth are both made primarily of water and it's this life-giving water that connects us deeply, even in death. It was as if the cloudy haze made it possible for me to step in and out of plains of reality. It took everything I had to steal the life from the water to become flesh again. It is tormenting and shameful to break free from vapor and become solid again. You have to stand before the world stripped of everything that once made you real and pray the living still find some worthwhile piece of you. People rarely ever looked at me or said my name in life. In death only a faint memory was needed for them to acknowledge me.

"Was Mother earth holding and caressing me in her cold embrace just waiting for the living to remember me before she spit me back out." I thought as I approached the group.

As they grew closer, I could tell the girls were on their way to school. They were clean and pretty, walking quickly to get out of the chill. Chris was bobbing and weaving between them trying to convince them to ditch class when he noticed me.

Chris blurted out "what the fuck happened to you? You look like you crawled out of a dumpster." The whole group stopped and gawked at me.

"Close, Danny's shit-mobile car" I answered in shame. I noticed Chris was not looking so good himself. He was wearing a new black eye. When asked about it.

He just said "My Mom got a new boyfriend. Good thing is he had some bitchin weed... until I stole it this morning. I was just telling the girls here they should ditch so we can get wasted all day."

The girls reluctantly agreed when Chris showed them the weed. We headed toward Marlene's' since it was deemed the safest place. On the way I was reminiscing about my friendship with Chris.

Chris was one of those guys whose body grew too fast and quickly became too tall for his age. I had been to his house a half a dozen times. It was like an abandoned fallout shelter. There were no pictures on the walls and only the barest essentials of furniture were left about the place. I never saw any food of any kind. His room was very spacious bedroom with only a lone mattress on the floor, no sheet, a blanket, and piles of clothes strewn about. I thought I had nothing, but he really did not. The one thing they did have was a nice collection of empty booze bottles neatly lined up on the counter in the kitchen. The only time I ever met his mother she was already drunk and going out at two in the afternoon. I never asked about his family. No one ever brought these things up. It was part of an unwritten street code. The things that were obviously fucked up in our lives were never spoken of. I knew why Chris had a mean temper and a lot of hate, just waiting for any trigger. He too lived inside the twisted dream others called reality. He was a lot like me, just another one of hell's soldiers in the making.

I knew Chris and his anger very well. One time when we were just walking along some guys in a truck did not like the way we looked and yelled some bullshit out the window. Instead of just letting it go Chris yelled back "Fuck you. You faggot fuck pussies!" Chris liked to say that particular curse and I always remembered it because it didn't make sense and always made me laugh when he said it. Anyway, these pricks must have had anger problems to because they couldn't let it go. They turned around and stopped in an effort to confront us on a more personal level. They must have been landscapers because they had shovels in the back of their truck which we preceded to grab before they came to a stop. Chris grabbed one ready to kill, and I grabbed one out of fear. As soon as the passenger in the truck got out Chris hit him full swing in the head with the shovel. A distinct smack sound rang out as the guy stumbled back and fell against the truck. His friend, the driver, now scared jumped back into the truck and put it into drive. The passenger door was still swinging open when Chris put a nice dent in the side of the truck. All the while Chris was yelling "You should shut the fuck up from now on!" I halfheartedly smacked the truck again for good measure. Inside I was scared to death and grateful I didn't have to fight. All the beatings I took had turned me into a coward. I was never a very big person and fighting back always made things worse for me. At the sign of violence, I would panic inside. But with Chris being so brave I did not want to appear weak. The injured guy managed to grab hold of the door and pull himself back in. He was crying about a broken tooth with a face full of blood when they drove away. Chris and I were laughing and taunting them

"We've got your shovels; come back and get em! Don't you need them?"

His temper issues aside Chris and I got along very well. He was smarter and stronger than any other member of the collection of rejects I knew. The way he could unleash his pent-up hate into an intimidating rage always made me feel safe. I loved Chris but looking back I wish we had never met.

Reunited with my lost friends a surge of life straighten some of the kinks out of my jagged walk as we headed over to Marlene's apartment. Of all the kids I knew Marlene was the closest to being normal. She still lived at home, had two parents, she was fed daily, still went to school and from my perspective lived a "normal" life. I think her parents' worked nights because I never saw them. We often hung out here because of that fact. Whenever I was at her apartment Marlene and her older sister were the only people home. Marlene was cute enough but her sister was a smoking hot 19-year old with a heart of gold.

When we went inside, it immediately felt different from the other times I had been there. I no longer blended in. The other times I was here I was still alive and felt welcomed. Now it felt like the very walls wanted to vomit me out. This place and the girls were bright, clean and full of life. I was filthy, gross, disgusting and full of death. My hosts could smell death on me and even though they wouldn't say it aloud their faces told the truth. Their eyes told me they were looking for a nice way to get me to leave.

We were just hanging out smoking pot when Chris noticed something in the parking lot next door. There was a truck with the entire back bed full of soda. Some Indian people who ran the 7-11 must have gotten a good deal or were too cheap to pay a service to deliver soda. Anyway, I was quite thirsty from the weed when Chris dared me to grab a six pack off the truck. I didn't want to do it but I thought if I could retrieve the soda maybe I'd feel welcomed again. I was contemplating the cons when Marlene's sister stood before me with her tight breasts poking through her shirt and the curve of her perfect butt descending from her cut-off shorts begging me for soda. I had to go!

I walked into the daylight. My eyes were blinded by the noon sun. I had roamed in the dark so long, now that I was in the light it felt completely out of my element. My instinct told me not to go through with this, but my hands felt tied.

"It's impossible to hide in the shadows in the broad daylight" was the only thought I had time for as I sauntered across the lot.

A fast minute burned away before I found myself next to the truck looking around with no plan. It was a do or die moment. I looked around once more and I said, "Fuck it"! I grabbed one of the six packs and started to walk away. For one tenth of a second, I thought I was getting away with it, and then someone started yelling. I ignored the yelling and just started walking faster.

I was an ignorant fool. I didn't even look back or run I just walked away. In my brain-dead state I paid little mind to the commotion. I had nowhere to hide so my best hope was to believe the yelling was over something else. I was taken by surprise when someone grabbed me. I turned around and recognized the face. It was Omar, a kid I knew from school. He looked as surprised as I did. We had not seen each other since that first week of school. Back then I could not turn around without finding him there wanting to be my buddy. He looked the same, I looked like shit. At that moment I hoped he would remember his previous infatuation and show mercy but he either did not recognize me or didn't care. He knocked the soda from my hand and punched me hard in the face.

I was stunned but not as much as Omar was. He stood in shock that I was not knocked down. My father did teach me how to take a punch. For all the wrong reasons I did not feel fear. For the first time in my life, I felt rage. I could see the girls watching and Chris was halfway down the stairs coming fast and angry. Like a starved dog to food, he loved to fight! Before Chris could make it through the parking lot, I punched Omar in the throat and kicked him in the balls.

Omar's was on the ground and his family was assembling outside yelling "We call police! We call police!"

The only thing that scared Chris was the police so out of instinct Chris ran. I didn't look back, I just followed Chris. After a short run we stopped to catch our breath when Chris said "That was fun but I wanted to kick that fucking guys ass!"

"Next time" I replied.

Chris was clearly bored and a little upset because he had to leave the "party" and he did not get a chance to fuck Marlene. Trying to salvage what was left of the day he asked if I had any money. I didn't have any money, but I had been carrying round the little bag of powder I bought from Pee-wee the last time I was at Mom's place.

I was not sure what the powder was or what it would do to me for that matter. The only reason I saved it was to hopefully barter with Danny for some food or anything useful. Since I had no idea where Danny went, I offered it up to Chris and told him I did not know what it was.

"I don't know what this is. Danny stole some pills from his house then he and mom mix them with some other shit. I really don't know man."

He asked if I bought it from Danny and I told him I had no idea to whom Pee-wee gave my money. It may have been Danny or Mom or Ken.

Chris was not interested in anything Danny was selling but the mention of Kens' name captured his attention. Chris grabbed the small bag for my hand "Ken you say?" he held the bag to the light and gave it close examination then he tasted a little of the powder. Chris perked up as the powder raced to his brain. "Fuck yeah; do you know what you've got here?"

I did not even remember having it "No" I replied not thrilled with whatever I snorted with Danny the day I bought it.

With an evil gleam in his eye, he said "This is a one-way ticket to sail all night!"

I did not know what the fuck he was talking about, sailing all night. The only thing I knew was the last time I snorted some of the crap Danny and mom mixed up, it was not pleasant. I had no real interest in "doing" any of the powder but having it made Chris want to hang out with me and I did not want to turn back into a ghost wandering alone so I agreed to do the mystery drug.

We needed a safe place to cut and snort so we tried Chris's apartment. Unfortunately, when we got there we spotted his mom's car in the parking lot. We could not hang out and do drugs, but Chris still wanted to collect some things. He did not want me to come inside with his mother home. I waited around the corner watching the shadows grow until Chris came back out with a shaving razor and a tape case. I was clueless why he wanted an empty tape case. Chris decided without any other good options we would have to use a public bathroom. Inside the bathroom of a gas station Chris broke the razor, removed the blade, and began to chop some of the white nugget into powder and then scraped the powder into two lines on the tape case. I rolled up one of my last dollars and after him I snorted it. It burned like dry ice. Then my face went numb, and the lighting seemed to change.

I was expecting the awful sick feeling I experienced the last time I did a line. This was defiantly something different. I could now feel something building up inside of me. The walls of the room began to enclose us. As soon as I stepped back outside, I could smell the night coming. I was sweaty, nervous, and a little scared as the drug coursed through my veins. The fear of the unknown effects this new poison might have on my flesh was quickly replaced by an indestructible sense of wellbeing. I felt something animalistic. Like a beast on to the hint of blood, my eyes widened, and I could feel my muscles tighten in anticipation of a fresh kill.

We did not have any place to go and even if we had a safe place we couldn't stay still. I didn't have any paranoia about the police catching us. I did however have an overwhelming feeling the universe was begging me to chase it. So, we ran all over the city that night like the wild unleashed creatures we had become.

Every so often we would find a quiet place to chop more of the nugget into lines. Chris was chopping and cutting with surgical precision when he told me we were snorting something he called "glass" but others called crystal meth. Chris knew a lot of the local druggies and according to him Ken had the best connection in town. Chris had done some odd jobs for Ken in trade for party supplies and knew Ken liked to trade crystal meth for painkillers or downers with Mom to try to come down and sleep. Then Chris explained a complicated system for naming all the distinct phases of the psychotic rollercoaster. There was pinging, ponging, zeeking, peaking, and six or eight other weird names and finally burning out.

I mostly remember feeling like I could pull the stars down if I just reached up and grabbed them. I threw caution to the wind and flew with the breeze. It was like standing on the surface of the moon and looking beyond the mortal world into something unknown. For once in my life I felt totally unafraid and never-ending. Just like the distant light of the stars I felt infinite. I knew even in death my existence just went on and on. I was the cursed undead but at the same time immortal. It felt good to be slightly more than alive. I was indestructible and nothing else mattered!

I spent the night hunting the darkness, but the beast could not be caught or held. While I was stalking the darkness time slipped by unnoticed. The sun began to slowly consume my wild dream. By dawn I was coming down and burning out hard. The vivid neon lights one by one surrendered to a blank white sky slowing consuming the night. We needed a place to crash so we returned to Chris's apartment. I was relived his mother was not home because I didn't have to sneak inside or go somewhere else. I was completely exhausted. A bare spot on the floor was all I needed to fall into a deep sleep.

When I awoke, I was afraid and unsure where I was and who might be there. I had something more than a hangover. My mind hurt, my thoughts were all disassembled and reassembled missing pieces. It felt like my flesh was being torn from the bone as it was fading from one plane of existence to another. I sat up. I rubbed the sleep and daze of confusion from my eyes. It was dead silent. My joints cracked and popped as I forced myself to my feet. I found Chris sitting in the kitchen digging in the ashtray for cigarette butts and smoking them. When he noticed me, he made a small cheerful noise and said his mother left ten bucks and a note. He didn't say what the note said, and I didn't ask. Whatever the message read it did not make Chris feel loved, he crumbled it in disgust and threw it on the floor.

I thought we did all the "glass" or "meth" last night, but Chris still had a tiny amount of powder left. He pulled it from his pocket as if it were his and glared at me before He cut and scraped what he could together, snorted it and licked out the bag. I had seen this look before in dogs guarding their food. I did not mind and did not protest. At this time, I had no seeded lust for the product but Chris on the other hand had developed quite an appetite for the powder. Within second of finishing what was left he decided we should go search for more. We went to the number one place drug dealers were known to hang out: the park.

To me returning to the park felt like the completion of one of my pointless circles. I was convinced I was trapped in a vicious circle when we ran into Danny. Danny and Jeff, some random homeless person Danny knew from childhood, were lying about like garbage when we arrived at the park. After a short conversation it was clear Jeff had done so many drugs (and whatever else he could get his hands on) that he was probably legally retarded. Jeff was compelled by some insane need to try anything to get high or die. According to him and Danny, they spent a great deal of their youth inhaling spray paint and ingesting household chemicals. Jeff should have been a poster child for the D.A.R.E. program. He was living proof that drugs gave you brain damage. Danny was by no means smart but Jeff was somewhere off the edge.

Jeff would slur things like "I saw this movie one time" and that would be it! He wouldn't even finish the sentence or even say anything else again for 5 or 10 minutes. He would enter into conversations with lines like "I lit a plastic chess piece on fire". It was a miracle he still possessed the faculties to even walk or speak such nonsense at all.

In my undead state I felt no pity for this guy, this zombie! He existed without purpose; he was truly a waste of space. Perhaps he was one of God's little jokes? Or perhaps just another reminder of what happens to the discarded.

We went to the park to ask Danny about scoring some more stuff and wound up waiting for some other guy to "maybe" show up. Danny says "no one's able to score right now because the police are coming down hard. They aren't fuckin round!"

Shortly after he said that the police went by and Danny got extremely anxious, so we decided to leave. As Danny was in particular hurry to leave it occurred to me that Danny was probably arrested and in jail during the time, I missed him. Chris was now very bored and aggravated about not finding any crystal, which I wasn't even thinking about anymore. Chris, Danny, and Jeff were all addicts and they needed some kind of buzz so they decided we should steal some beer.

The simple plan the idiot convention devised was for Danny and Chris to distract the checkout clerk of the 7-11 while Jeff grabbed a case of beer, walked to the front and then just ran out with it. I would stay outside "to be the lookout" or at least that's what I told them. I was no dummy. I didn't want any part of any plan to try to steal anything. The last time I stole something I got punched in the face.

Honestly I didn't think anyone was dumb enough to go through with such a foolish plan; but scumbag Jeff was just that dumb.

When we arrived at the 7-11 it was just before dusk. I went inside to "scout it out." I bought some gum and looked around. There were about three or four other people inside shopping. I went back outside and told Chris what I saw. I thought they would want to wait until the store was empty but Chris said the other shoppers would help distract the clerk so without any further prodding the boys went inside.

While I was waiting patiently outside, I didn't even look around like I was supposed to. I just watched and waited thinking Jeff would either chicken out or more likely, he'd forget what he was in the store to do. After waiting a few moments I was surprised as dumb-ass Jeff came running out trying to hold onto a case of glass bottles. The moron, instead of taking cans, he grabbed two twelve packs of glass bottles which escaped his fumbling grasp and were now rolling and breaking across the concrete. I reacted immediately. As I ran, I grabbed up two or three of the bottles rolling through the lot. Just as I was passing Jeff in the middle of the lot Chris ran out and grabs what is left of one of the boxes. Danny followed shortly behind Chris, but he trips over Jeff as he's running out, who was still lying in the parking lot scrambling to grab some of the stray beers. The clerk comes out after Danny yelling loudly in Arabic or some other tongue I couldn't understand. Just like before I did not look back. I just ran into the night.

After running a fair distance trying to catch Chris, he finally stopped under a bridge in the storm drain. I was huffing and puffing trying desperately to catch my breath when I reached him. I had a beer in each hand and a giant grin on my face. Chris and I had a good laugh over the idiot twins falling over each other. We each had a half of a beer killed by the time Jeff and Danny came hobbling up. Before even finishing his first beer Chris had decided alcohol would not feed his hunger. He smashed the beer against the concrete and decided to head for Mom's looking for drugs. Without any intention of doing so I found myself dragged into the pointless circle. I prayed I did not have to repeat a night in the car with Pee-wee while everyone partied inside.

When we arrived at Moms, Ken was just about to drive away when he saw Chris and called him over to the truck "What are you kids doing with that beer?"

Chris was not amused by ken's humor. His only interest was scoring more drugs. "Fuck beer I'm looking for some better party supplies, can you help me out?"

Ken laughs, "It just so happens I was looking for you. I need a few people to do a job in the morning and I'll let you dudes party with me tonight in a hotel room if you promise to do some work in the morning." With nothing better to do we hastily agreed. We were about to get in the truck when Ken insisted, we ditch Jeff. Chris simply told him to wait around the corner till we got back. Jeff went like the brain-dead zombie he was. Chris, Danny and I all jumped into the truck and we sped away. Who knows how long Jeff waited around the corner? It might have been days. He was so far gone he did not even remember life anymore.

I was glad it was only a short drive to the motel. Danny was staring at me, and his overexcited greasy smile made me nervous. When we went inside, I sat as far from Danny as I could. Once we were settled in Ken made a call and then produced a large bag of the crystal powder. He cut two long lines out on a mirror; snorted one and handed the straw to Chris. Danny looked on with a sad desperation as Chris inhaled the other line. I tried to act like I wasn't paying any attention to them. I didn't care about the exclusive drugs reserved for Chris and Ken. I had a tired growing on me that a thousand nights of sleep could not fix. I was in the perfect state of limbo, drinking and smoking pot, lying on a real bed.

I was about to rest my over weary eyes when Kens "girlfriend" arrived. She was a real *classy* girl. You could tell by the way she flashed us all as soon as she arrived. We were all pretty buzzed by this time but it was no surprise when Ken asked us all to take a walk for a while.

We stumbled around the block a few times. I was reminded of the times back home stumbling drunk through the snow with my friends there to catch me when I fell. "There is no snow in hell" I thought as I tripped and fell face first into the concrete. I looked up at the dirt and filth that surrounded me. No one was there to catch me! In fact, no one was there at all. I stumbled to my feet briefly before falling again against the nearest wall. Sitting up I began to wonder "have I become so alone that the last few days were nothing but a delusion, have I gone insane?"

I did not have to wonder long. As I sat there lumped against the cold wall, drunk as fuck, with the whole world spinning around me, a distant voice was getting closer.

"What are you doing dumb fuck?"

I looked up to a silhouette in the street light. It was Chris, he returned to save me from this drunken nightmare. For what reason or how long I'd been there I do not know. I was just glad not to be forgotten or worse insane.

When we returned to the room Danny told us Ken had to give his girl a ride somewhere and we should stay there. I was totally wasted and passed out on the floor with no problem.

# CHAPTER 6

## The price of rebirth

Once again with the new day came the vicious pain; retribution for a life wasted. I was fixated on a tiny stream of light bleeding out from underneath the door in an otherwise dark and filthy room. I could smell the vampires lurking ever closer to me in the pitch black. The light danced and taunted my frozen eyes. As I peered into it, I could see an escape from hell. I was trying to find the strength to leave this place and walk into the enticing light at the end of the tunnel when the door swung open. The bright morning light flooded the room chasing away the vampires. I cowered away from the light and held my eyes.

A voice boomed out of the all-consuming light. "Get up you fucks knobs, it's time to work." I struggled to make out the image in the blinding light. Ken's silhouette becomes clear and I remember the deal we struck the night before. Like a suicidal jumper, I regret my decision just before I hit the pavement when it's too late to back out.

After a kick in the ribs and a 5 minute face bath in the sink I peered up into the mirror. I looked like shit, period. I ran water over my head and tried to pull back my greasy tangled hair. I wished my hair wasn't so long, the tangles rip from my head taking bits of flesh with them as I try to straighten it. The hair tearing from my scalp and bits of bloody flesh in the cold water only got worse. I couldn't let myself look in the mirror anymore.

It felt good to be given another chance to live as I dragged my rotting corpse into the daylight. The cool morning air filled my lungs. No matter how much pain you carried from the night, or life before, you always felt grateful for that second chance to live. Even if you're buried in resentment and hate, the moment when you spit the dirt from your mouth and cough out the dust from your lungs to breathe again always feels great. You don't question why fate toys with you. You just inhale and let it fill the cold, dark, emptiness . . . it's the exhale that make things so much better.

Like sheep being led to the slaughter we got into Kens truck to start another unknown journey. The pecking order was quite clear. Chris always rode up front with Ken and Danny and I always rode in the back. I did not know or care where I was being taken. Ken broke the circle I was stuck in and drove up into the hills. Time slowed as the cold wind and its defining silence joined Danny's awkward stares.

The day was changing and getting hotter as we continued our ascent into the hills. The altitude and our surroundings changed from the filth of the city to clean forests. The further we drove from the city the more alive I felt. The city can be so suffocating. All The dark corners of the city cried out for the life they once held. Their screams were so far away now that I could no longer hear them.

We arrived at a small cabin deep in the woods on a secluded lot. No one appeared to be home. While passing a joint around Ken told us that he had purchased some wood and we were to fill the truck. Whoever's cabin it was, someone had taken a considerable amount of time to cut split and stack large piles of wood.

I was too stoned to notice at first but as the sun grew ever hotter I noticed Danny and I were both burned out with bad hangovers cooking in the sun. Ken and Chris however had energy to spare. After half the truck was full of wood Danny and I were ready to drop. Danny in fact was lying on the ground when Ken decided in was time to recharge the troops.

We were taking a smoke break when Ken laid out four thin lines on the tailgate of the truck, one long and three short. Danny was shitting behind a tree at this point. Ken did the long line then Chris did one and handed the straw to me. I already felt terrible: what did I have to lose. I snorted it and handed the straw back to Chris. Chris did half of the line that was left and called Danny over. My head went numb and I could feel my dead skin fall away. The breath of life I got from leaving the city was nice, but this was like being reborn as Jesus. I felt like the universe flowed through my veins. Time was irrelevant when high. My mind raced and entertained thoughts of flying somewhere beyond the mortal plane. A grandiose idea of immortality danced with insanity. I imagined I had lived a thousand life's before and would live again and again and again. We loaded the rest of the truck in what seemed like a fraction of a second.

The job, for now, was over but I was still flying high when we crammed ourselves back in the truck and left. I could see the clouds crash out of the sky. I could smell the sun and taste the air. I didn't know where I was and didn't care. I was packed in the back of a truck like cargo; still melting into the world swirling past me when we finally stopped. After another long drive in the hot sun I knew I was far from home.

We had arrived at an upscale looking cabin. Ken exit the truck spoke to the home owners and then we were instructed to start unloading wood to a designated spot. Once ken felt we piled enough up, it was back in the truck. We made several stops at big high dollar houses. At each stop we unloaded a portion of the wood and at each location Ken collected one hundred dollars or more. These fine folks had no idea what a fair price for firewood was or how much wood was in a "cord". The entire truck load was about a "cord" but ken told each of our customers they were getting a "cord". It didn't bother the homeowners they were getting ripped off; in fact most of them stopped us from leaving as much wood as we wanted to. We still had plenty wood left in the truck at the end of the day.

The sun was beginning to set when we arrived at a fenced in ranch. We drove onto a large piece of mostly bare land. It had a nice house overlooking a small valley. In the valley there was a truck camper resting on cinder blocks. Off in the distance I could make out some corrals and what appeared to be a stable.

"Where are we?" I asked Danny.

"Ken's place, well his parents anyway." He replied with a smile, clearly happy to be out of the city.

Ken stopped the truck next to the camper. We were told to unload and stack the rest of the firewood here next to a small fire pit. As we unloaded the wood Ken walked up to the house. When Ken returned he said we worked hard that day and he wanted to do the same tomorrow. We could stay here and party by the fire tonight if we would work for him again tomorrow. We weren't really given any other choice when Ken added the disclaimer that he wasn't going back to town till the day after tomorrow and wouldn't be able to take any of us back until then. He had almost a case of beer and a bottle of some cheap awful whiskey. We agreed to stay, of course. Nothing mattered to me anymore, I certainly wasn't going to walk into nowhere.

The sky was a cascade of colors as the sun was slowly devoured. We started a nice fire and watched the stars awaken. After a few beers Ken left to get "smokes" and did not return. We sat and drank the rest of the beer. The sun had long ago left us here alone when Danny, who drank most of the whisky, passed out in the dirt and threw up on himself. Chris and I just left him lie there in his own puke.

Hours passed and a few too many beers later my surroundings looked like a wasteland. I was burning out hard. The only desire in my heart was returning to the dear, sweet comfort of the black emptiness. The only light I could see beside our slowly dying fire was a faint dim glow coming from somewhere inside the house. I felt very alone among the rocks and wind. I threw more logs in the fire and huddled closer to the flames. The drugs and alcohol were clouding my reality. I slipped in and out of consciousness. I was hypnotized by the flames and lost in the fire. Ken disappeared into the dark and Chris went from sitting in front of me to sleeping in the truck. His feet could be seen sticking out the window. I assumed Ken went inside the camper.

I dozed off and when I came to; the fire had burned down to mere embers, and it turned so cold outside in the dark that I had to find some shelter. I crept inside the tiny camper to ask Ken if I could sleep on the floor. It was dark and smelled awful. A sick blend of whiskey and piss hung in the air. I nudged the only person I could make out in the small, cramped darkness. Fast as a bullet someone rolled over grumbled a half burp and swung out hitting me hard in the face.

"Get out burp; grumble" the voice in the dark commanded.

I slumped back from the punch, stumbled and fell back outside. In the darkness with blood running down my face, I found what appeared to be a horse blanket. I wrapped myself in it and fell asleep.

The next morning, I awoke drenched in the piercing awful pain that kicked me every sunrise. Chris was sitting up in the truck smoking a cigarette butt that he dug out of the ashtray. Danny was still lying motionless in the dirt. "Maybe his rotting corpse was finally ready to turn to dust" I thought as I sat up still wrapped in the blanket. The fire, long burned out, no longer provided any warmth. The morning sun burned my eyes. My face stung. Flakes of dried blood rubbed off as I tried to comfort my wounds. Somewhere in a blur of memory I remember the stranger inside the camper.

Chris emerged from the truck and now sat poking at the fire. Chris noticed my bruised face but did not inquire about how it got that way. I asked Chris if Ken was still asleep in the camper.

Chris laughed at me "He went up to the house right after the whiskey was gone. Ken would never sleep in the shitty camper".

I was thinking there must be something wrong with my rotting brain. Had I taken so many drugs the monster that hit me last night was just an apparition? Or perhaps I stumbled, fell in the dark and dreamed the rest. I sat shivering trying to clear my head when my questions were answered. The door of the camper burst open.

A scummy, dirty man stood in the doorway. He stood before us in his once white thermal underwear that had turned gray and brown. Even worse there's bits of fabric missing from here and there exposing the dirty flesh underneath. He had a thick unshaved face and some of his front teeth were missing. I thought we looked rough; this guy was downright gross. The awful smell from the interior of the trailer last night was him.

His stench strangled the breeze as he bellowed out. "Who the fuck are you pukes!?"

Danny popped up in surprise and Chris jumped to attention; always looking for a fight.

"Ken brought us here last night," Chris snapped back.

"Ken, huh? Where is my asshole brother?"

Like a dimwitted animal it was easy to change the focus of this foul beast. "In the house" Chris pointed in the direction of the house on the hill.

Just then you could see Ken in the distance coming our way. As he got close he yelled out "Ready to work, fuckers?"

When Ken reached the campsite he threw me a can of cold soda and saw my bruised face. "You boys get wild down here last night?" Ken asked as he glared at the stranger.

The stink bag immediately protests "Who are these kids and why are they here?"

Ken snaps back, "Fuck off, dickhead", looks back towards us and says "Don't mind my brother Bill; he's a drunken loser; now get in the truck we've got work to do". We piled in the truck and drove into the hills.

I took turns holding the cold can to my bruised face and drinking it. The long ride in the back of the truck and the cold soda eased my pain a bit. The day was a mirror image of the one before. We loaded the truck at the same place and unloaded it at various high dollar properties. The only noticeable difference was Danny was no longer wearing a shirt. He threw it in the fire pit that morning after waking, realizing it was soaked in puke. At the end of the day Ken dropped us at the park. Through the window I saw Ken give Chris a small bag of weed as our pay. I overheard Chris protest and beg Ken for more "glass" but Ken told him he was shit-out-of-luck. It was all gone but there would be plenty more in the future.

Ken gave us enough pot for two or three bowls. Chris was burning out and very irritated. He did not want weed. People who smoke weed are nothing like the meth heads. Meth heads are hard core addicts. Addicts feel like they are going to physically die without another fix. Chris was feeling that way now and it made him terribly angry. Without the drug of choice in hand we made do with what we had. Chris found an empty soda can in the trash, fashioned a crude pipe out of it and we smoked up.

The weed did not pacify Chris's rage. He was kicking walls and talking about beating and robbing random people walking by. The only way to get a new fix was with money and we had none. Danny was a true parasite. He attached himself to anything he could feed from. Danny fed the fire in Chris's mind and the two of them together were preparing to rob the next victim that walked into the park.

I still only had one foot in hell. I did not have the undeniable need for the euphoria that Chris and Danny shared. For me that would come later. At this point in time, I should have been the voice of reason but I was silent. I no longer cared. Compassion was one of the things I traded to the devil in exchange for the privilege of walking among the living. I walked in-between life and death every day. Not caring about what I had to do to survive or who got hurt in the process. That was just the price I paid to be reborn. In many ways in order to survive I had to give up choice.

Chris's lust for drugs was strong but there was still one temptation that was stronger. Lucky for the general public, before the boys could pounce on some unfortunate victim, Marlene and Lisa showed up. They said we looked like hell and we all laughed. Danny made some sick comment about Marlene looking quite "Fuckable". Shortly after the words left Danny's mouth Chris's trigger got what it needed. Chris immediately punched Danny square in the nose, knocking him to the ground. Danny was lying in the dirt, crying and demanding his share of the weed.

Chris just spit on him and kicked him in the ribs while the girls made cruel remarks like "You suck Danny even your momma didn't want you". Chris continued to taunt him by swinging and kicking at him until he ran away. Danny left half lumped over, still crying and mumbling.

The "fight" with Danny was more than enough to make us feel uncomfortable at the park so Lisa suggested we go to the circle church to kick back and smoke one. I always just followed along, especially when pretty girls were involved. When we arrived at the circle church Chris filled another bowl with our day's pay. It felt surreal being in this place again and listening to the girls talking about things normal kids do. I was barely alive. They both knew me before I looked and smelled like hell yet they both sat here like old times never changed. The girls talked about the mall and their classmates in school. Chris and I sat politely while hiding our resentment for this type of conversation from the girls.

Chris and I had grown to hate "the normal life". We had more than our share of resentment for the "normal people" that we felt didn't suffer as we had. We hated them for all the things we longed for. The hatred we shared was the only thing that bonded us together. Chris knew the bruises on my face told my story. I too wore a forbidden mark that I was only proud to bear among others who wore the mark. I was not a child anymore. I had that beaten out of me. I was just another victim.

I was not sure of anything anymore. It had been so long since I was home. I was not sure where that was anymore. I could not remember my last meal. But at that precious moment in time, there with Lisa I did not feel hungry, cold or dead. I never wanted that moment in time to end and neither did Chris. When the girls started getting restless and wanted to leave Chris began packing another bowl.

Marlene looked at him and said, "Bring that with, my parents are out and we can get something to eat and kick back at my house."

Food was a thought I had learned to live without. I say the thought of food because when you have no choice and you're starving, the cravings that can't be fulfilled drive you mad. There are a hundred million things a person can consume to stay alive and the living dead (like me) get their sustenance from horrible places. I was so caught up thinking about eating actual food I walked right past the apartment complex with the truck I had stolen the soda from.

Like an angel flying into my hell, Lisa never judged me for how I looked or smelled (and I was very scummy and dirty.) Marlene only put up with me because I was Chris's friend. Marlene's sister was not home. Marlene loved playing homemaker for Chris so she made us grilled cheese sandwiches like a good mom would. Chris and I were more than happy to pig out and eat our fill. After eating Chris and Marlene went into Marlene's room to fuck. Their absence left me sitting awkwardly with Lisa. I barely spoke as we watched some pointless crap on TV. She however talked almost nonstop and I listened; hypnotized by her eyes. Time passed far too quickly. Chris and I had to leave before Marlene's parents came home.

I followed Chris back to his apartment. When he saw his mother was home, he did not even want to go in and there was no chance his mom would let me in. Chris didn't need any extra bags in his life and I knew he wanted to ditch me, go inside and forget another day. I begged Chris to show some mercy. I told him the only other place I had to go was Danny's car and after what happed at the park, I doubted I would be welcomed there. Chris never had any siblings, but he did have a big brother moment in life that day. He looked down at sunken eyes set upon a bruised face now in tears. Chris knew well the consequences of double crossing the devil when he stole back enough compassion to sneak me in. Chris went inside and opened his bedroom window which I later squeezed through.

Once I was inside Chris's fearless demeanor changed. The one person I thought was unshakable was afraid of his mother. Chris was intensely explicit that I remain absolutely silent and hidden in his closet. The small closet reminded me of the little scrap of space that my father afforded me when I still lived at home. The small fuzzy memories of home led me to wonder if anyone was missing me. My thoughts were distracted and drowned out by the muffled sounds of music and sex that started leaking through the wall. Even though I had little knowledge of what sex was; I imagined it was Lisa and I making the noises I didn't understand. I was burning out big time and the small comfort of being inside was all I needed to fall hard into a deep sleep.

The next morning Chris woke me with gentle taps on the closet door. "My mom is gone, you can come out".

My face was still a little sore and my body hurt but at least I wasn't hung over today. I was a little dazed but extremely grateful not to wake up abandoned outside again. I asked Chris if he ever got in trouble for being gone from home for so long.

Chris wasn't used to people caring about his life and took a moment before He said "No she only complains when I am here."

"You're lucky", I said as I thought of the beating I'd get if I showed up back at home after being missing for days.

"Yeah, lucky" he replied in a sad sarcastic tone.

We were sitting in the kitchen contemplating the new day, digging in the ashtrays for smoke-able butts when Chris pulled a sizable roach from one of them. "Breakfast . . ." he said as he lit the roach and inhaled "It's the only breakfast you'll find around here" he exhaled a large billow of smoke and laughed. I looked around at the empty beer bottles lined up on the otherwise empty countertop. We smoked the roach, rubbed the death out of our eyes and began a new day.

Chris said his mother wouldn't be back anytime soon so it was cool if I wanted to get cleaned up. I took a quick soap free shower since their bathroom was as empty as their lives. There was no soap or shampoo of any kind. I dried off with a small hand towel that did not smell too bad. My crappy pocket comb once again ripped the tangles of hair from my head. The water washed away the dirt, but it couldn't wash away the shameful remorse. Death was pulling me back into the pointless circle. I was once again waiting in the cold, black in-between; never quite here or there. I just lived in a daze drifting in the breeze going wherever.

# CHAPTER 7

# The girl who never lived

With little money, no drugs, and no plan Chris wanted to go back to the park. I hated being drawn back into the pointless circle. I wished I was still innocent or naïve enough to believe we gravitated to the park because somehow it reminded us we were still only children, but the hard adult truth was that it was the best place to score more drugs.

On this sour day we didn't find any drugs. Instead, we found Lisa alone and crying. Lisa was badly bruised on her face, arm, and leg. When she saw us she immediately ran to us and clung to me. I hoped maybe she finally noticed how I felt about her, but in her shaken state she would cling to any friendly face. She tells us how her mother found some weed in her room and completely flipped out. After ripping all the evil posters from the walls her mother decided it was in everyone's best interest to have Lisa institutionalized. After being forced in the truck, Lisa jumped from the moving vehicle. Lisa, like me, finally decided a desperate life on the street was better than living at home. I did not press her for details. We all had wounds and none of us liked salt thrown in them or having to relive any of our nightmares. I didn't know anything about Lisa's home life. I just assumed that because she was so pure and innocent that she was loved. Now that I knew her wounds ran as deep as mine I felt a greater connection with her. Deep wounds preferred to live in a state of semi-denial.

My recent trip up into the vast hills had me daydreaming of camping when I was still an innocent child the year before. And just by speaking aloud "I wish we could just go camping" I hatched an idea that just grew bigger. We fantasized about going up into the hills and carving out a new society of our own. We spent the day hunting down kids we knew and persuading them to donate camping items by telling them we were having a big "camp out" party and they were all invited. Phillip, a spoiled rich kid whose folks had given him everything but attention, gave us a small tent and two sleeping bags. Some kid Lisa knew wanted to fit in, so he gave us his backpack. We ended up at Marlene's apartment where she supplied us with a small bag of food. It was mostly junk food, some Crackers, half a jar of peanut butter, a couple of sodas, and a bag of chips. Chris had a few dollars and used it to buy hot dogs, buns, and some cigarettes. We were supposed to meet up with the handful of house kids (ones who still lived at home) who donated stuff back at the park. That was never going to happen simply because we were smart enough to know a big crowd would draw too much attention. Besides, they did not suffer like us. They were not anything like us. Just because they were loved and would be missed we hated them. At the same time we showed them mercy by sparing them from the true horror of the street.

Like foolish children we headed toward the closest mountainside. We didn't think it mattered which direction we went out of town. We were surrounded by hills. The direction we chose turned out to be a very lengthy one through town. It was getting dark when we finally reached the edge of town. We knew the setting sun wouldn't allow us much time as we headed up into the hills. We settled for a spot with a small clearing that we felt was far enough from any homes to see our firelight. It was very hard to tell in the darkness. The only thing we had to go by were the lights coming from inside homes and streets so when we couldn't see any more lights nearby we figured we were far enough away from civilization to not be noticed or discovered. Chris dug a very small fire pit with his bare hands and a large stick. Lisa gathered sticks for firewood and I set up the tent. We managed to get a small fire going just as the sun disappeared. I felt like a kid again as we cooked hot dogs on sticks and ate them on plain buns. It's a fine meal that we washed down with one of our few sodas which we drank one at a time. It felt silly passing around the can like soda winos.

It was a full Moon that night. I remember how it lit up the valley as if this great celestial body was looking for something below. I was gazing up at it wondering what it was looking for when the cross all lit up on the top of one of the peaks across from us caught my eye. From anywhere in town you could always see the large cross up on the hill lit up at night. I couldn't help but think the moon was shining its light on this valley because God was looking for the girl who fell to earth. I didn't believe he was protecting me anymore but I still believed he was watching over the faithful.

"Someday maybe I'd walk up to that cross high on the hill and confront God." I laughed to myself. A terrible chill came over me but on this night, I didn't feel as cold and desolate as I did the night at Ken's ranch. Lisa was the light my life needed. With Lisa still clinging to me and smiling I felt warm and content.

Lisa was very tired and went into the tent to sleep shortly after eating. I wanted to follow her but I knew this wasn't the time to tell her how I felt. Chris and I guarded the campsite and talked into the night. Our conversations were never about silly childish shit. I looked up to Chris because Chris never talked down to me. I was used to adults feeding me lies and pretending things were different from the obvious right in front of me. Chris was the one person in life who never lied to me. His views of life were cynical and bitter but he taught me the basic truths of being either a sucker or a con. If you weren't taking advantage of others, then you were just a sucker. I did not necessarily share his views but in a world where corporate greed and corrupt politics danced upon the graves of compassion and decency it was hard not to see a great deal of validity in his views. The American dream according to Chris was a pointless race to see who could sit atop the biggest pile of money. Thieves and liars were at the tops of those piles and the bodies of the suckers were underneath.

We never discussed the future since there was rarely any hope in that. It only held more desperation. It was better to let someone else worry about tomorrow. NOW is the only time that is real. Time twisted and leaped ahead out of turn. The night was gone. Chris and I talked the whole night away. When the morning snuck up on us Chris decided to head back into town but promised to return with more supplies.

I was glad when Chris left. I thought Lisa might notice me and how I felt about her now that it was just the two of us. After what felt like an eternity, I decided to wake her. I opened the flap of the tent. In the daylight I could once again see her bruises. I was reminded of the cruelty of the world. I had to let go of all the thoughts I had of fun or happiness. Reality has a way of killing innocence. I did not know how to react. I sat at the opening of the tent contemplating if I should still disturb her peaceful rest when she opened up her eyes. She was truly stunning in the early morning sun. Her blue eyes smiled at me and she asked if there was anything left to eat?

We still had some snacks and hot dogs left. We didn't want to start the fire back up in fear the smoke would give away our hidden campsite. So we ate raw hot dogs and split a soda. When you are truly hungry any meal tastes like a godsend and I thanked God as I glanced at the cross up on the hill. Now that Chris had gone, Lisa no longer masked her fear. She huddled up next to me and hung her head and asked

"What am I going to do?" I could hear her voice breaking.

I tried to comfort her with a half-brag "I have been out here for a while now! Tossed out into the world to be forgotten but I am still here. As long as we're still breathing it's a good day and I won't let any bad things happen to you." I said trying to be gallant but in reality was still quite naive.

She broke down in tears "Bad things happened to me? You're too late there's nothing bad that can happened to me that hasn't already!"

Silently I sat next to her. I had no idea of the twisted fucked up things that go on every day. I thought at worst maybe she was kicked around. I was not prepared for what she was about to tell me. I put my arm around her and try to soothe her pain with a half hug. I said nothing. I did not know what to say. An open ear was all she needed. The flood gates opened, and all of her pain came washing out. Between sobs she told me her life story.

Her father had killed himself eight months ago, after she threatened to tell of his late-night visits to her room. After his death, gagged by her own shame, Lisa kept the dirty little secret to herself. Her mother's alcoholism spun out of control as she blamed Lisa for her piece of shit husband's death. Lisa traded nightly visits for daily beatings. Recently her mother found a new boyfriend. I have heard abused women often look for the same crap in the next guy. Well, she found it. And this time when "Daddy" came knocking Lisa refused to keep any more secrets.

She tried to tell her mother but was accused of trying to destroy her mother's life and called a lying whore. Lisa was told over and over she had driven her father to suicide. Her mother became obsessed with the idea Lisa was trying to do the same to her. In a raging fit she burned Lisa's back with a red-hot iron, which she now shows me by lifting her shirt? It is still blistered and filled with pus.

Seeing it was so grotesque it makes me gasp, "Oh my god!"

To which she replied, "I don't believe in God" and continued her tale.

Lisa was not really sure where her mother had planned to take her yesterday morning. She honestly believed that her mom was going to drive somewhere secluded and kill her. She just panicked, jumped from the truck, and ran. She hid in the park until we came along.

As I looked towards the sky, I saw the cross on top of the hill and I began to question why God failed to protect so many of the innocent. I did not consider myself innocent; I was rotten to the core, but Lisa was still pure in my eyes. She had fallen from heaven, broken her wings and God did not seem to care. She was far too wounded to fly so I decided to take her into my deadly embrace. I could not lift her back to heaven but at least I cared about her. I believed I could protect her from the rest of the putrid filth that lingered just beyond the shadows. While looking into her eyes I told her with confidence "Nothing will happen to you while you're with me. I'll kill any dirty fuckers that come near us!"

She smiled a little and we just sat there for a while until she broke the silence, "I wonder if Chris will ever come back?"

I could see a different look come over her when she spoke of Chris. So I asked "Why; do like him?" My heart broke when she said she had a crush on him for years. I felt stupid for believing anyone among the living would ever feel something for the living dead. I was just rotting street garbage and I could tell she did not believe I could be her hero. Now that she had purged her misery she just wanted to go back into denial. I wasn't about to dig into her wound's any further, so we went about playing house.

We spent the day making our campsite a little cozier. In the burning bright sunlight I was spellbound by her beauty. I did not see the bruises or the dirt. I only saw her. Her eyes mesmerized me as I listened to her every silly, foolish word. At one point she asks me if I ever think about marriage, kids, and all that since we are playing house. I tell her "I'm already dead there is no life for me!" She laughs. I am not sure if it was because she thought it was a joke or because she believed it. I did not tell her how I felt or my story. We just went about pretending we are having fun camping. Long term abuse victims are able to hide their injuries longer because their tolerance for pain grows very high. That day I could tell Lisa was at her threshold and I tried to comfort her best I could.

Later, near sundown, Chris returns and he is not alone. Marlene is with him. Apparently, it's Friday and Marlene can stay out late. They brought more snacks and soda, also Chris has half a bottle of tequila his mom "lost." They even have a couple joints. Lisa drinks heavy gulps from the bottle right away to kill her pain. We spent the night laughing, smoking, and drinking. The stars light up the night sky. In the starlight Lisa looked so radiant that the world around her looked like a better place. Lisa was drunk and clinging to me trying to keep warm. As I looked into her eyes, I silently cursed God for letting this happen to her. I could see in her eyes that something was missing from her soul, something stolen that could never be returned. I never really hated God for letting bad things happen to me, but I couldn't rationalize how someone as sweet and angelic as Lisa would be undeserving of God's love and protection. All the things I thought I knew about God began to fall away and were replaced with angst.

At one point Chris and Marlene fucked in the tent while Lisa and I sat awkwardly silent by the small fire. Lisa leaned closer to me in the cold night. I felt her shaking. She is cold and the alcohol she drank was not sitting well. Thankfully, Chris and Marlene finished up and left to walk back into town. I ask Chris if he is coming back. He just laughed as they disappear into the dark woods. Lisa was very drunk and falling asleep, so I gently carried her into the tent and covered her with both blankets. She does not look radiant anymore. She looks tied and pale. Her shine and her strength were fading. I knew exactly how it felt to ride a temporary high just before the bubble bursts and reality slams you back to earth. After gently tucking Lisa in, I returned to the fire.

The fire burned away and finally out as I stared into it contemplating all that had happened. I did not care for my soul anymore, it was nothing. I stopped worrying about what might happen to me the night I died. Now that she was here with me everything changed. I felt compassion again. I worried about her. I did not want her to rot away like I had. I was scared again, and all the questions of reality were beginning to soak through into the twisted dream I'd been living.

I prayed for her in the dark before I crawled into the tent. I felt like we were lepers cast into the wilderness. I tried to fall asleep next to her. I was very cold as I lay next to her with no blanket. I was afraid to reach out and comfort her. She sobs in her sleep, and I want to touch her but I was afraid I might be mistaken as an uninvited guest.

All I could do was whisper "You'll be OK I won't let the world hurt you anymore" as I touched her hair. Tears ran from my eyes as I laid there feeling weak and powerless to help her.

I stared into the dark, questioning my God, my faith, and myself. Maybe I was a demon bred in hate or maybe an angel fallen from grace? I did not know what to believe now that Lisa was in my life. She changed everything. The nightmare I lived in where I did not exist was shattered! I now had to exist or there was no way to save her! She made me want to be alive again.

I awoke alone. I hated waking up alone and with Lisa missing it felt extra bitter. The early morning sun was slowly turning the dark comfort to oven heat inside the small tent. I did not want to open the tent flap. I was fearful that I might have scared Lisa away. I was not ready to face another day alone. I was relieved when I emerged to find Lisa sitting by the burned-out fire pit. She was staring into it, as though it still burned. I could relate, wishing my life were not so burned out.

She did not break her fixed stare on the blackened coals until I told her, "I can't let you suffer we need medicine, bandages, more food and water. We must go into town."

She looked back at me with panic "I can't go! She will find me and . . ."

I stopped her and reminded her of my promise to keep her safe. She rose to her feet and began to cry as she embraced me. I held her there and kissed her forehead. I wished this embrace was a sign she loved me, but her fear of being alone could be felt in her body as she held tighter. Perhaps the thought of staying there alone was more terrifying than being found by her mother, or perhaps it was the hunger building up within the both of us. Either way I eventually convinced her to go back into town with me.

We had no money, so I stole aspirin and some bandages from a busy drugstore. I knew that she could not survive on the street. She was starting to look like just another victim. I wanted her to go somewhere safe, but Lisa's paranoia wouldn't allow it. She was in a frantic state of shock all day. She would not allow me to tend her wounds; she took the aspirin but denied her scars or the noticeable limp she now walked with was real. She was impatient to get back to the safety of the camp site. She hid in the shadows as I scavenged for supplies. I never shared my true feelings or fears with her. We both went about the day in denial until we returned to the campsite.

When we returned to the campsite, we found everything destroyed. Nothing was stolen, but instead shredded, ripped, and torn. Bits of the tent were everywhere and what was left of the sleeping bag was smoldering in the fire. Our snacks were ground into the dirt. Our last soda was dumped out. The crushed can lay there amongst the debris. We only had half-baked ideas of who had done this. Lisa's imagination ran wild. She thought her mom somehow found out where we were and came here and destroyed the campsite. I did not know what to think. Maybe Danny was still mad about not getting his share of weed and had somehow followed us. Maybe one of the house kids that we ditched found it?

Unbeknown to any of us at the time, there was a small illegal pot field just up the hillside. Either the police or the owner of the weed had trashed our campsite. In any case our stuff was trashed so we had to leave the forest.

Back on the streets we had to find some place inside, fast. Lisa's paranoia was at an insane level and growing worse by the minute now that the campsite had been destroyed. Lisa insisted cameras in the sky were following her and at any minute her mother would leap forth and kill us. We headed for "Mom's" because it was the only place I knew. When we arrived, it was past dark. The family: Peewee, Mom and Jim were already pretty drunk. Peewee let us in with contempt in her eyes. I explained we needed a place to crash or just hang out for a while.

Mom instantly said "Fuck no! No runaways are staying here!"

Jim could smell the desperation and interjects "Maybe they can work for some money like the rest of us."

An evil glint came over Mom's face "Yes" she says, "maybe you and your cute little friend can earn some money by entertaining us?"

Lisa (still naïve) asks "How?"

I cut her off by saying "I don't think so."

Peewee staring with contempt at Lisa says, "Come on, don't you want to fuck your skinny little friend for us?" Lisa's face went instantly red, and she ran outside. I turned quickly and followed her out of this nut house.

"We'll take just you honey. Come back when you change your mind." Jim said as he closed the door. Their demonic laughter echoed through our heads as we walked into the night.

I confided with Lisa "I'm sorry I don't know what I was thinking. Those assholes are the only people I know with their own place, and I don't really even know them. The truth is I don't have anywhere to go. We'll have to come up with someplace on our own."

"That's ok it's not your fault adults are assholes! We don't have to be inside; I just need to go somewhere and rest for a little while. I'm so tired of walking around" she said as she put her arm around me.

We had to find someplace safe. All the places I once took refuge were no longer safe. I did not even want to tell her about Danny's shit car. Paranoia is a cruel master. It makes you go deep into the dark, to the places light itself is afraid to go. I remembered one such place; an abandoned mini mall we passed by when we went camping. It was a small complex with the front glass windows all broken out. With no other options we went there.

We were not the only ones seeking shelter. Inside there were drunks and junkies sleeping and drinking. Someone was mumbling under their breath as we crept though the structure. The vampires and zombies did not seem to notice us. The vampires were too busy injecting fresh blood into their veins and the zombies were drowning in the bottom of a bottle.

We found a small room towards the back. It seemed the drunks and junkies kept mostly near the front of the building where some light from the street kept it dimly lit. We went into the dark where no one wanted to be. We curled up in the corner. I pulled a scrap of dirty cardboard around us both for warmth and camouflage. A long day of walking had made us both very tired, but I found it impossible to rest. The grumbling wino eventually stopped but the silence that followed became an invisible monster of infinite size. I was sure it would crush me if I dozed off. The silence of the night would be broken briefly as cars passed by. I opened my eyes as the headlights reflected across some of the interior giving me a quick chance to check for safety. In those brief moments of light Lisa would look at me, smile and hold me tighter making us both feel a little better.

When morning broke it was quite cold inside the concrete tomb. We went outside, past the wino zombies and junkie vampires. In the bright morning sun, I can clearly see Lisa. I wondered to myself if I was meant to be here? Was it my destiny to save Lisa from the nightmare I was a part of or had she come to save me? Was it our destiny to escape from hell together? Why were we both lost and thrown away? I desperately wanted things to make sense again but they didn't. I shook the confused thoughts from my mind. She was not dead like me. She carried a heavy sadness but there was still hope for her and right now I was that hope. I had to find a way to lift her back up to where she belonged. Her hair was a mess now, entangled like mine. Lisa's clothes were soiled from camping and sleeping on the ground. To most she looked like just another reject, some street trash, but to me she still looked like the most beautiful angel I had ever seen.

She stopped to tie her shoe when I noticed the wet spot on her back where her wings should have been. The blisters from her burns must have broken and the pus was beginning to mat up in her shirt. Lisa was in too much pain to deny anything was wrong. She no longer needed to be convinced something was very wrong. I told her I had to do something about her open wounds. We decided to head for the park and its public bathrooms.

In the woman's bathroom I helped her peel her shirt off. Our eyes locked and she could see the desire in my heart. That's when she asked "Why didn't you ever make a move on me? Do you think I'm ugly? I'm I too much valley girl not enough heavy metal for you?"

Still a little embarrassed I wanted to I tell her I thought she was beautiful and that I had always thought that. Instead, I mumbled "I'm just shy."

She whispers "You don't have to be shy anymore" and she catches me by surprise with a passionate kiss on the mouth. As quick as she kissed me she spins around to expose her burned back. I was stunned by the kiss and drowned in the moment briefly before the sight of her burns brought me back to reality. I cleaned her wounds the best I could and applied the bandages I stole the day before. I gave her my shirt to wear while we washed hers in the sink. We then decided to see if Chris was home. Lisa's mom did not know Chris or where he lived so Lisa felt safe going there. With a little luck we hoped we could shower and eat there.

We walked hand in hand. I had never before felt wanted or needed like this. I imagined this must be what love felt like. She liked me! The shock and excitement of my first kiss swimming in my mind must have gotten my guard down. We were walking in the clouds when just as suddenly as she kissed me; reality once again crushed us hard into the earth.

Like glass shattering, tires screeched on the pavement behind us, breaking the silence of our peaceful world. We turned to look. It was Lisa's mother and her new boyfriend. Lisa just stood there frozen in shock as her mother jumped from the truck and grabbed her still bruised arm. Lisa cried out in pain. I tried to separate Lisa from her mother but was punched in the stomach and thrown down by her mother's boyfriend. Her mother screamed at me as she pulled Lisa inside the truck "Stay away from my daughter, you degenerate." Lisa was kicking, screaming, and reaching out for me. I tried to get up but was kicked in the chest. With the wind knocked out of me all I could do was lie there and try to catch my breath as they drove away.

As they took her away, beyond the horizon of my reality I screamed! "Fuck, Fuck, Fuck!" I cursed at the same sky I had loved only moments before. I was once again abandoned with the rage that grew from a belief that God hated me. I staggered to my feet and continued towards Chris's apartment. Not only did they take Lisa they also had my fuckin shirt. I would have to make do with Lisa's wet shirt.

Lisa showed me a place beyond the pointless circle I was trapped in. I could not just walk away. I forgot about Chris and changed direction towards home. Lisa had my heart and I had to follow it. I had to know if she was ok. Twisted thoughts of her being slaughtered in the woods swirled in my head. I went back to the apartment complex that Lisa and I had once called home. I went around to the empty lot right behind Lisa's apartment. Through a hole in the fence, I could see my dad's truck all washed and clean. Lisa's apartment was dark and closed up. Once again, I didn't know what to do.

I was so tired I could feel the roots break free from the soil to grab and pull me under. I knew there was a nasty old mattress stuffed into one corner of the lot because Chris bragged about tag teaming some girl on it. It was not hard to find but the spot it was in was surprisingly secluded. All the surrounding apartments had eight-foot-tall fences running around them and there was one corner where two complexes came together at odd angles. The odd angles created a small space in-between and in that space under the shade of a tree I found the filthy mattress. I was so exhausted from walking and lack of food that I had no trouble falling into a deep sleep. My dreams were haunted by thoughts of what may have happened to Lisa.

When I awoke it was dark. I rubbed the terrible dreams out of my eyes, stumbled to my feet and headed towards the hole in the fence. As I approached it, I could see two figures sitting on the stone slab. I was a little leery when I saw it was Phillip and Danny smoking a joint.

As I walked up Danny instantly pipes up "Hey guy, where's the pot you owe me?"

I did not know where this shit was coming from, and I told him "I don't owe you anything. And as far as the pot Ken 'paid' us with, Chris took all of that. I'm just like you, bummed out and fucked over."

Danny smiled and handed me the joint. As we smoked, I could see the lights in Lisa's room come on through the hole in the fence. I took a big hit and went through the hole to get a closer look.

I tried to sneak up close enough to Lisa's window to get a peek inside when I was spotted. I could hear Lisa's mom yelling, "Get the hell out of here you junkie scum!"

I could see the boyfriend going for the door leading outside so I ran back towards the fence. He chased me through the fence and halfway across the lot. He was not nearly fast enough to catch me and probably wasn't really trying. From a safe distance I could hear him yelling "She isn't even here. Stay away or I'll call the cops!" I felt defeated and banished to my pointless circle.

When I was chased through the fence Danny and Phillip ran off as well. I could tell by the direction they were headed where they were going. It was always better to not be alone, so I too headed for the park. The park was a very different place at night. I did not care for the hate filled unwelcome stares from the family crowd during the day. The only thing worse was the leers from the undead at night. When I did not find the boys right away, I just wanted to use the amenities and disappear back into the shadows.

I was leaving when Phillip showed up laughing at me "You ran out of there so fast I thought you'd catch fire." After I explained Lisa feared for her life and ran away, Phillip told me Lisa's mom took a bunch of stuff from Lisa's room to the Dumpster earlier in that day. He handed me the "Slayer" cassette tape that I had given to Lisa earlier that year. I grabbed it. Surprised by how fast I grabbed it Phillip said, "You can have it I don't want it."

I was already worried about Lisa and this new information had my brain spinning in a blender of despair! "No sign of Lisa though, huh?" I pressed for details.

"Nope" was all he said.

Later I went back to Lisa's apartment but there was still no sign of her. I was just a few dozen steps from my home. I was SOOO hungry that I almost went there. No matter how much nostalgia I felt for home I could not go back. I was not the same person that walked away. I wasn't a naïve, mindless sheep filled with life, unaware of the butcher's axe. I was so much more aware now and like all wild creatures had learned to fear the hand of man. On pure instinct I ran back into the shadows.

It was the most conflicted and confused night of my life. I had selfish motives when I wanted to find something meaningful in my pitiful excuse for a life. I wanted Lisa to love me and at the same time I did not want to drag her down into my filth. I struggled with my own beliefs as if God were testing me. Maybe I was meant to be Lisa's savior or maybe I was a demon luring her to death. I hoped my love for Lisa would be enough for God to forgive my wretched soul and let me back into his favor. For the moment I was out of ideas and energy. It was too late for me to change the day. I headed back towards the only place I thought I might find some company, Danny's car.

# CHAPTER 8

## Once you get close, you're in too deep

When I arrived at the steel coffin it was abandoned. "Just as well I deserve to be alone" I thought to myself as I sat alone under a nearby tree.

I was about to leave when I saw people coming. I was somewhat relieved to see it was Danny headed this way, but I wasn't exactly thrilled to see Danny had company. They were talking so loudly I could hear their conversation as they approached. Its lame ass Jeff, he had apparently stolen a bottle of cheap whiskey among other things. I could see Danny and Jeff taking turns pulling off the bottle as they crossed the forgotten lot that the car rested in. As they reached the car, I was thinking about fading back into the shadows when Danny noticed me sitting under the tree.

"Holy fuck! What are you doing hiding in the dark dude!" Danny blurts out nearly dropping the bottle.

"I'm not hiding, I got nowhere to go man, so I'm just hanging here. Is that cool buddy?"

Danny instantly smiles when I call him buddy. "Fuckin cool by me, wanna drink?" He slurs while putting the bottle forward.

I hate myself right now and the bottle swears she has all the love I seek. I toke an extra-long drink from the bottle before handing back to Danny. "Thanks buddy I needed that."

In between drinks Danny and Jeff were taking turns smoking hits of Anbesol, yes Anbesol the tooth numbing liquid. It smelled awful and only a fucked-up brain could even think of such a ridiculous idea. I hated myself but was not interested in joining them. I was truly glad the two brainless zombies were fixated on their insane method of getting high. They paid little attention to me or how much of the whiskey I was drinking. Not long after the bottle was gone Danny passed out against the car. Jeff took several pulls at the empty bottle before he eventually stumbled off into the darkness.

I crawled into the back of the car. I sat alone, spinning in the back of the lifeless shell of a car. I felt like a passenger on a journey to hell. Swirling downward to my demise I pulled at Lisa's small pink stained shirt trying to stretch more of it over my dead skin. I no longer felt like breathing I just wanted this perpetual nightmare to end. The small shirt was choking me with guilt over what may have happened to Lisa. I tried to protect her and failed. I loved Lisa but I was alone, cold, hungry, and afraid. I was powerless to help her. Desperation has a way of devouring any sense of hope or purpose and shitting out self-preservation.

Early the next day I was startled when someone pounded on the top of the car. I was half hoping it was the police or the angel of death ending my nightmare. I sat up and was surprised to see Chris. "What the fuck happened to you? I looked all over for you guys, when I went back to the campsite and found it was all trashed. Fuck, I thought you guys were eaten by bears or some shit!"

Rubbing the sleep out of my eyes with despair in my voice I replied, "I wish I had been eaten by a fuckin bear!"

Chris noticed I was wearing Lisa's pink shirt and asks, "What the Fuck are you wearing?"

I told him about what happen to Lisa while pulling at the shirt trying to make it fit. I told Chris how they stole Lisa wearing my shirt away and all I had left was her wet shirt when they rode off. I was embarrassed to show weakness, so I skipped the part where I got knocked down.

Chris could care less about Lisa or my problems, He only lived in the now. He interrupted my ramblings "I work for Ken full time now," as he nods towards Ken sitting in his truck at the edge of the lot. "I knew I'd find Danny here but finding you is even better. Ken has a job for us, come on let's go!" The car feels and smells like a coffin in the early morning sun. There was no doubt left in my mind. I had become the living undead. Once again, some unknown force pulls me from my grave, brings my flesh back to life again. Again, I must bear the pain of the day I was not meant to see.

The sun was unforgiving as Chris kicked at Danny and insulted him with an assortment of curses as we made our way over to the truck. "Morning my motley Crew", Ken laughs as the band played on the trucks cheap stereo. I had a ruthless hangover and struggled to climb in the back of the truck. Once in it I tried my best to fall back asleep. I assumed we were going to drive into the hills and load and unload wood all day but this time Ken drove into a rundown industrial part of the city. I didn't have any clue or care where we were. I did notice a small diner out of place among the assortment of abandoned buildings, factories and warehouses. All the structures here looked like the great beasts of yesteryear gathered together here to die.

We pulled into one of the lots. On this particular lot there were two buildings, a small storefront/ office near the road and a medium sized warehouse building on the back of the lot. The rest of the fenced-in lot was covered with blown trash, empty barrels, hundreds, maybe thousands of broken pallets stacked high. Various bits of debris, dusty and dirty were randomly scattered about like someone left it 20 years earlier and never looked back. We drove a small loop around and parked near the storefront. Ken and Chris were deeply engaged in their conversation, completely ignoring Danny and I. Ken pulled keys from his pocket, opened the front door and Ken and Chris went inside. Danny and I just sat in the truck because we were not privy to whatever was said inside the cab. Chris must have thought we were because he was frustrated to have to come back outside and yelled at us, "Come inside you dumb fuckers!"

Just Inside the door was a small room. The front was lined with a row of full-length showroom glass windows overlooking the street. The opposing wall had a long countertop running along the entire length of the room. The counter had room behind it for salespeople or whatever. There was a drawbridge type thing in the middle to allow passage behind the long counter. Beyond the counter and through a door there was a small hallway leading outside and to two other doors. On the right there was a small shop of some kind. Remnants of rusted tools and a vise bolted to the bench were all that were left now. Through the left door there was an office that still contained a 1940 style desk and chair. The office also had an attached small bathroom with a sink. I did not often have a chance to use private indoor plumbing. I made a beeline for the bathroom as soon as I saw it. The water from the sink sputtered and spat brown liquid until finally running somewhat clear. The toilet was brown and filthy from hard water stains.

When I came out of the bathroom there were lines of crystal meth and beers on the desk. "You're up" Chris said as he handed me the straw. I did not really want to do more drugs but the time I spent sober felt like a slap in the face. God was just taunting me with the truth and things I could never have. Drugs were the lies I needed to hear to survive. I snorted my line and everything in my world made a drastic sharp turn.

Time twisted and bent as it was sucked down the spiral and up my nose. Days could be weeks; months could have been hours. The drugs were quickly changing something in my brain. Things became increasingly more distorted. Even as I think about it now, I still cannot be sure of how much time I spent "working" for Ken at the shop. Time no longer meant anything to me. Day or night, it did not matter; from here on out the only thing that consumed my mind was the next line and what I had to do to get it!

I was high as a kite when Ken announced his new business plan. He told us he had made a deal to buy this lot for the purpose of converting it into a reconditioned battery shop. Ken explained how lots of car shops had old dead batteries laying around. We could get paid to remove the old car batteries that had lost their charge. Then you take those batteries; wash them, add new acid, recharge them and slap on a new sticker to be resold. Ken's father had a string of these shops and was ready to give Ken a shot at his own shop. But before we could get things started, we had to clean the store front and clear out any debris left in the warehouse. Ken's plan was very convincing. He genuinely believed this was his big shot at life. He only had to set up one last "business deal" to retain cash for batteries and we would all be in business together. Even a wise man can be misled by golden, shiny plans only to find nothing but dirt. I was the living dead, so I believed and daydreamed down that river without reservation.

I was so busy working I did not notice the days speed past me. It was a lot of work cleaning and painting the store front. The small warehouse was far worse. Inside the warehouse there was one small, well-insulated empty room, probably used for noisy air compressors, and the rest was full of more busted pallets. It appeared the previous owner was in the business of reconditioning pallets and probably went broke. There were not any tools left but all the workbenches, stacks of pallets, and barrels with replacement boards were still here waiting the next shift. Ken wanted the whole warehouse cleared. Once we cleared everything out, Ken had us make two rows of the best pallets on the floor.

We were never paid and rarely ever fed. No one ever complained because we all believed in Ken's plan, and we had an endless supply of crystal meth, soda and beer. I didn't like being drunk and wired at the same time. Mixing the two always made me feel like a marionette with its strings all tangled. Mostly I drank a lot of Pepsi. I remember it well because I drank so much soda and never ate that I would get sick and vomit out black syrup. Somehow that became part of my normal routine. Do some work, do some lines, drink some soda, vomit, wipe face, do more lines, do more work, drink more Pepsi. I really do not know how long this vicious circle went on. Every time I came to the part of the circle where I had to decide to get out or go round again I kept going around. I believed something was at the end of the spinning tunnel and if I kept pushing ahead eventually, I'd get there.

I really believed we were going to be a legitimate business. In theory it all made sense, just make old batteries new for profit. I daydreamed of taking over the business one day, working hard for an honest day's pay and all the other American dream bullshit. I remembered Lisa and daydreamed about enough money to find and rescue her from whatever terrible fate. Then I feared she may already be dead. I thought about calling the police but what were they going to do besides laugh when I told them "An extremely paranoid girl on drugs believes her mother is going to kill her!" I wanted to leave and look for her, but I had no idea where she was. Hell, I did not even know where I was! It bothered me a lot that I could not be her rescuer because I was so lost that I could never be found. I desperately wanted to help Lisa but I felt there was nothing I could do.

We were going into legitimate business, well sort of. Ken lived his whole life scamming, scheming, and making deals on the side and under the table. Ken made one legitimate deal with his father; the money he made from the wood scam was enough for Ken's father to gain enough confidence to lease Ken the lot and the equipment needed. At the same time, unknown to me, Ken made another side deal with two "Russian" Brothers. The battery shop was to be merely a front for their crystal meth lab. Apparently, the smell from these labs was quite strong and often brought unwanted attention. Our new business partners believed the smell could be explained away by telling people it was just the smell from the acid and recharging batteries. Ken found a perfect location because no one ever did complain about the odd chemical smells.

The first time I met the brothers I thought they were the property owners. They came to the lot one day and while speaking to Ken, I overheard them say they were happy things looked good in what I thought was a Russian accent. I do not know for sure if they were

Russian or even brothers. It was just that they spoke some fucked up broken English; they both dressed very similarly and never, ever were called by name. So, I called them the Russian brothers. Ken talked with them briefly in the warehouse building, gave them some cash which I assumed was rent and they left.

I would not find out what we were really up to until it would be too late to back out. I was so dead inside I kept paddling closer to the eye of the whirlpool wanting to be pulled under! I just went along with the flow. I never cared where the money for the drugs or the drugs themselves came from. I was just the undead wandering without significance until I was brought back to serve my new master.

Once we finished cleaning the place up, Ken had to setup what he called "a meeting" with a guy whose name turned out to be Guy. We were told we needed cash to buy batteries and Ken was going to ask Guy to invest in the business. Guy liked to party so we were all invited to "the meeting". We were all pretty excited that we would soon be open for biz. It also had been a while since anyone beside Ken left the shop. In the back of the crappy old truck with the wind blowing through my hair I started daydreaming about Lisa and somehow finding her.

# CHAPTER 9

## The worst is yet to come

We drove to a cheap hotel near an airport. It was the kind of place people did not go to for the amenities. As we walked to the room a jet was landing overhead. It flew over so close it felt like you could grab it, and after it passed the sound was loud enough to knock you down. When we got to the door Ken used some silly code knock, but Guy still demanded to know who was there. Ken told him to quit fucking around and open the door.

The door opened to reveal an old man. Guy was, by my guess, in his mid-fifties. A once large, powerful man was now wasting away. Guy had retired early, quite wealthy and didn't mind throwing his life savings away now that he had contracted throat cancer. The doctor told him his outlook was grim (which you could hear in his voice). He spoke in a low, distorted tone due to the flesh missing from his frail neck. The scars from his most recent surgery were hidden under a large bandage he wore across his neck. Another plane was making its approach to land, the building began to rattle and shake as we entered. I was delighted to find the super-hot twins were there doing tiny lines off the coffee table when we arrived. They both were all dolled up; dressed even sluttier than usual.

I forgot we were here for a "meeting" when Ken threw a large bag of crystal on the table. Guy was taken aback by the sheer amount of powder before him. Guy bought drugs from Ken before but never any quantity this large. His eyes lit up, "Holy shit! This is the new stuff?" he asked Ken. Ken nodded "Check it out, best yet, 100% pure". Guy chopped and snorted a large line. When his heart went into overdrive he produced a large money roll, counted out a couple hundred, handed it to Ken, and then gave each of the twins a twenty. Without being told the girls rolled the twenties into straws and began to chop lines out for themselves.

We spent hours snorting, drinking and partying. All the while Guy was grabbing the twins and asking for sexual favors. The twins pretended it was all just in fun and resisted (in front of us). But when Guy insisted everyone but the twins go on a beer run I'm sure it was more than lines Guy was doing while we were gone. When we returned the girls were gone and Guy was now wearing his bathrobe. No one speaks of it, but we all had ideas of what transpired. Hours and many lines disappear, time blurred until Ken said, "It's time to go."

I didn't want to leave ever since the twins left Guy, had been making "Too good to be true" promises. In my desperate undead state I was easy to con and I believed him. He did not promise anything sick or obscene. He promised me I would get food and a place to stay in exchange for helping him out around the house. He promised he could give me back all the things I missed, clean clothes, shelter and food. If that were not enough he also promised to supply any and all the drugs I needed. The thought of sleeping inside on a bed instead of on the dirty old ground was the one thought that made me say yes to his deal! I suspected nothing could go wrong. I was desperate and undead, still craving life. I wanted to live again. In my mind I thought he just had sex with the twins and never once did I ever think there would be any danger to me. I was still a virgin, and I had no idea how lust ruled the male mind. Besides drugs, the only desire I ever had was for Lisa and that was pure hearted not perverted.

The rest of the crew, however, knew what was in store and they urged me to go with them. As a true friend, Chris whispered in my ear "Guy will try to fuck you". But the drugs and alcohol made Guy's lies irresistible. The zombie in me did not want to wander the streets anymore. The human left in me just wanted something better. The drug addict growing inside me wanted to be closer to drugs without all the demanding work. The naive child wanted so much to believe that there was good in everyone. At the pathetic center of my dead soul, I just wanted to be of some value to anyone. Lisa was gone and with no hope of finding her she may have as well been a dream. Ken seemed almost pleased to leave me there, but Chris was shaking his head and speaking with his eyes in a last ditch effort to talk me out of staying when the boys left.

Not more than ten minutes after the boys left Guy says, "I'm tired." He needed to rest, and he wanted me to help him out of his socks.

"Forget about your socks just pass out", I told him.

He began to swear and curse in the same frustrated, angry tone my father used when he wanted me to do something. He says "I'm too old and too drunk to bend over and remove my socks and I can't sleep with them on." He goes on to whine about how "you made this deal to help me out and the first thing I asked you to do, you refuse?"

I didn't see any harm in helping him and really wanted him to shut up so I could sleep. I knelt before him trying to help when he brutally grabbed my hair very hard and asked "Is this your first time?"

(My previous ignorance slaps me), "What!" I exclaimed and began to rise when he grabbed my hair now with both hands and tried to force me toward him.

"Such pretty hair" the disgusting fuck says. I was trying to come to terms with what was happening all the while his limp dick was hanging in front of me. He was still trying, with all his drugged out might, to force me closer. I resisted and broke free. I turned in full panic and ran for the door. I was struggling with the lock when he hit me from behind with something heavy. The force of the blow propelled me forward. Last thing I remembered was my face slamming into the door then falling to the floor. Then the empty void surrounded me.

The blood flowing from my head wound into my eyes and nose brought me back from the beyond. I was on the floor struggling to regain consciousness. I could feel him on top of me trying desperately to get his dick hard with one hand and pulling at my pants with the other. The warm blood running from my head was pooling up under my face, reminding me that I still had some life left. I had to either fight death or let go and embrace darkness forever. Lisa's voice cried out in my mind, "You can't let it end like this! I need you" I had to dig deep to find the strength to live again. I grabbed out for something, anything. I latched onto a glass ashtray that had fallen off the dresser. I gathered every ounce of hate in my heart, turned the hate into rage and swung. BANG! I hit him somewhere in the head. He fell back silent. The blood running into my eyes made everything red and blurred. Nothing would come into focus. I pulled my pants up and crawled a few feet to lump myself against the wall. I sat stunned and confused.

After what felt like days compressed into seconds, panic, shock, and adrenaline set in. "What the FUCK just happened?" I thought, still holding the ashtray. I held it up so I could try getting a better look at it and hopefully bring reality back into focus. It shakes back and forth in my hand. I used my other hand to steady the object so I could see it. Blood drips from the glass. Dazed and very confused I rose to my feet and began to survey the scene. I froze in place when I saw the money roll that strayed from Guys pocket lying on the floor beside him. The money seemed less than fair compensation for the day's labor, but it would have to do. I threw the ashtray down, grabbed the money, wiped some of the blood off my face, spit on the still motionless Guy and left.

The shadows comforted me as I slithered between them and ran. I had no fucking idea where I was. I was completely lost and feeling like a very small fish in a very big shark tank. Anyone who doesn't understand addiction won't understand why I made the next bad choice in my life. I had a pocket full of money and a romantic idea of saving a girl. I still question why I didn't chase that impossible dream. I had just been raped after a prolonged drug binge. To say I wasn't thinking straight would be an understatement. I wasn't thinking about Lisa, I wasn't thinking about the wound on my head, I wasn't thinking about Guy lying dead in the hotel, I was only thinking about how I could get some more crystal. I had become a zombie, living only for the lure of the next high. Naturally I sought out the only dealers of death I knew.

I walked several blocks away and found a pay phone to call the battery shop. Ken answered a little shocked since there are only a very select few that had the phone number. I told Ken something had gone wrong and I begged him to pick me up!

Ken just laughed, "We all fucking tried to tell you what would happen."

I interrupt, "That's not why I called . . . I think Guy's dead!" Panic was now evident in my voice. I did not want to say more over the phone, so I begged "Please Ken I've got money, lots of it".

Ken went silent for a second then replied with a serious voice, "Where the fuck are you?" I relayed the cross streets, and he told me about a pancake place a little ways up the road. "Go there and stay there until I get there" he now demands of me. I desperately wanted to wash away this nightmare. I wasted no time going to the diner.

The waitress gave me dirty looks as soon as I walked in. I took a table by the window and put twenty bucks down on the table. An extremely pretty but clearly overworked redhead named Michele came over to my table and grabbed the money. When she first headed toward my table, she held a hatred for all the filthy homeless coming in here for one cup of Joe, and chasing any good tippers away but when she looked at me and the apparent wound on my head her heart opened.

She smiled awkwardly at me trying not to show her pity, "Are you ok?"

I wasn't thinking about the blood or wound on my head when I assured her, I was fine "Living on the streets can be hard, I have money and just need to sit down for a bit"

"Ok you can stay but you have to order something, so what will you have?"

I had to think about it for a moment, crystal meth destroyed my appetite. Food was something my body no longer wanted. I order a soda and some toast. The few customers that linger during the graveyard shift look at me in disgust as they eat their food. I figured I had better try to freshen up if I didn't want to draw any more attention to myself.

I retreat to the bathroom. One look inside the mirror was like gazing into hell. My skin was a pale yellow and it felt like bugs were feeding on me underneath it. My teeth felt lose and I had dark bags under my sunken eyes. The crack in my skull stopped hemorrhaging when it finally clotted in my tangled and knotted hair. My face still had bits of dried blood on it. My clothes now resembled rags; stained and torn. I truly looked like the damned. I tried to clean the blood from my face but I couldn't stand the image in the mirror, so I bought some smokes from the vending machine and returned to my table by the window.

The plate of toast and glass of soda are waiting. My undead body treats food like an enemy. I cannot bring myself to eat more than a couple bites of toast before I feel nauseous. It is not just my stomach that doesn't feel right. The entire dinner feels different. The clean plate, the soda in a glass, the people eating all fit this surreal nightmare, but I do not remember why I am here. A deadly silence stifled the air as I flic at my lighter trying to light the shaking cigarette in my hand.

I only smoked half that cigarette before I noticed Ken pulling into the parking lot. He did not come inside, and I didn't care. Being out in the open public eye was overwhelming. I was pretty sure the waitress was in the back calling the cops when I left. She came out trying to stop me in concern for my injury but I was so nervous I forgot about the twenty I put on the table when I came in and thought she wanted money, I gave Michele another twenty and mumble "thanks I'm fine" as I pushed past her and left.

I jumped in the truck before Ken high tailed it out of there. Once clear of the diner I told Ken "I think I killed Guy."

"What the fuck do mean you killed Guy?" Ken looked puzzled like he couldn't figure how a little scrawny one hundred pound kid could kill anyone.

After I told him what happened he decided to go back to the motel. Ken wanted to find out if Guy was really dead or just left for dead. I couldn't see the room from where Ken parked. I figured he didn't want his truck seen when he parked at the far end of the parking lot next door. I stayed behind while Ken went to check it out. The early morning sun was beaming directly at me. I was burning away inside the truck along with Ken's dirty laundry and assorted garbage. The heat and awful smells rising were too much, I couldn't hold it all in, I ran behind the truck and vomited everything in me out. The sickly smell of alcohol makes me dry-heave. Eventually I pulled myself together and crawled back into the truck. I smoked the rest of my cigarettes just to get the taste of puke out of my mouth. I was crashing hard and impact was imminent.

After an eternity of sweating out the nightmares running through my mind Ken finally returns and says, "You're in big trouble kiddo!"

"Oh God, is he dead?" I asked, now in a full panic again.

"Where's the money roll Guy had?" was Ken's only reply.

"The money? Yeah, I got it right here" and I handed Ken the money, I didn't even think about it. My mind was racing and I couldn't think straight, I was in full panic, freak-out mode. Ken could tell I was vulnerable and he used it.

"Good", Ken smiled "As long as you've got the money it's all cool. I won't tell anyone what happened and you'll be safe just as long as you never tell anybody about what happened here".

Relieved I reply, "Like I want to tell anyone some gross old guy tried to rape me."

I was so relieved I didn't even realize that Ken never said whether Guy was dead or alive. Ken cut out a fat line to calm my nerves. I snort it and the numbing blur set in. The great nothing was washing away all my cares about Guy or the money. My only thoughts were of never leaving the safety of the pack again.

On the way back to the shop Ken rambled on about Guy foolishly confiding in him. Guy's cancer treatments were not working. The only thing he had left was a clock ticking away the seconds until he died. Guy did not have any family and even if he did, he would never let someone else get his money. He was determined to spend his money on himself. Guy took all of his savings out of the bank so he could basically party himself to death. Ken used this information to produce a plan of his own to get Guys money.

Ken planned to feed the old guy overpriced drugs till he hopefully had a heart attack. Ken saw it as a no-lose situation. Ken had access to plenty of drugs and liked to party. Guy was an easy mark; He had no idea the street value of drugs. He always paid too much and turned around to give them away in his party lust. Ken also knew Guy liked young people, boys, or girls, and he used this as well. Ken supplied the motel room, the drugs (which Ken did most of), and the girls hoping the combination of young lust and crystal meth would be deadly to Guy's ancient system. And when Guy died of "natural causes" ken planned to take all the money the old fart had left. Ken always rented the "party" room in advance so he would have a key to get back in when guy was dead.

Ken's plan did not include me deciding to stay there or me bashing Guy in the head. But this way was even better for Ken because Guy hadn't dropped dead as soon as Ken had planned. This was the third time Ken set up Guy's party arrangements and Ken was running low on drugs, money, and patience. Ken didn't have a plan B so my phone call fell into his lap like a godsend. My rotting brain told me I had really done the world a favor. The world now had one less twisted old fuck. I envisioned Guy's corpse dragging me down into the earth. I was brought back from my hellish delusion by Ken's voice "Fuck Guy! He partied himself to death!" Ken said, quite pleased with himself and the way he tricked me out of the money. I laughed but inside I still felt remorse, not for the rotting bastard, Guy but for me. I had gone from petty theft to murder. Murder? I thought to myself. NO, not murderer! I convinced myself it was self-defense; after all I really had no choice. Besides, I thought none of this mattered since no one hunted the undead or cared when we killed each other off.

When we returned to the shop Chris and Danny were both immediately making jokes?

"Have fun with Gay?" they taunted as they made blowjob and fucking motions.

Ken in a loud voice, yells at them, "Shut the fuck up! Anyone brings Guy's name up again and I will kick your fucking head off!"

The boys instantly stopped in shock. No one had ever heard Ken talk so loud or so angry. In the office Ken cuts lines out on the desk and after he did one, he began to count the money. It was just shy of five grand.

"You did good kid" Ken smiles and cuts me out a big line. As I snort it, he says, "Now we're ready to get this place up and running. We need a bigger truck to haul batteries so tomorrow I will go into to town to rent a bigger truck. You three make sure the warehouse is ready."

By the next day, any thoughts of Lisa, Guy, or anything besides getting high were far from what was left of my mind. Finalizing the shop and the warehouse were all that mattered. While working I wondered where my desire to live went. I still felt trapped in a pointless circle, but I no longer wanted to get out of it. I still believed we were going into a legitimate business, but I didn't think about spending profits retired in the country. I did not care at all about money. The only desire left in me was for a never-ending supply of drugs. I still did not even know the real reason Ken set this all up. Later that same day the Russian Brothers showed up to collect more money from Ken. I still thought the money paid was for rent. In reality while we were off collecting batteries the brothers would be bringing chemicals and lab supplies in to make more crystal meth

# CHAPTER 10

## Into hell we ride

The next day we crammed into the small U-Haul truck that Ken had rented the day before. We drove away from the coolness of the ocean through the hills and into the desert. I had the unlucky seat next to Ken. Ken was driving and the stick shift was between my legs, so I had to sit kind of sidesaddle each time Ken shifted. The day, just like the plush hills, faded into a dark barren night in a very lonely desert. We drove all night with rarely any other vehicles in sight. The night air felt so good. The sanctity of the night and the landscape made me feel like I could shed my old life away. Like this lone truck in the middle of nowhere my new life was only a meaningless speck on a never-ending horizon. The darkness blacked out any thoughts about Guy, my family, or the life I once lived. But the stars, they reminded me of Lisa. Somewhere unknown and so far away yet burning so bright I could not dispel her image from my mind.

A pitch black night and a never ending road have a way of hypnotizing a person into a deep sleep. As I fell in and out of consciousness Lisa haunted my dreams. I wanted the feeling back that I felt with only her. I dreamed of Lisa, my angel, flying down to the lake of fire to try and pull me free. I was bound by fire as I grasped desperately on to her, but I couldn't be pulled free. I told her to fly on without me, but she would not leave. It was evident the only way to free her was to destroy myself. I let her go and submerged into the flames. If the fire would not release me then at least she could fly away to mourn in a better place. I felt the flames consume me as I was awakened to a new day.

The heat was now rising with the sun coming up over the horizon directly in front of us. I felt like a condemned outcast. I was not given a new life. I was cast into hell to pay for my sins. The sun was God's light burning us for our sins. And this was just daybreak, what other suffering would the day bring, I wondered?

After a few more hours of endless nothing I could see something coming into view on the horizon. Civilization got slowly closer until we arrived in Yuma, Arizona. Yuma is a not so small oasis town with a very large army base. Ken's dad had made a sweet deal with an old army buddy who was stationed on the base. Not only would we have more than enough batteries to get business started but we were also getting paid a rather hefty sum to "dispose" of the dead lead.

Once we were inside the base the soldiers looked at us like we were the enemy. I did not blame them. They lived in a world of neat clean edges and discipline. We lived on the opposite end of the spectrum, in a world of chaos and disorder. We were directed to a hanger and once inside the structure I quickly realized there was a big problem. There were a lot of batteries we were supposed to dispose of. Ken had been too cheap to rent a proper sized truck, or just did not know how many batteries there were. Either way, the truck he rented was way too small. The army men didn't care about our predicament though they did have a good laugh while they completed their assignment. We did not have to do anything. A small squad of men with a forklift loaded the small truck in no time. One of the officers handed Ken a check and we were off. The truck was overloaded and resisted like a beast with a broken back when we rolled out of there.

We made one stop at a gas station before we left town. Ken bought us each one soda and a pack of cigarettes to share. After a good stretch and long overdue trip to the bathroom we crammed back into the somehow shrinking truck.

Before we pulled out Ken asked, "How'd you all sleep last night?"

Danny pipes up right away "I slept great against the window."

"I don't remember sleep", Chris grumbles.

I replied "I had to move every time you shifted so it wasn't me".

Ken pulled the last of the meth he had from his pocket cut out three small lines on a cassette case and told Danny "It's a good thing you got some rest because there isn't enough for you."

Ken, then Chris, then I, each in turn did our line. Oh the sweet numbing haze in my mind thickened as we drove back into the unrelenting cruel desert.

The trip back was truly going to be a long road out of hell. The now overweight truck would only go 35 to 40 miles per hour. We drove the whole day chasing the sun. It felt as if the windshield was a giant magnifying glass, and God was using it to fry us, like a child would do to ants. God was making sure his light was once again focused on our journey. I never hated the sun more than I did that day.

By midday no one had anything left to drink. We were all coming down hard. No one spoke; we all just grumbled silently. Every so often someone moved, and we all pushed and shoved for one more inch of comfort until settling back into our silent discontent. Everyone was sweating profusely and the blower on the truck only blew more stifling air out. My head was pounding from being so dehydrated. My wretched corpse could not feel anymore decayed. Everything hurt. Hours felt like days.

There is a point you reach in the desert where the radio stations die and leave you with the empty air whistling through the window. The only thing good about the crappy truck ken rented was the fact it had a tape deck. The "Slayer" tape I once gave to Lisa had been through a lot; thrown into the dumpster, later retrieved by Phillip, and finally returned to me. "Hell Awaits" was sounding stale when the cassette could take no more and was eaten or melted. It was a bitter-sweet moment, I was glad not to have to hear the same songs grind away over and over. On the other hand, it was the only thing I had to remember Lisa.

The silence that followed was agony. Angered, Ken pulled the tape from the deck and threw it out the window. I watched in the side view mirror as the tape smashed and tumbled down the road. I was reminded of the day Lisa was yanked out of my life. As I watched the tape quickly disappear from the mirror into oblivion I wondered where she was. I prayed that she was OK, and I vowed to God, I would save her if I were granted life once more. I was beyond delusional as the sun set. I could hear Lisa whispering just beyond the hills leading me back from the land of the dead.

It was past dark, and God's light was long gone when we returned to the hills of California. The journey home had taken us twice as long as it had to get there. The truck literally bore the burden and it showed as it struggled with the inclines. We would cheer out when the truck would clear a summit and we could ride sweet gravity back up to speed. The ride in itself was quite scary! The weight would propel us at high velocity only to slow back to a crawl up the next hill. It was daybreak, when we finally arrived back at the shop. And upon pulling in we immediately noticed Bills crappy camper was now parked on the lot.

# CHAPTER 11

## Love thy brother

Nobody liked Bill, not even his family; they pawned him off on one another like the plague. The deal Ken made with his dad had changed to now include his drunken, loser brother. Ken was obviously annoyed about Bill being there, but he had only one thing on his mind right now. After pulling in, the first thing Ken did was to call for more drugs. It had been one hell of a ride and the nasty water from the sink was fought over like gold. Ken was not the worst boss; he did know how to reward the troops after a hard battle. We spent the rest of the night partying.

Not long after Ken returned with more drugs I went outside to pee because Danny had been in the bathroom so long, I was afraid to go in after. I was hidden in the shadows when I saw the Russian brothers pull into the back of the lot. They did not make their presence known but I was curious why they were here so late, so I crept to the edge of the warehouse. Inside I saw the brothers, along with a new guy unload some boxes. One of the brothers' said something in a foreign language to the new guy and they got in the van and left without their friend. I was intrigued by this but not enough to stick my nose in uninvited. Drugs were luring me back to the shop anyway.

It had been one hell of a fucked-up day. It is not easy to crawl back out of hell but I did it. I felt like Dante emerging from hell after defeating death but in truth the drugs and alcohol were pulling me deeper into the earth. Six feet up is a long way to go when you are buried in a grave of delusion. The weight of addiction was like heavy earth that kept me from my vow to look for Lisa. The whole idea of finding Lisa was just a daydreamer's lie, a lie that I told to myself in order to hold on to something real. I did not have a clue where to even begin such a task, let alone complete it! But I felt some comfort telling myself this lie.

It was not long after sun-up when Ken decided party time was over. It was time to get back to work. Ken had a remarkably simple and effective motivational approach to management. None of the workers got any drugs until the task was completed. People always work together better when they share a common goal. People often discredit drug addicts by assuming they are stupid or lazy. Addicts are the most resourceful people on the planet because they have a simple unpolluted goal that they must reach at any cost. Ken knew this simple concept and he knew how to use it to his advantage.

The sun was blazing as we made our way outside. No one was prepared for the shock when we opened the back of the truck. The army guys were not fucking around, the truck was packed to the limit with batteries. We had expected just 12-volt car batteries. There were a lot of regular 12volt batteries but under them were buried massive black boxes. We all speculated they must be tank batteries. None of us had ever seen (nor imagined) a battery that big. The contract was to dispose of batteries. It never specified what kind. At the sight of the massive lead boxes Ken knew this was clearly a task that needed more manpower. I had forgotten Bill was here somewhere, but Ken hadn't and rudely woke his worthless ass demanding he report for duty.

We all burned in the hot sun unloading the batteries. Since we had no forklift, we had to unload everything by hand. This gave Chris and I the perfect opportunity to show Bill, who we now nicknamed Dildo that we did not want him around. Chris and I were up inside the truck and whenever we found a cracked or damaged battery, we would deliberately tip it when handing it down to Dildo so the acid would spill out on him. He probably didn't remember hitting me, but I remembered and for reasons I didn't know, Chris hated him as well. Revenge tasted sweet and I enjoyed the twisted pleasure I derived from spilling acid on him, all the while acting like it was an accident. He complained to Ken.

Ken just laughed and told him "If you don't keep fucking working, I'll throw you and your crappy camper off the lot!"

Funny how alcohol will make a man put up with so much. As long as Bills' half-drunk he did not even feel the acid burning him until later when he freaked out and Ken had to rinse him off with a hose. At that point Bill snapped and complained to Ken "I'm going to tell dad that you've got a bunch of minors doing drugs down here and some stranger making God-knows-what in the back room of the warehouse"

Ken taunted back "You do that Bill" as he sprayed him in the face with the hose. I was in the back of the truck, so I never had a chance to see what the new guy was making but once again my curiosity peaked when Bill brought it up. Bill grumbles an assortment of curses as he went back to his hovel. The truck was half empty, so Ken decided that was enough for today. We went back to the office to do more lines.

Ken's lifelong intolerance of Bill had now grown into a paranoid rage. Ken was infuriated about the possibility of Bill fucking up his big life plan. Gears were already in motion and Kens' new partners were not the kind of people you disappoint. Ken was sweating out the ideas of what might happen to him when he decided something had to be done about Bill. Ken was one slick bastard when he took Bill a "peace" offering bottle. When he returned from delivering it, he wore a malevolent smirk on his face "We will wait till later when he passes out and we will pay that prick a visit."

It was a grueling day, and my rapidly decaying bones were breaking. I was lumped in the corner rising only to take my line. Ken was scary mad and was not shy about sharing his dark intent. When Ken became fixated on something he made it happen. I was trying my best to not be there, to fade back into a dark corner and scratch at the bugs under my skin that were constantly feeding on me. The itching was incessant. In hell there are no corners to hide in. Later that night Ken asked Chris and me to follow him outside. Danny was already passed out from one of the two bottles of whiskey Ken bought earlier. Both bottles were originally meant for Bill. Ken hoped whisky could buy his brothers blind eye but when Bill pushed back earlier it was clear no offering would buy his allegiance.

I followed Chris and Ken outside but as we headed towards Bill's camper, I was held back by the bad mojo the camper possessed. I stopped to light a smoke near one of the many stacks of pallets. Ken and Chris were so focused on their task they did not notice I stopped following them. They walked in and out of the shadows as they crossed the lot. I was blending into the darkness about one hundred feet away from the camper. In the distance I saw Ken and Chris emerge from the shadows and enter the camper. All the years of Ken hating his worthless half-brother now came to a pinnacle at this moment in time. I turned away looking towards the road for any sign of life. There were no cars or people anywhere in sight. The streets were empty. I turned back towards the still camper. Nothing was happening but I stood frozen staring at the great nothing before me, waiting. I could feel the emptiness eating away what was left of me when I heard noise coming from the warehouse.

I went around a corner to peek at the light burning in the warehouse. There was a terrible smell in the air that kept me from going closer. My mind was fried. I had forgotten why I came out here and was just "Zeeking out," the phase of the high when any small thing can distract you from reality and pull you in. I was literally creeping around like an insane specter when I looked towards the camper and saw Ken was now outside the camper. He was sitting on the ground just outside the entrance with the door hanging open.

Chris caught me by surprise when he walked up out of the darkness, "What the fuck happened to you? You totally missed it. That was fucking awesome!" Like a kid on Christmas morning, he was ecstatic. Chris had blood splatter across his face. His eyes were charged and lit up, so I knew something violent happened. Chris handed me the bag of meth that Ken always hung on to like it was his most prized possession. "Ken wants you to go inside and cut out some fat lines."

With drugs in hand, it did not matter anymore why I came outside. I did not want to know what happened in the camper. Addiction always takes president. I did what I was told; I went inside and cut big lines out on the desk.

When Ken and Chris walked in, Ken immediately kicked Danny in the ribs and said "Get up, I got a fuckin job for you".

Danny grumbled as he stumbled to his feet. Ken and Danny each did one of the lines and they went outside. Chris and I stayed in the office. Chris did a line and went into the bathroom to wash the blood off his face and hands. When he came out he took over chopping and cutting more lines. While we waited for Ken to return, Chris did more lines revealing nothing of what happened to Bill. I figured Chris must have beaten him up. Ken returned and we partied away what was left of the night without Danny. But near dawn I went outside to pee and noticed Danny asleep next to a small hole he had been digging in the back corner of the lot behind the cover of Bills camper. I did not think much of it other than I was glad Danny was digging instead of me.

As the sun began to light up the world, Ken went to check on Danny's progress. There was not much progress since Danny had gone back to sleep without Ken's supervision. Ken was not happy about that. He expected the task to be complete, and after giving Danny a hard punch in the chest, he instructed Chris and me to help Danny finish digging.

Danny never knew when to quit. He still resisted and whined "Why do we gotta dig a stupid hole fur anyhow?"

Ken was thoroughly irritated, he got right in Danny's face and said, "Because I got stuff to get rid of fuckhead!"

No one said a word. After that we went right to work. Chris, Danny, and I spent the morning digging. We only had one shovel so two of us had to use broken boards. Once we had a rather large hole Ken told Danny and I to go finish unloading the batteries from the truck into the warehouse.

Once we had the truck unloaded Ken told us to set all the 12-volt car batteries out in long chains on pallets in the warehouse. While Danny and I did that, Ken and Chris took the truck to pick up two massive battery chargers. Kens dad was supplying the enormous battery chargers and as far as his dad knew we were setting up a legitimate battery reconditioning store. If Ken wanted to keep up the charade, he had to not only pick up the chargers and batteries he also had to set them up and use them. Ken returned with the chargers, half a barrel of acid and several boxes of short wire links that went from one battery to the next. I refilled all low batteries with acid and linked them together while Ken and the boys moved the chargers in place and wired them in. Then we connected the lines of batteries to two massive electric chargers. The idea was to charge the batteries and disconnect them from the charger, any batteries that still held a full charge after 24 hours, would be cleaned, have a new sticker put on it, and resold.

By late day we had all the batteries linked up. All that was left to do was to turn on the chargers. A stranger emerged from the small secluded room in the back and took great interest in what we were doing. As Ken was checking the connections, he explained to me that a cross connection would cause a short circuit and with the amount of juice flowing through the lines it would probably cause an explosion. After overhearing Ken's words, the stranger, who will now be known as the chemist, because of the mad scientist shit he had going on in the back room, approached. The smell of noxious chemicals surrounded him. In a thick accent he told Ken, "Never turn on charger when I'm here working or there will be an explosion." He had serious concerns someone might kill him by accident, so he and Ken went to make sure that the breaker that ran the massive chargers was off. The breaker was located inside the main building, and when Ken and the chemist went inside the shop, I could not help but sneak a peek in the back room while they were gone.

There were big jars of pharmaceutical drugs; not the little pill bottles you get when you go to the doctor but rather the large industrial size the pharmacist has. I can't remember for sure, but I think the label read Pseudoephedrine I believe it's a common cold/ flu remedy ingredient that is now available over the counter but back then wasn't. There were several chemicals like hydrochloric acid, iodine and ether mixed with out-of-place things like heating oil and drain cleaner.

It did not look much like a lab, with the exception of several round glass jars cooking a strange confection of what appeared to be the pills and heating oil. I wanted to get a closer look, but the smell was so strong it made me a little dizzy and I turned back. I was still naive enough to be unsure what they were making. I kidded myself by imagining it was some new experimental battery acid. I wasn't that dumb but believing that was easier on my mind then believing these were the same chemicals keeping me at the end of a very short rope. I used to believe Danny and Jeff were crazy for huffing spray paint. Deep down I knew those weren't experimental battery acid ingredients, but I wasn't ready to believe the truth.

That night while we were doing our usual all-night party, Danny was starting to have second thoughts about what he had gotten himself into. He was asking all kinds of questions that were wearing Ken's patience very thin. When Ken had enough of Danny persisting, he announced "Tomorrow's is a big day, we will be open for business and if you don't relax Danny, you'll find yourself permanently cut out." Ken went on to state "If anybody else wants out now is the time to either get on board and shut the fuck up or get the fuck out." I was not leaving; I didn't have anywhere to go and besides I still wanted to believe we were starting a legitimate business. I desperately wanted to hold onto the foolish dream that someday with hard work I could live a normal life; paying bills and all the crap that went with a mundane life. But deep down I knew the next day there would be no lighting the "Open for Business" sign. There would be no John Q. Public types arriving in droves to spend their money on our used batteries. By "open for business" Ken meant the chemist was finishing up and in his place, there would be a huge batch of meth. I knew that because I had overheard the chemist use the phone when I was in the bathroom earlier.

In the cover of darkness, the brothers came to collect their friend. Ken had a short meeting with them in the warehouse before they left. Ken returned to the office with more drugs than any of us had ever seen; possibly more than most addicts will ever see in their very short lifetimes. At first I did not know what to make of the unprocessed meth he brought inside. I was only used to seeing small amounts of the processed product. There were all these long cigar shaped crystals which we were instructed to cut and chop with great care so not to lose any.

Addicts never trust anyone so it was only natural for Ken to think he may have been cheated by the chemist. Danny was lowest on the pecking order and by far the dumbest so he was the brave soul chosen to try the first batch. We went about preparing the product while we anxiously waited for something, anything to happen to Danny. Ken was impatient and insisted Danny should indulge and have some more since he was so unhappy earlier. Chris and I knew what Ken was doing but Danny didn't. After watching our ignorant little Guinea-pig not show any signs of harm we all cut lines out for a "test". It was so fresh and pure it made Ken's personal drugs seem like garbage. We had so much in front of us that even Ken was overwhelmed and let us do all we wanted. I didn't go crazy like Danny and Ken, but I did enough to launch into space. We spent hours, maybe days floating back to earth locked up tight in the office cutting and weighing hundreds of little bags and large bindles. After we cut and weighed it, we had to count how many we had.

We started counting by ones and after several argumentative yet comical stalls and restarts I suggested they count out piles of 10 and then give them to me to total up. I was not sure some of them could count past ten so I hoped this way would be faster and easier. They agreed and counted out the little piles until we came up with four hundred and twenty small bags and one large full bag.

"Four hundred and twenty times twenty a piece that's um" Ken was struggling with the math

I interjected, "Eight thousand four hundred".

Ken tried to scribble the equation out to double check but still couldn't do simple math. "Yep, you are the new bookkeeper, kiddo" he told me. Now that it's all cut and weighed out, Ken put in a few calls to the ever-growing, needy population of addicts. There were so many among the living that couldn't wait to get in line to join the dead.

We had no problems unloading that first batch. Back then crystal meth was very new. It delivered a longer, cheaper high than cocaine and was four hundred times as addictive. Drug lords hate profit loses and often lose a lot of product trying to smuggle it into any location. Our benefactors were tired of taking loses and hoped that crystal meth was cheaper and safer to "produce" here then to have something else smuggled across the border. The living were crying out for a cheap high to suck the life out of them, and thanks to us, it was about to be readily available.

Ken told Chris and Danny go out to the warehouse, gather up all the empty chemical containers and waste product and throw it all into the hole we dug and bury it so the police couldn't find it in the garbage. There was a lot to bury since the process produces about 6 pounds of waste for every pound of meth. Ken told me to drive his truck up front and wait inside it.

I admit I was little scared why I wasn't helping Danny and Chris. After a short wait ken got in the truck, slightly nervous I asked "What's up boss?"

Ken could read the uncertainty on my face, "Don't worry. I don't want the others to know I'm going to gone for a while, I need you to take some stuff back to them so they don't go doing anything stupid, like wandering off"

Ken drove up the road to a gas station and went inside. When he came out he handed me a bag. Then he reached in his pocket, pulled out one of the bags of drugs, tossed it in the bag, and told me to head back to the shop. The gas station was more than a mile from the shop so I had plenty of time to look in the bag. Inside it was a carton of cigarettes, a bottle of whisky, and a two liter of Pepsi. I went about my task without question, walking in another pointless circle back to the shop. When I think back now I can't help but wonder if maybe Ken was trying to give me one last chance to walk away from death. It didn't really matter, I was chasing the immortal high now and nothing could stray me from the path that led to it. I did however think about keeping all the meth for myself, but thoughts of the boys finding out and killing me derailed that train of thought.

While Ken was unloading the first batch and partying, we were stuck with the task of recharging, washing and relabeling enough batteries to make the shop look legitimate. Ken would leave us just enough drugs to stay complacent until he returned with more drugs. If he returned and the tasks he demanded weren't done, instead of drugs you would get a beating, which Danny took on a regular basis.

Chris desperate for his fix would typically negotiate an arrangement that got things back on track.

Once all the meth was almost gone Ken had no choice but return to the shop. Ken called a meeting with the brothers. When they arrived Chris and Danny were still outside trying to complete their daily tasks. It always amazes me how quickly any group of people will assimilate the small and quiet ones.

When the brothers came in one of them asked Ken "Who's the kid?"

Ken replied, "This is my bodyguard, a real cold-blooded killer!" I looked at them in silence with my best steel eyes.

"Killer . . . huh?" The smaller one said as he shrugged his shoulders and looked at the other.

They all had a good laugh and then larger brother replied, "You Fuck with us, and we show you killer, huh!" He paused then looked over at Ken and in a no longer joking manner said "Where's my fuckin money?"

Just like that I was in the circle of trust. They wasted no more time on frivolity and got right to business. The chemist's estimates of volume and value were way off and the only person who had any real precise knowledge of the actual street value was Ken. Ken had been dipping into the profits pretty hard and was now sweating when he offered up five grand in cash and a handful of excuses about the drug being new. Lucky for Ken no one else knew the value and the brothers were very happy with the five thousand. They hailed the first small test batch a huge success and decided the next batches would be much larger. They haggled over the exchange of money and set up a time for the chemist to return. The brothers also made it clear to Ken that the only time he would have contact with them in the future was when a new batch was done. The brothers made it crystal clear that when they came to collect their friend Ken better have the profits from the previous batch or the partnership would come to a rather violent, abrupt end . . .

At first Ken made all the drug deals. But shortly after the second batch was done Ken's paranoia grew so overwhelming he was terrified of leaving the comfort of his office and his big pile of drugs. Ken decided to make us handle all the direct sales and deliveries. He believed if we got busted we wouldn't be charged with a crime since we were minors. Ken still took all the orders over the phone but he didn't want to be involved when it came to the actual exchange of money so Chris, Danny and I took turns walking the phone orders to a gas station more than a mile away. Ken had only had a handful of regulars but they were constantly calling. More than once we passed one another making a delivery. It felt familiar going around and around in the newest pointless circle. Ken would give instructions like "Look for a guy with red hair in a blue truck" or "a lady will be waiting by the payphone" and whoever was up had to walk way the fuck down to the gas station, make the exchange with some stranger, and then walk back. Eventually I knew all of the random strangers that made up Ken's clientele.

Even though the phone rang all night, the pace which we were unloading the drugs wasn't fast enough for Ken. He decided to have Chris and Danny sell directly to the public while I continued to make the big drops at the gas station. Chris didn't like doing direct sales to strangers so he recruited Phillip to work the park to help him keep up with the demand. Unfortunately Phillip wasn't very smart and bragged all about the drugs and the money he had on him. Dumbfuck was jumped and beaten to death. His corpse was found in the park.

After Phillip was found dead we were all having new fears come to light. I never put any thought into my own safety but now the dangerous nature of the game we were so innocently playing was looming above us waiting, to take its next victim. I never felt safe again. I only dealt with the regulars. Some of them were like me; skinny and yellow with scars on their skin from trying to scratch the bugs out but the rest of the clientele were not like me at all. They were mostly big scary looking guys. I was just a decaying carcass but the drugs in my pocket commanded respect from those who knew what it meant to be cut off from the supply.

Even Danny was treated differently which must have gone to his drug fried brain, because one day he decided not to make his sales and tried to disappear with the meth instead. He might have gotten away with it if he was not so dumb. Danny showed his ignorance when he crossed paths with Marlene in the park and bragged all about the meth he had and his plan to go party at some motel. Danny thought maybe the power of the crystal would be enough to make her want to join him. But she liked pot, not powder and she hated Danny. Later when she met up with Chris she told him all about it and about the motel where Danny was planning on hiding.

When Chris returned to the shop he told Ken about Danny. Ken went ballistic acting like a couple hundred in missing meth would break the bank. I knew the true reason Ken was so upset was because one of his puppets had cut the strings and ran away. Ken's biggest fear was now the remaining puppets getting ideas from Danny's betrayal. Ken knew right where the motel Danny was hiding out in and for the first time in weeks Ken left the sanctuary of his office to go and get him.

You could say that the drugs brought out a devious nature in me. When Ken left I was sitting at the desk going through the drawers when I found the cash box. I was sitting alone reflecting on the fucked up mess I was in when Danny's disloyalty did give me an idea of my own. "I could steal the money, but I couldn't just run off with it, Ken or one of his people would find me. I need a way that no one will suspect me." After a minute or two I came up with the best plan my super baked mind could think up.

I took a battery which we had plenty of, and removed the "guts", leaving an empty shell that I planned to fill with all the money we had on hand. Once all the cash was tucked inside I planned to hide the fake battery among the others, and fake a robbery before Ken returned. I believed that if I stuck around after the money was missing no one would suspect me with empty pockets. Later I could retrieve the money and escape. Part of me still believed I could leave any time I wanted, but I didn't know where I would go with no money and no life left in me. It wasn't summer anymore and it was cold on the street at night. I managed to find a suitable battery, removed the lead, cleaned it out, and looked for a place to hide it among the ranks of all the other batteries. Just as I found the ideal space to stash the fake battery, Chris and Ken returned. I would have to wait for another time to steal the money.

I ran back into the main building just in time. They burst through the backdoor dragging Danny, already bleeding from the nose. Ken rolled the chair from the office into the back room. Under Ken's instructions Chris and I tied Danny to the chair. Ken went back into the office to do more meth while he decided Danny's fate. All the while Danny was pleading with Chris and me, saying he was sorry and could step on the new stuff to double it and make back the missing money. Chris just punched him in the face and told him to stop talking.

As Danny whimpered Ken returned and said, "I'm very disappointed in you Danny. I gave you everything and you spit in my face. Now I have to make an example out of you!"

Chris had no idea the example was for him. He was too caught up in thoughts of violence, his favorite activity. Chris couldn't wait to get started as he grinned and said, "Yeah, yeah you fucker you really put your dick in the shit this time!"

Ken looked at Chris and simply told him, "We'll do fat lines as soon as you guys are done with Danny." Ken did not say or seem to imply what exactly we were supposed to do to Danny but that didn't matter to Chris.

I will never forget the look in Chris's eyes as he beat the life out of Danny. Nobody but me liked Danny, and Chris hated him. Danny was always leering at Marlene and making rude sexual comments. Chris had fought with Danny several other times, but this time was different. In the past Danny would always cower and cry until Chris would let up. But this time Chris would not let up. I stood by and did nothing, perhaps frozen in fear that this would be my fate if I interjected, but in truth the ghost I'd become didn't feel anything anymore. Chris's eyes gleamed as he grinned from ear to ear in sheer pleasure. Each time he hit Danny, Chris felt some kind of vengeful joy, Danny definitely felt something, but I felt nothing. It was somewhat like watching violence on TV, I didn't create the program, but I didn't change the channel either.

No one knew what the end game here was but when Chris got bored hitting Danny; he decided to dump battery acid on him.

Up till now Danny was taking the beating and telling Chris "To go fuck himself" among other classic tell offs, but after the acid

Danny started to scream and plead with us, "Don't kill me! I don't want to die!"

I figured this was the breaking point that would end this. Which it probably would have been but Danny tries to appeal to Chris bravado by saying "you can't be mad at me for wanting to fuck Marlene, she's a fine piece of ass"

Chris fucking snaps like a twig in a hurricane. Marlene had dumped Chris shortly after we went full junkie. The thought of her with anyone else explodes in his mind. Chris grabbed a chunk of wood and bashed Danny in the head repeatedly until Danny was silent. Then, like nothing happened we went back inside the office to do more lines and tell Ken it was done.

It was strange and surreal. I just watched a man get bludgeon to death and yet I felt nothing as I sat there stained with Danny's blood. Chris was still smiling; blood splattered across his face "I hate that fucker! That was fucking awesome."

Ken cut out two really big lines; we did them and went back into the other room. Ken looked over what was left of Danny's now still and lifeless shell. Ken nudged the body and exclaimed "I want his fuckin head. Put the rest in the hole and bury it before dawn", with that said, Ken untied Danny's limp body, pushed him off the chair, and rolled the chair back into the office and closed the door. I didn't know if Ken finally tipped over the edge he'd been teetering on or if he was trying to see how far our loyalty to him would go. I looked at Chris, puzzled, but he didn't seem to share my bewilderment.

Chris seemed excited about our new task. We had no tools to speak of, so I thought maybe Bill had something in his camper. We went out back and into Bill's camper. It smelled even worse now than it had the first time I had been inside. Chris turned on the light. A small dim bulb ignited, I could see the bed was stained with dried blood, a lot of blood.

"Holy shit!" I gasped.

Chris replied, "Yeah that fat fucker bled like the pig he was!"

Without me asking him what happened to Bill (because I really did not want to know) Chris went on to explain, "Ken couldn't do it, so I cut his filthy throat while he slept. You should've seen his face when I cut into him, and he started to wiggle about. Ken had to hold him down with a pillow until the bastard stopped squirming."

I started feeling nauseous when Chris produced a small hatchet he found buried in the mess. As we walked back to the main building, I couldn't keep my moral denial in any longer. I fell to my knees in the corner, vomited out all the sick black truths and went back inside.

The scene inside was gruesome. Chris knelt over Danny hacking away at his neck until he had cut all the way through. Blood was flying everywhere in the small room. I should have been horrified but I was not. I did not look away until we dragged what was left of his corpse to the hole. There wasn't much room left in the hole when we dropped him in, and Chris remarked "Now Dildo will have some company." I had desperately wanted to believe the hole was for the chemical boxes and waste product, but with Bill's hand sticking out of junk I could not lie to myself any longer.

I looked down at my bloody shirt, then into the hole and I thought to myself "What am I doing? What have I become? Am I just a cold-blooded killer now? Is this just another one of my bad dreams?" I threw my shirt in hoping to bury the horrible truth along with it.

Chris, seeing what I did now realized just how covered in blood he was and followed suit by throwing his shirt and pants into the hole. High as a kite, under the moon light, almost naked, Chris and I filled in the pit.

It was still before dawn when we went back inside. We put Danny's head in a box and left it on the counter in the shop. We threw dirt and battery acid on the bloodstains on the floor and tried to scrub the mixture around. When we returned to the office Chris took a sink bath with a rag. Since Ken lived here full time, he had a small box of clothes in the office which Chris and I had to borrow from. Chris rummaged through the box, grabbed some clothes, and threw me a shirt.

I stepped into the small bathroom and looked into the mirror. I avoided looking into mirrors because I did not like the zombie looking back at me. My skin was pulled tight against what was left of my rapidly decaying body. I was so thin my bones pushed hard to escape. I had scratched away large patches of skin trying to eradicate the bugs underneath it. My eyes were dark sunken pools without a hint of life. My clothes were so dirty it looked like I just crawled up from the grave. I washed the blood from my face and hands and put on the somewhat clean shirt.

When I finished and went back in the office, we all acted like the new day rising could just erase the night before. The only thing Ken said about it was now Chris and I had to pick up the slack. Chris and I both would have to take more meth out with us, and I had to now wait at the gas station most of the night. It was reminiscent of sitting in front of the bank so long ago. I could only return to the shop if I ran out of product. The only thing Ken did any more was sit in the office, get stoned, answered the phone, and of course make the meet with the brothers.

As time went by, Ken's hunger for money faded and he remembered his lust for other things. Ken often had sleazy call girls visiting him. Ken was now shooting up, since snorting and smoking no longer got him off. He often had junkie prostitutes in the office with him for hours or even days. He now had all the drugs and sex any man could ask for. As long as the drugs kept being produced; all the money in the world now meant nothing to Ken. In fact, we had all gone past the point of users, well past the point where the drug changes the chemical make-up of your brain. Rational was no longer an option, only the constant need for more remained.

In the beginning I would sell a little of my personal stash to buy soda and sometimes even food. But now that Ken was shooting up, he only entertained his new vampire girlfriends. He never partied with us minions. Chris and I now had to beg for, cheat people out of, and steal the drugs which we were heavily addicted to. Time had no meaning and I couldn't remember anything about my life before drugs. Just do my deliveries and get my fix, that's all I could think of or do. I was truly dead hanging around the gas station selling drugs when she found me again.

# CHAPTER 12

## And then there were none.
## in a flash it's over

I had walked alone for so long among the dead I almost didn't want to remember life or Lisa. But there she was standing before me once again. She looked more angelic than ever as she peered into my hollow eyes.

"I've been looking for you; I couldn't stop thinking about you alone on the streets. What happened to you? Where have you been? What did they do to you?" she pleads for answers from someone that has none.

"Who" I reply, my mind was a rotting blank.

"My mom and her boyfriend did they hurt you? You look terrible, are you sick?" she persists on trying to get water from a dry well.

"What? No, I'm fine. I've just been busy" I said but in truth I was surrounded by death and decay. I wanted to get away from the gas station and perhaps Lisa as well, so I started walking. Lisa was the only person alive who still saw the human left in me. The smallest fragment of life left in me remembered the times when we were still innocent children running off to get high behind the bushes.

My escape somehow became a rapid descent into a cage. I had not forgotten the times on my fall when she showed me compassion no matter how disgusting I looked or smelled. I had not forgotten her lips on mine. I often daydreamed of that kiss, but I felt nothing but shame for not coming to find her. I was excited she was still alive, but I was so dead I couldn't stand the thought of her becoming like me. There are times early in an addiction when the addict tells themselves they can quit any time and be fine. I was way beyond that point, I felt like Hell's gates might appear at any second. I did not want her to be there when it happened. I continued to walk away ignoring her like the undead slave to drugs I had become. I did not want her to get too close, I was soaked in trouble and death's hounds were on to the scent. Still unfamiliar with the smell of death she follows me like a pup.

She told me her mom put her in some treatment facility. She played their mind games and when she got home yesterday, she went to do the laundry and ran off looking for me. I had promised myself I would look for her a thousand times but let the drugs lure me away every time. I was just another junkie and I hated myself for not keeping my promise.

"Me? Why me? I'm nothing! I'm just another one of the living dead!" I told her.

"NO!" she insists. "You're not the living dead! You're my angel! Remember you promised to take care of me? When no one else cared, you did! I need you!! We can still escape from all this! We can run far away, where no one knows us."

She latched onto my arm, desperation cracking her voice, tears bleeding from her eyes, as she pleaded with me. I stopped in my tracks for a moment, turned and stared into the eyes of my true love and from the tears that now ran from her eyes the dreams we once shared washed back into my mind. I remembered back to when I was still alive before everything spun out of control. "That was then," I thought to myself. "I was a cold-blooded killer, a demon, a junkie, and worst of all soulless. I had given up on living all together. How could this beautiful beaten down girl still believe I was her angel?" She had me questioning everything about my existence. I was so broken, so beaten down, so lost, and so forgotten that I did not believe there was any hope left for me. The blood she gave brought something inside of me back to life. It was love, the love I had so desperately needed to bring me back from the grave. My dark bubble burst and all the mirrors that reflected an unfamiliar face shattered and rained ten million shards painfully down upon me.

Maybe, just maybe, if I could save her God would forgive me and let me back into his light. I felt I was forsaken and damned for what I had done and for what I had become. But Lisa, dear, sweet, innocent Lisa did not deserve this hell. She was the angel flying down to try to pull me from the lake of fire. Then I remembered the day I found the cash box. I no longer needed an elaborate plan to steal the money. The idea of Lisa and I having a normal life was all the motivation I needed. I would take Lisa with me back to the shop and wait till morning when Ken was the most vulnerable and just take the money and run. I did not want to take Lisa to the shop but felt I had little choice and Ken never turned girls away. For obvious reasons young girls always trumped Ken's paranoia. I deeply regret the fact that I couldn't think of anywhere safe. I didn't want to risk losing her again. I couldn't face the fear of letting her go again. I had to keep her close, somewhere I thought was safe from her mother's grasp.

I couldn't go back to the shop without selling out, so we went back to the gas station to sell the remainder of my stash. After a few hours we returned to the shop together. I introduced Lisa as "A friend from school." Ken was preoccupied with one of his whores and paid little attention to Lisa. He just exchanged the money for another bag and sent me back to my post at the gas station. Together Lisa and I went back to the gas station. After a few hours I sold all the drugs and returned once more to the shop. In hindsight I wished we had just run away then and there. I had more than a couple hundred dollars from the deliveries in my pocket.

Since the circle of trust was getting smaller by the day Ken set a large mandatory buy limit. I now only made big drops to a select clientele. I guess I was greedy and didn't think a few hundred bucks would be enough to secure a proper escape. We had to get very far from here, maybe even leave the country and that wouldn't be cheap. I didn't tell Lisa I had planned to steal the money. I just told her I would find a way to buy the life she deserved. She had no idea of how deep I was in. I had been involved in three murders and I was surely damned for it. She only saw her angel and it felt so good to be wanted. Little did I know how condemned I was or the price I'd have to pay for my sins?

When we arrived at the shop Ken was already upset because the next batch of meth was almost ready, and we hadn't sold enough to pay the brothers yet. Lisa and I were sitting on the floor for less than 5 minutes when I was given a familiar address across town and two more bags to drop there. Lisa couldn't walk any longer on her still wounded leg and she told me with a soft voice she couldn't walk around any longer. Ken heard her and quickly agreed she could stay there while I made more deliveries. I may have been a little ignorant about sex, but I knew why Ken's paranoia towards strangers was subdued by his sexual desire and my Lisa was so young and pretty. I tried to whisper a warning not to stay in her ear, but Ken was extremely impatient about gathering all the money by dawn. Ken grabbed me by the arm and picked me off the floor to remind me who was in charge. Ken assured Lisa she'd be ok and that I'd hurry back.

"Don't hurry too much", Ken warned me "The police like to grab runners." It wasn't my well-being he was thinking of.

The city never seemed very big until that night. That night the blocks stretched out and seemed to go on into infinity. I just wanted to get back. I ignored Ken's words and ran as fast as I could. I figured the early morning hours would be my best chance to steal the money. I knew everyone's routine; the chemist would finish up his latest batch, which meant the brothers would be there tomorrow for their cut of the money. The cheap cashbox where Ken kept the money would be nice and full. I had to act before they arrived. Ken was usually pretty smacked out by daybreak. I ran through the cold night dreaming of Lisa and my first kiss which now seemed like a different lifetime. I was going to break free from my hell and rescue Lisa. Together we would find the happily ever after that was reserved for the chosen few. I truly believed if I could steal enough money, I could buy my way back into life.

By the time I returned to the shop I had convinced myself I was not stealing the money, only collecting my pay for the weeks or months that I put in. It was very late, nearing dawn when I walked onto the lot. It was dark and still as I made my way inside. The faint sound of music playing on a clock radio led me through the dark. The only light was coming from inside Ken's office. A dim light was creeping out from the bathroom. There was just enough for me to make out Ken's silhouette passed out in the chair. I was right about Ken. He was always pretty out of it when I returned from my deliveries. I put the money on the desk and was about to sneak away to find Lisa when Ken startled me and mumbled "Your girlfriend is outback sick or something. She puked in here and I had to drag the little bitch out back." I freaked out and rushed to find her.

Outside in the darkest hour of the day just before daybreak I frantically called her name with no response. I found her slumped against some debris behind the building. Shaking from the cold or so I thought. I sat by her and gently held her face to turn it towards me. She had thrown up on herself and the stink of vomit filled the air. Her eyes were rolled back in her head as I held her and pleaded "Lisa wake up. Are you ok!?!" She was completely unresponsive.

She was growing cold and started shaking violently. I ran back inside.

"What the fuck did you give her?" I demanded from Ken!

"Just tequila and some lines," he said in a smug slurred tone.

I panicked, thinking "Lisa's never done meth." I rushed back to her side with some water in an empty beer can. She looked even worse now and I tried once again to wake her and to get her to drink water to no avail.

I ran back into the office, "We have got to call an ambulance!" I pleaded with Ken, who was now preparing another spike to get his fix. He clearly did not respect the seriousness of the situation and was more concerned with the police showing up. He grabbed the phone before I could dial. His paranoia took over as he pulled away the phone so hard that the cord ripped from the wall by mistake.

"Now look what you made me do, dumb shit!" and he punched me in the face knocking me back into the wall.

I rose to my feet. With blood leaking from my face, I still tried pleading for compassion, "Please, Ken, we have to help her!"

"Get out! I need my fix" is all he yelled back. When I persisted, I awoke the demons in Ken. His eyes glared as he hit me again now with full force. I could feel my jaw and teeth crack as I slammed against the door landing in the hall. Ken kicked me and slammed the door leaving me bleeding on the floor. In a full panic for Lisa's life, I ran into the streets desperately screaming at the top of my lungs "Help me! I need help!! Please anyone help!" It was dead quiet there was nothing and no one in sight.

I feared for Lisa, my love, so I rushed back to her. She was not shaking anymore and at first, I thought this was a good thing. As I held her in my arms, I could feel how cold she was. I tried to keep her warm, but it was not working. I was in a full state of shock and did not know what to do. I was only a kid! I did not know CPR or rescue breathing. The only thing I knew at the moment was how powerless I was to help her. Panic took back over, and I tried briefly to shake her back awake. She was slipping away when I pleaded with God. "Please God hear my plea for Lisa. Help her! Save her! Please take my rotten soul in her place! I'll burn over and over! But let her live!!!" I begged and cried but my prayers were in vain. As the sun began to rise and spread its light into the cold yard, I could now see my red tears of blood streaming down her pale blue face. She was not breathing anymore. I realized that she had passed away as I held her. In an effort to try to trick death into taking me with her, I held her as tight as I could. I closed her eyes and kissed her for the second time.

In my mind the Devil collected Lisa's soul in place of mine. I knew I was an agent of evil but now that I knew the true devious nature of the beast, I felt humbled and betrayed. I played right into Satan's hands leading my only love to the slaughter. In an attempt to make some kind of bargain, I spoke again to God. I never lost faith that God existed I just did not believe he ever cared for me. This time I told him "I'll clean up the filth putrefying society in exchange for Lisa's passage into heaven." I did not need God to respond. With or without his blessing there would be hell to pay for Lisa's lost soul.

Still holding tight to her dead body, I realized there was no good or God left in me. I was never her angel. Lisa was my angel all along, she tried to save me. I had my chance to join her in the light, but my drug addiction pulled us both into hell instead. I was damned and there would be no salvation, no absolution, and no love for me! The only thing left in me was a dark and bitter hatred.

I vowed to her, "From the shadows I will push the demons into the light!" Everyone had to account for their sins. Ken had killed Lisa, me and who knows how many others with his poison. I had to stop this madness. The dead were calling from the grave for a flag bearer to deal vengeance upon the world and end the misery we were inflicting on society. I was reborn as an instrument of God with the sole purpose of collecting past due payments on delinquent sins. With pure hate and vengeance on my mind, I let go of Lisa and I went into the warehouse.

I did not know every detail of the meth-making process. From what I did see I gathered this much. The pills were smashed up and cooked with the methanol in the round beakers to liquefy them. The liquid produced is an acid that has to change into a base in order to solidify into crystals. The step of changing acid to base was the most unstable and the most dangerous. The chemical reaction produced a lot of combustible gas under pressure. If the pressure wasn't released just right the whole thing would explode in your face. Hence the name crystal meth, crystal from the finished product, and meth from the methanol added at the beginning. I could smell the venting taking place when I asked Chris to step outside for a moment.

These days Chris was helping the chemist in the hopes of learning the recipe. Chris loved meth and the dependency showed on his rotting corpse. I spoke with Chris knowing that this would be the last time I saw him. I thanked him for looking out for me and protecting me. I told him he was my best and only friend.

"Yep! Like death and destruction together forever" he replied.

That's ironic I thought "Death and destruction" that's all we had brought to this world. I didn't know what else to say so I lied and told him Ken wanted an update on their progress. I loved Chris but he only loved violence and he was by no means a decent person anymore. "I'll be saving him from this junkie hell" I thought as I watched him go back inside. Chris and the chemist were both so busy working in the back room they never even noticed when I crossed the lines on a chain of dormant batteries strung out on the floor. With tears running down my face I cranked the dials on the chargers. I closed the door and looked over to the hole where we buried Danny and Bill. Looking at the grave, I assured myself Chris had to pay for his sins and my way was better than a slow grind in prison. Passing by Lisa again I couldn't bring myself to look at her but I stopped with my head hung low, begged her for forgiveness, and assured her that her tormentors would soon be in hell. I'd make damn sure of that!!!

I stepped inside to check on Ken. I stood outside the office door. It was silent. The sun's rays were viciously piercing through the windows. The light hurt my eyes and I thought to myself "God's watching me clean up this mess." I walked over to the breakers, paused for a moment to think of the permanent chain of events throwing the switch would create, and I threw the switch that would turn the massive chargers on. The tranquil morning was broken as a massive explosion shook the building and shattered the windows. A fireball of broken glass, debris, and dust instantly filled the air. The force of the explosion was so great that I was thrown to the ground as the back door flew off its hinges, striking me down against the hard floor. Ken ran from the office, right past me still lying on the floor, to stand outside in awe as pieces of flaming batteries were starting to fall back to earth. I used the opportunity to grab the money, stuff it in a bag and run off in the confusion. I never looked back.

After a few blocks I could hear and see emergency vehicles of all kinds racing to the scene. I hid as they went by. "Foolish," I thought, "Like anyone will notice me, I'm just another piece of human garbage."

I went to the one place I thought would be safe and I prayed. I did not pray for me because I believed I was damned but instead for Lisa, Chris, Danny, Guy, Bill, the chemist and even Ken. I knew I was damned, and I wanted to kill Ken. But this way I figured he would have a lot more to answer for. I figured when the police found all the meth and the bodies buried on the lot Ken would get life in prison which would be a more fitting punishment than death.

Ken never did answer to the police. That coward bastard cheated me one last time. After I ran off, he returned inside. Even after he realized the cash was gone and the warehouse was now a fucking crater his thoughts were still ruled by his addiction. With the sirens growing closer he ended his own life by way of the biggest spike he had ever done. He was a true junkie to the end. I will never know if he meant to die or if he just wanted one last big fix before the police arrived.

I walked for hours until I found myself at a familiar place where I felt God might see me. I sat exhausted and alone with the money for a long time thinking of what to do. I was starting to come down and all my sins weighed heavy and painfully on my tired body. I decided the best thing to do was to bury the money and go home. Maybe somehow, I could just go home and pretend this nightmare never happened. It was hard digging with my bare hands. I could not stop thinking about Lisa and regretting every wrong turn I took in my life that led to her death. I was digging at the earth with my bare hands unsure if I was, I digging my way in or out of my grave? One last time I completed the pointless circle and returned home. I was shaking pretty bad as I made it up the stairs to the door, I once called home. I knocked without response, so I crawled into a ball there on the patio and fell into a long overdue sleep. I hadn't saved Lisa or myself, but I believed that I had saved the world from a demon drug that consumed its victim's whole and didn't let go until they were dead.

# CHAPTER 13

## Back into the light

Somewhere in the darkness I could hear Lisa crying out to me. She wants me to come and find her. I find her surrounded in black, silent, and floating. Still pale and blue, her eyes stared through me.

I try to tell her, "I'm sorry, I'm so fucking sorry I couldn't save you!"

My pleas are answered by a stranger's voice as Lisa disappears. I pry my crusty eyes open. There's the familiar bright light that always burned my eyes. My body felt like cement, solid and unresponsive as I tried to sit up.

I'm held in place as someone said "Just relax, you're in the hospital. You've been very sick. You need to lie still and rest". My eyes painfully strain before things come into focus. I look around at the sterile clean room. I'm in a hospital gown and tubes are pumping fluids back into me. I was still very tired and unsure of who I was or why I was here. The strange woman before me asked "Who's Lisa?"

"What?" I replied still confused and half dead.

The nurse explains, "Lisa? You keep calling out for her and apologizing. Who is she?"

"Who is she? She was... everything" I whispered as tears rolled down my face and reality slammed back into my head, and I remembered my love left dead in the dirt.

The nurse told me she had to inform the doctor I was awake.

When she returned, I asked her "How long have I been here?"

"You've been here for a few days now. You were in really bad shape. You were dehydrated and hooked on meth when they brought you in" she explains as she unapologetically plunged a needle into my sore flesh "I'm giving you this for your pain and then some people want to see you". I couldn't imagine anyone, but my parents would want to see me. I wondered, what I will tell them. Were they still mad at me?

The nurse propped the bed up and I sat up nervously as the door opened and two men I had never seen before entered the room and displayed their badges. All this time I thought I was invisible and that no one noticed the dead. I was wrong. A waitress from the diner down the street had seen and remembered me constantly walking back and forth from the shop. She also saw me flee the scene the morning of the explosion.

The detectives go on to tell me that Guy isn't dead. Ken went back to Guy's hotel room and found him still alive; he had promised Guy he would get the money back from me. Of course, Ken never told me that because as long as I thought Guy was dead Ken could use it against me. Guy went to the police after Ken didn't retrieve his money from me and stopped taking his calls. His statement turned into a drug investigation. They had more than enough evidence to hang me. Beside the fact that one of my regular costumers was an undercover cop, there was my shirt in the shallow grave and the pants I was wearing when they found me were stained with multiple victims' blood. On top all that most of bill's camper survived the explosion, even without the murder that place looked like hell. The police didn't know everything, but they knew enough. I was fucked and I didn't care anymore. I gave them some of the missing puzzle pieces, but I never told them about the money I stole or where I had buried it

As soon as the men left, a small group of hospital staff came in. While one nurse told me to relax, and everything was alright the others strapped my arms to the bed. I had no will to fight them as I began to detox. The demons being chased from my body however were not going without a fight. A river of sweat poured from my body and my nose was crusted full of snot. My body twisted and convulsed in agony as I cried out for one last fix. What little was left of my fragile psyche was crushed into bits. More than once I begged for death to come and release me from this anguish. The drugs were eventually driven from me, but they left nothing but damage behind.

As soon as I was well enough to leave the hospital I was arrested. Cameras flashed and people shouted as they dragged me in full restraints from the hospital to the jail. I was oblivious to it all. I was not really sure about anything anymore. All these strangers yelling and screaming at me did not know me, or what I did for them. They didn't know how I'd saved the world from the plague of drugs about to kill their young. Even if they had known what I'd done for them nothing would change the way they felt towards me. The quick and easy facts and a monster to hang in the name of their own indifference were all that the people wanted.

Once they found Danny's decapitated head inside the shop; the public wouldn't sleep safe again until all the monsters were destroyed. Unfortunately, I was the only monster left. There was a quick trial and I confessed to all of it. Even some stuff I did not do. Bill's death, Ken's death, even Lisa's death is pronounced murder and, it was all pinned on me. I heard the prosecutor's ridiculous theory so often I even began to believe it was my entire fault.

I was found guilty as Lisa's mother shouted "Burn in hell, you bastard! You deserve to die!"

None of my family members showed up at the hearing. Instead, they disowned me. I don't blame them; after all the media had half the world thinking I was the antichrist. I was a true-to-life "monster", a demon from hell. Danny's "missing" head, the butchered bodies buried on the lot and the "Satanic" music all added up to one juicy headline. The press loved pushing the satanic cult angle. I spent my days locked in a cell awaiting sentencing. I prayed for answers, but God and the Devil had equally forsaken me and left me there alone to pay for my sins.

Because of my age and my drug fried mind I was sentenced to an institution instead of prison. I didn't know at the time, but one member of my family had not disowned me. My well-off grandfather still had an incredible amount of sympathy for me. His son had a lot of shortcomings and he felt guilty about the repercussions now arising. He had spent a large amount of money to keep my rotten flesh from the wolves in the California prison system. With the help from an expensive lawyer, I was to be transferred to an institution for the mentally ill back in Wisconsin, my home state. While the trial went on, I left the jail almost every day but now it was over I was stuck in my cell all day and night while my travel arrangements were made.

Most people in jail are housed with other inmates in a large general population cell but because of my age and my violent crimes I was kept in what's called an observation cell. It is a very small cell. It had two concrete walls and one wall with a partition made of Plexiglas with bars behind it. Behind the glass and bars there was a thin walkway and a small camera placed in the corner. Finally, there was the solid steel door with a small window to open and slide your food through. There's room for one steel bed rack, a toilet and three or four steps worth of space left to pace back and forth. I was suffocated by emptiness. I had already spent months inside this tiny box alone with what was left of my shattered memories. I suffered over and over as I relived my nightmare past over and over again.

I wondered about the money endlessly. I am sure no one ever looked for it since most of the people who knew it existed were dead. The Russians probably figured it was seized by police or destroyed in the explosion and the police were clueless. I still remembered quite vividly those few minutes of chaos. The debris was still falling, but the smoke and dust in the air would never cloud out the memories of Lisa lying dead in my arms. She haunted me every minute of every day. Her ghost screamed at me because I could not save her. I awoke many nights screaming back at the empty air trying to release her memory from my tortured brain. Only to have my caretakers tell me to shut the fuck up!

The day of my transfer a sheriff came to my cell with three deputies in tow. They shackled my feet and my hands, then placed a belt around my waist which they attached the hand cuffs to. After I was secure in the restraints the sheriff pushed me down sternly into my bed and said, "If you give me any trouble, I will kill you on the spot". Then they picked me up by the shackles and carried me to the car. It was extremely painful, but I held back any feelings of trying to fight or struggle because I had simply no fight left in me. I spent the next 53 hours shuffled from one police car to the next. I begged to stop to use the bathroom, but it seems the farther I went from the crime scene the more horrific and demonizing the crime I committed became. At the first exchange one of the officers asked the other if I was the kid who killed his entire family in some satanic ritual. By the time I reached the Midwest the rumors of what I had done were out of control. They thought I had killed dozens of young girls on some drug crazed satanic frenzy. Because of the stories, not one of my escorts would allow me to use a bathroom. I was treated worse than an animal left to go in my pants when I could no longer hold it.

It was well past dark when we finally arrived at the Milwaukee Adolescent Treatment Center or Kiddy jail. We pulled into an underground garage, and I was dragged from the car with my own piss burning into my skin and I couldn't help but wiggle in discomfort. My current jailers had taken this as justification for one last jab at me before they gave up custody. They threw me down and punched at me before picking my limp body up and dragging me in through the doors back into the light.

# CHAPTER 14

# The caged rat

While I was being checked in my new caretaker complained that I was soaked in my own urine. The Transport officers told him after stopping to use the bathroom several times I pissed myself anyway, in some sort of last defiant act. The man checking me into the institution didn't have any sympathy for me but he didn't like dealing with people soaked in piss so he mumbled "He really showed you guys" in a sarcastic tone to the officers as he signed the release papers. I was taken into a locker room, released from my shackles and told to strip down. After a humiliating cold shower in front of two grown men, who demanded I scrub lice shampoo all over my body before I could escape the freezing cold water, I was given a very thin robe and escorted to see the facilities doctor.

I was left unguarded and alone with the physician. A very obese older man with terrible breath and skin introduced himself as a doctor then asked me to disrobe. He made me stand before him naked while he asked me routine health questions that I had no answers to. The most upsetting question is how old am I. I think about it but I don't know. He forcefully fondles my genitals and made me bend over the exam table to "check for contraband." I felt raped and violated. I wished I were still in my tiny jail cell. After this ordeal was over, I was given underwear, paper slippers, and a two-piece blue denim suit. I was then escorted to a small empty room with the walls covered in carpet. I was left locked in the room for hours before a group of people came for me.

A man introduced himself as Doctor Nosferatu. He asked me who I was and why I was there. I was still craving the life of constant highs. All the drugs I so foolishly ran through my body had burned out my emotional regulator and shattered my personality.

I responded with the only truth I knew "I'm the living dead and I'm here to eat your souls and take you all to hell!"

Totally unshaken, the doctor replies "That's very troubling do you think you can behave so we can take you to your room?"

I was puzzled and confused and didn't know how to respond. I felt threatened and outnumbered. I just wanted to cower in the corner, so I did.

"He's not ready we'll come back later" the Doctor says to the others, and they exited the tiny room.

I had just started to doze off when the door opened again. "Would you like to use the bathroom?" A female voice asked!

I peered up. The neon light flooding the room from the hallway was blinding compared to the dim 25-watt bulb in this room. I cannot quite make out the figure in the light but her soft voice reminds me of Lisa. I smiled and in a small timid voice said, "yes please". Two large men blocked out her silhouette as they entered and escorted me to the bathroom. I was hoping to see some sign of life but as we passed some windows, I couldn't see anything but darkness on the other side. After watching me use the bathroom the men grabbed my arms and carried me away. They took me off the ward I was being held in, to a totally different building on the grounds. Once inside I was dragged into a large office where a man was apparently waiting for me.

"Do you know why you are here!!?" The angry man demands from me while the two guards stand behind me. Not waiting for an answer, he proceeds "You are here because you are the scum of the earth, the lowest form of life, murdering druggy filth, society has no place for you, you should be rotting in prison but instead they send you here to me! I don't like drug dealing filth and I don't care how the fuck you got here!" His anger raged as he stared through me.

He was a high-ranking official at the institution and recently his own daughter became addicted to cocaine and lost her life on the streets. He was looking for reason in her death when he heard the second-hand twisted tales about me. He had found the scapegoat punching bag he was looking for. He clearly wanted to hold me personally responsible for his shortcomings as a father. I didn't have any response to the rhetorical questions he demanded from me. "What could my daughter find in filth like you that she'd sell her body and soul for? Answer me you degenerate punk! Why did she leave me?" His rant went from hatred to tears and I sat in silence because I understood his rage, I related to his feelings of loss. My silent eagerness to be punished just made things worse. The man became so agitated while spewing more hate he punched me several times in the ribs forcing me to fall into the guards. They picked me back up. The only sympathy I got from them was in the form of a gentle reminder to the angry man not to leave any marks on my face. Then again later when they want to cover their asses, they stopped the madness by declaring "We've got to have him back by the five A.M. shift change." The angry man pounded his fist on the desk disappointed play time was over. The guards had no remorse for their participation. They acted like the mindless zombie I was once, obeying a master without question. They dragged me back to the small room with carpet on the walls.

The next time the door opened I rushed and attacked with all my force. I was a caged, delusional, abused animal backed into the corner. My fight reflex naturally kicked in. The scared animal in the corner would take no more. It was time to show some teeth. I took them by complete surprise as the adrenaline in my system was raging at full power. It took six grown men and one very overweight woman to restrain me. I was dragged, kicking, and screaming, into a new room with a metal bed frame bolted to the floor and several leather belts hanging from it. I was put into what's called five-point restraints. They forced my legs apart and strapped down both my feet with thick leather belts. Then they held down my arms at the opposite end of the bed and strapped them down. After that they put a fifth strap around my waist. They held a pillowcase against my face to keep me from spitting on them. I couldn't breathe and would have passed out but the pain from the women sitting on me was feeding my rage. I squirmed and tried to wriggle free from the immense pain. My ribs could not take any more. I already took several punches and now this three-ton bitch was crushing my ribs into my lungs. It was a relief when they finally managed to strap me down and she got off me. They left me there in the dark for days. My abused animal mentality had reaffirmed their belief I was a dangerous convict.

While I was strapped down the silent minutes crawled by until my body began to ache. Discomfort slowly changed into panic. I writhed and pulled at my restraints, but they would not budge. My twisted mind was consumed with the thoughts that I had gone deeper into my own hell. I hadn't had any normal social interactions with people in a long time. I only had brief encounters with my keepers. Like a neglected pet, I was only dragged from my cage to perform a trick. I was beaten for not knowing how to behave even though I'd never been shown how to act. After failing to understand what's expected from me, I was tossed back into the cage; only to repeat the cycle again and again. I had become something far less than human. I must have angered God, and this was my punishment for trying to interfere with his plans. Whatever deranged thoughts went spinning around inside my head would never be treated here. I learned quickly to keep my head down and act like the trained animal they wanted me to be. I did what I was told and kept my mouth shut.

I don't remember a lot about this time in my life. I was severely lost in a delusional frame of mind. My soul and sanity were distant relatives that rarely came to visit me anymore. All my friends were dead. My hand in their deaths pushed my mind to the brink. The long days in a tiny solitary cell before, during, and after my trial pulled my mind over the edge into insanity. At sentencing when the judge read my charges aloud, I felt like I was standing at the gates of heaven before Peter. When he finished reading all my sins, I was denied entrance and cast into hell. It wasn't difficult to accept my fate because I believed I deserved it.

The detention center I was held in wasn't exactly what most people picture when they think of hell. There was no lake of fire or anything like that. Instead, it was very blank. Everything was nothing and nothing was everything. There was No color, No music, No fresh air, and No freedom of choice. A world where nothing bleeds into nothing and lets nothing remain is truly Hell. The hallways, the rooms, the daily routine, they all contain the bare minimum. Everything is white and sterile. My room had two beds that were attached to the wall. Each bed had a three-drawer dresser/ open door closet type thing that was also attached to the wall. The room didn't have a window, just rows and rows of concrete blocks. My entire worldly possessions also: nothing. The clothes on my back were not even mine. There was a stale routine for every insignificant detail of life. I woke up, ate my meals, showered and went to the bathroom at the same time every day. Weekdays we left the ward six hours a day for class. Class consisted of silently working through problems in a workbook. The class had some girls from a different ward, but you could never speak aloud to them. Passing notes was futile. You would get banned from class which meant you had to spend a day in the Quiet room instead. Six hours in there and you were begging to learn something.

I shared a room with another kid at first. His name was Chad. He was a farm kid whose dad liked to take punches at him so he, in turn, took punches at other kids. During one of his fights, he had apparently hurt some kid pretty bad. He was found guilty of battery and was sentenced to rot in here; or at least that's what he told me. Once a day we had one hour of Quiet time where you had to remain in your room and do nothing. That was easy to do because there was nothing in your room to do. My roommate came up with several dumb games to pass the time. One was called "torpedo" where he called out to the kid directly across the hall and when the kid came to the doorway, he'd spit on him. When he got a hit, he would say "I sunk your battleship." You would think a game this stupid would end when the other guy got spat on once or twice, and learned his lesson, but after the first couple times they just tried to pop into the opening and spit on each other until that got old. This went on for weeks. I thought the game sucked to play and did not participate but it was fun to watch. That game finally got old when the kid across the hall ultimately figured out the only way to win. Not play.

My roomie didn't like the nothingness chewing away at him, so he made up another dumb game. "WrestleMania!" was his next brain-fart. This guy watched way too much wrestling at a young age. In his newest game he wanted to wrestle against me. He started one day doing TV wrestling threats like "This coming Sunday I'm going to annihilate you" all the while talking into an invisible microphone. To make things worse he even had named himself "The cow puncher". "I've knocked out cows back on the farm" he would brag. "More like the bull fucker" I'd taunt back thinking he was only playing. Sunday came and during Quiet time when no one was supervising us because the whole "Quiet time" was just a ruse to keep us in our rooms during shift change. He came at me grabbing me in private places and thrashing about. He caught me off guard when he had me pinned on the bed when I lost it. I flashed back to my father beating me, Guy trying to rape me, and then to the monster inside me that killed and dismembered my friends. I let the monster free from his cage and fought back. I managed to kick Chad off me, knocking him to the floor. All the pent-up rage I held came rushing out. I was tired of the world kicking me and I would tolerate it no longer. I was a cold-blooded killer. Once my demon smelled blood there was no way to put the beast back in its cage. I grabbed Chad by his hair and pounded his head against the floor over and over again until blood was gushing out. I didn't stop until his body went limp. It's a common flaw in the "MIGHT makes right" theory; sometimes the quiet little ones stab you in the eye. The kid across the hall laughed as they dragged my blood-stained body away to the restraints. After days in restraints and weeks in isolation I was returned to my room. I never saw my old roommate again and they never gave me another one.

Every day was a numbing blur one into the next into the next for what seemed like an eternity. One of the few other days that I do remember was the day one of the new orderlies refused to give

153

me my after-lunch cigarette. They liked to keep the psychopaths hooked on cigarettes. My jailers made cigarettes the primary reward and punishment for compliance to their rules. Six times a day I was allowed one little crutch. It was the only thing I had left in my world and some new fuck wouldn't give me my smoke. I don't know if he was messing with me to be funny or just an asshole. Either way, I didn't break any rules, and I didn't take kindly to him fucking with me. I took all the chairs in the day room/ cafeteria and stacked them in the furthest corner of the room.

The new orderly taunted me and joked from the safety of his booth saying, "What ja going to do climb your pyramid out of here monkey boy?"

I was not that crazy. I wasn't building anything; I was stockpiling ammo. I knew what was coming next. When two orderlies came around the corner to drag me away to the restraints, I had no intention of going without a fight, I began to unload. Chairs were flying through the air one after the next and I was holding my ground pretty well until I ran out of chairs. Once again, I was dragged away to be strapped down, except this time they threw in a few good punches to let me know they did not like the rain of chairs or my disobedience. Just like the times before I was left strapped down for days on end. Just like the other times, I promised to behave and in time returned to my room.

I lived the stale life day in and out for the next few years. I can't say for sure how many years because I didn't keep track. I never had any visitors or mail. No one tells you it's your birthday on the inside and I had forgotten myself when mine was. Just when I thought I couldn't take the isolation anymore the fear of being alone forever began to break me and I started to hear voices. At first it was just whispers from the dead somewhere down the hall. Then it was phantoms just outside my room, and finally they found their way into my head.

Time disappeared as I went round and round in my pointless routine until I turned eighteen. I remember my 18th birthday because that's the day I was transferred from kiddie jail to an adult facility. Just after breakfast the guards escorted me to the holding area. I was told to put on an orange jump suit, and I was once again shackled at the feet, wrists and waist. I was never told where I was going. I was just told to get in the squad car. I was taken to Winnebago metal health institution. I'd grown too old for MATC and labeled too mentally ill for jail. I remember the two-hour drive well. I had not been outside in years. The sun was shining and the officer driving me had the window down. The air smelled so sweet. When we stopped at traffic lights people stared at the freak in orange with hands and feet shackled. I was too busy enjoying the blue sky to notice the world's subtle changes.

# BROKEN GLASS

Broken Glass. Broken Glass in my window.
I can see distorted images of a Twisted World.


Broken Glass. Broken Glass on the floor.
I can see shimmers of sunlight dance across.


Broken Glass. Broken Glass in my mind.
a thousand pieces of shattered dreams.


Broken Glass. Broken Glass against my flesh.
The shards and my skin become one.


Broken Glass. Broken Glass stained with blood.
The light from the Broken glass is shown.


Broken glass. Broken glass.

# CHAPTER 15

## Behind the wall of sanity

When I arrived at the institution it felt like I had never left Milwaukee. The same muffled echoes of madness rang out among the concrete walls that greeted me. The same absence of color surrounded me. The same stale air recycled through my lungs. I was left in a small room with carpet on the walls just like the time out room back at MATC. I thought I was in for more of the same endless boring routines just in a new room. I imagined spending the rest of my days here, just slowly grinding away the minutes until I gradually ceased to exist.

A lot of things were changing in the metal health care industry. They stopped doing surgical lobotomies only a few short years before and doctors were now in favor of so many new chemical lobotomies. There were and still are a lot of federal and pharmaceutical company dollars on the line to test and find drugs to "cure" the mentally diseased. I was a perfect candidate to test those drugs on. No one cared if I lived or died, and my past certainly proved my insanity. I could never understand the double standard when it came to drugs. I was constantly told about the evil of "street" drugs and their negative effect on my mind, body, and life but no one ever questioned the equally horrible side effects of the prescription drugs I was forced to take against my will.

The first prescription drug I was introduced to was Thorazine. A doctor came into the room accompanied by two male staff members. I was restrained by the two men while the doctor told me he was giving me something to relax while I made the adjustment to my new surroundings.

"Relax? Why I'm not tense?" I replied puzzled by what was happening.

Without answering my question, they firmly held my arm and injected the liquid into it. The cool liquid chilled my veins as it ran its course. I felt the effects almost instantly as the world began to move in slow motion. "Caaaan yuuuooo wwwaaallllkkl?" a strange voice seemed to ask. Before I could think of leaving the room, I realized I already left the room. It felt like I was floating, but in reality, I was carried by the staff. I couldn't understand my own thoughts and I found myself melting into the chair I was placed in. I sat drooling on myself, unable to move. I could tell other people were in the room, but it was like we were all in some heavy fog. I don't remember how or when but at some point, I was taken to a room with a bed and fell into a very deep sleep.

Somewhere within my subconscious I found myself with Lisa. We were lying on the side of a very tall hillside gazing up into the warm midnight sky, enchanted by the stars. The wind caressed our flesh while the trees whispered a forgotten song. The look in Lisa's eyes was one of peace and tranquility. She aches to be with me. I want to believe a world of hate can fade away as I close my eyes and reach out to kiss her. I reach into empty air. I opened my eyes and see her transform into a corpse. The corpse then collapsed into dust. I found myself crying in the spot where I had left her body. I scream to find myself awake in Hell. Alone and sweating in the dark I tried to get up, but I was sharply held back by leather restrains that bit at my wrists and feet. I guess my new keepers wanted to remind me of whom the master was and that I could expect the same medieval discipline methods from them just in case I'd forgotten. The Thorazine had clearly worn off and my sudden clarity was very scary.

I don't know how many hours passed before they came for me. I was so weak and sore from being strapped down when they finally let me out of the restraints I could barely stand up, let alone walk. I was placed in a wheelchair with my wrist strapped down and wheeled into a bathroom. A cold shower with the nasty smelling shampoo for lice was enough to get me back to my feet. After being deloused I was given pajama type bottoms and a matching shirt. They didn't give me any socks or underwear, but I was given a pair of paper slippers. I got dressed and strapped back into the wheelchair, then wheeled into an office to meet with my new doctor.

A very tall thin pale man entered the room and introduced himself as Doctor Vohn. He looked over some of the papers from the thick file sitting on his desk. After studying them for a very brief moment he looked over at me and asked, "Why do you think you're here" and then he spoke my name aloud. This took me by great surprise because I couldn't recall the last time someone said my first name to me. I only heard my first name spoken aloud once or twice in the last five years. My keepers always used my last name when referring to me.

One of the demons buried deep in me was summoned by calling that name. For one brief second of clarity the demon replied "Who are you to speak the name of the dead!"

"The dead?" Doctor Vohn replied. "That is very interesting" and he spoke my name again.

I did not like hearing the name of the person I no longer was and the more he said it the more agitated I became. I wrapped my hands around the rails of the chair I was still confined to.

Doctor Vohn obviously noticed this and asked "Does it disturb you to hear your own name?"

I'd had little to no interaction with other "humans" for several years now and whatever twisted thoughts left lingering inside my mind were bordering between shattered personalities and full blown madness. I had been living in my own nightmare (literarily and figuratively) for a long time. I couldn't escape the prison of twisted fantasies and guilt built, for me, inside my head. I sat silently in my chair and refused to play his game. Choosing when and when not to participate in "therapy" was the only control I had in my life. After getting no further response from me, the good doctor decided that the best thing to do was keep me sedated and strapped in my room for another day . . . or two . . . or three. He said he wanted me to be able to trust him, so he could diagnose and resolve all my problems.

"Why would I trust anyone in a world filled with deceit and cruelty" I thought to myself.

The needle went in, and I faded away into an endless void deep in my subconscious. In my state I believed all my dead friends were somehow still alive trapped inside my head. The weight of my sins only grew heavier with the passage of time in my solitude. The pressure crushed my memories into ghosts. Their voices spoke to me in the dark, they argued with me, they pleaded with me, and they begged me for things I could not give. Sometimes I let the spirits run rampant. Other times I fought them back into their graves. It was difficult to tell where my mental problems ended and the effects from all the prescribed drugs started.

I was so stoned and drugged out that I had dreams within my dreams. The dreams within dreams bordered on the edge of the absurd and no longer made any sense. In one I could eat the air and drink the blood of machines. In another I understood the secrets of skin diving into pools of brick while building stars of Jell-O in a sky of chairs. My mad dreams were always different, in another nightmare; I licked the walls of a bomb shelter while crying paper dolls dissolved when I caught them smiling plastic ovens. I listened to the dirt in the great skyway of Atlantis and ascended into melted plastic only to emerge in a cardboard prison in ashtray hell.

The next moment of semi-clear thinking I had was not until days later, when the fine Doctor Vohn came back into the room. I had been strapped to the bed for so long I feared I was becoming part of it. The doctor had the nerve to ask if I wanted to stay here like this or get up and walk around. Everything hurt from being strapped down for days on end. The demons got tired of trying to scratch their way out and eventually subsided. I did not want to fight anymore. I just wanted to go back to the nothing blank life I had come to know. I was afraid of the fiendish plans they might have in store for me. I was told if I agreed to ingest whatever poison pills he might prescribe, and behave myself, I wouldn't be strapped down anymore. Of course, I agreed to the deal. The pain from being restrained was torture. I was unrestrained, given a paper cup of poison, and given the grand tour of my new home. As soon as I got a good look around, I was convinced I had fallen further down into hell. When you look up from the bottom, the path to redemption often seems unreachable.

I was escorted by two orderlies, one nurse and the doctor. I walked out of the cruel room I was restrained in and went past three more rooms just like it. These rooms were called observation or "quiet" rooms. Apparently, they had an abundance of naughty patients in need of a special place to get some alone time. The quiet rooms were located at the end of the two hallways of patient's rooms that made up our ward. Right in the middle of the two hallways and immediately adjacent to the quiet rooms was the "control" or staff room. The control room had thick glass windows all around and a locked steel door for the staff. The ward was co-ed. One of the long hallways housed the men and the other hallway housed the women. Each side was complete with separate showers and bathrooms. There was a large room with cafeteria tables and attached bench seats right in front of the control room. Everything here was very similar to the institution I was accustomed to, except for one major difference. This place had a small room with two couches and a 19-inch TV bolted to the wall in one corner. Television was one of the luxuries in life that I had learned to live without (and to this day I don't watch much of it.)

After a short tour I was given something that looked like a regular toothbrush, only this had a tiny nub instead of full length handle, one sheet, one blanket, one pillowcase and one pillow, (at least they call it a pillow; it was more like a bag of wet sand.) After a basic explanation of the daily routine and ward rules I was shown to an empty room right at the front of the hallway next to one of the many quiet rooms. My door had been removed and I was told if I behave, I'd eventually get a room with a door and some regular clothes. It was Friday night. Besides meals and pill times, there were no structured activities until Monday morning. Thankfully, I already missed supper, because the pills they blackmailed me into taking made me nauseous and lethargic. I made my bed, and I laid in it, trying to sleep. One of the rules was you're not allowed to go into other patients' rooms, and they are not allowed in yours. Rules offered little comfort to the nightmare of some unknown crazy coming in my room to kill me in my sleep. My only sense of safety came from hiding under my blanket. For the rest of the weekend I only came out of my sanctuary to use the bathroom, eat and take my pills. I avoided other patients and spoke to no one until Monday morning.

Monday morning after breakfast while most of the other patients who had outside privileges cards, were off on the morning run, I met with someone who would become the only ray of sunshine left in my life. Her name was Lynn and she was my drug counselor. A pretty female hadn't talked to me in years so she got my undivided attention.

"Welcome to the Gemini program. I'm Lynn I will be your counselor and we will be meeting once a day Monday through Friday. We are all here to try to help you." She spoke with a soft gentle tone. Her blue eyes were just like Lisa's. I fell for Lynn the minute we met so I spared her from my demonic urges. She asked me the standard lineup of stupid questions; "Why are you here," being everyone's favorite.

I'm sick of that question and told her "If you don't know why I'm here? I sure as hell can't tell you."

My honesty invoked a small laugh, before she continued "Ok let's not concentrate on what got you here. Let's talk about what you are going to do to get out of here?"

Her words hit me like a brick to the face "Get out of here? What . . . what do you mean get out?" I replied in shock. I'd never even entertained the idea of being released.

She repeated herself "We are all here to make you well enough to rejoin society. So, I ask you again. What are you going to do to help me, help you?"

I was still dumbfounded by the thought of release. I never thought I would ever see the light of day again! "I'd do anything to get out of this hellhole" I told her.

She leaned in toward me, looked me straight in the face and said "Well then, we must start with how you got here? What did you do in your life to end up in here?"

At this point I could not answer her. My mind had blocked most of my monstrous past out. I was content to live in a fantasy world. Worlds deep in my mind were filled with my dead friends. I wasn't ready to face my past, or leave the fantasy, so I had no answers for Lynn that day. The only answer I could think of was that the dead were sent to this special place in hell to decay and rot; and I didn't want to tell her that. She told me to think about what she said and ended our meeting. Our time together was always very short, only about fifteen or twenty minutes a day. She had a lot of other patients and not a lot of time. Lynn was always polite and cordial but her compassion for me never seemed quite genuine. Besides talking about my addictions her primary task was to monitor my daily mood and behavior. Monday through Friday she met with me and took little notes. Judging by her questions she seemed interested in my wellbeing, in truth she may have been more interested in the adverse side effects that I constantly suffered from as a result of all the medication. She reported to a doctor that I rarely ever saw, the doctor in turn would change my prescription based on her notes and I would find new pills in my daily cup of poison.

I kept to myself and in time I slowly became adjusted to my new surroundings. The Haldol I was currently on, kept me just comatose enough to not be considered a threat. Little by little, I gained enough trust to be assimilated into the rest of the flock of crazies. When I was deemed "safe" enough to move out of the room with no door I met my new roommate Jim.

He seemed normal enough at first but then when you got to know him you quickly realized why he was here. Jim had terminal indecisiveness. Put simply he just couldn't make up his mind. It sounds silly and perhaps not the kind of thing to label you insane but he was truly crazy all the same. For instance, he would ask to borrow five cents to get something from the vending machine, which I would give him. Then he would return, less than a minute later, to give the nickel back only to ask for it once again. Then return it. This would continue until someone broke the cycle. He did this with everything. They had to put him at the end of the food line because he held up the whole line repeatedly trying to return food. I was severely damaged but not stupid. I had a good relationship with him because once I figured out his nonsense, I was smart enough not to fall into his traps. If I didn't ask anything from him and said no to him eight thousand times a day we got along fine.

As my level of trust went up so did my privileges, until the day came when I got my one-hour patient privilege card. This card granted me the privilege of going outside for hour a day supported.

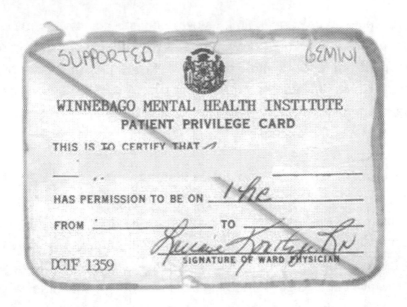

WINNEBAGO MENTAL HEALTH INSTITUTE
PATIENT PRIVILEGE CARD

THIS IS TO CERTIFY THAT

HAS PERMISSION TO BE ON _____ the _____

FROM _____ TO _____

DCIF 1359          SIGNATURE OF WARD PHYSICIAN

(That meant with supervision). Some patients had unsupported cards and could go out without supervision; I never earned one of those. I clearly remember the first morning I was allowed to join the others on the morning walk. This was an enormous reward to me. I had not been outside in years, except for my ride here in the back of a squad car, locked in chains. Since it was my first week out, I wasn't allowed to run. I had to walk right next to the guard. I followed along with the group down a beautiful path that led to the lake. The air smelled so good. I had forgotten how you could smell the oncoming of winter in Wisconsin. That clean crisp air spoke to me. It reminded me that things were never permanent. Like the season I could smell changing, I hoped I too could change.

After a few weeks I was allowed to join the running group. The running group had only three members; two guards and Brian. Brian was a very large muscular skinhead with a swastika clearly tattooed on the back of his head. The first day I was allowed to run with the group I was overexcited! As soon as we got outside, I bolted like a bullet from a gun, even though I had been warned not run too far ahead. I wasn't trying to escape or be difficult. I had been caged for too long. I could hear my long-lost friends in the wind. I was just trying to catch them. The guards must have thought I would burn out quickly because they did not chase me until they realized I wasn't going to slow down or stop. Brian started yelling "Run rabbit run!" I took that as a challenge to evade capture and I ran as fast as I could. I was smiling at the sun. I could hear my friends in the wind laughing just ahead of me. I felt like a rabbit running free. But this rabbit spent too much time in a cage. My legs were not what they used to be, I soon stumbled and fell. As soon as I stood up, I was tackled.

While I was being held against the cold earth the friendly laughter of the wind changed to cries of the dammed buried deep in the earth. When Brian and his escort jogged past, I heard Brian say "Foolish little rabbit you can't outrun the dogs". That was the end of my outside time for the rest of my stay. I was immediately switched to a different drug. Apparently the last one didn't have enough sedating effects.

My recent run for it earned me not only the privilege of being once again strapped down, but also the respect of one person here. My new wanna-be best friend Brian. When I got out of isolation for trying to escape, Brian was itching to talk to me. I was not allowed outside anymore but I at least I was no longer afraid to live again.

One day during lunch Brian sat down across from me and asked, "What's up little rabbit?"

I didn't want him to think I was weak so I replied, "living in the shithouse what's up with you?" in a hard tone while I stared at my meal.

"What the fuck where you going to do? Run home little rabbit?" he asked and laughed. It wasn't a cruel laugh but one of kindness.

I let my defenses down a little and told him "I just wanted to chase the wind. I have been locked inside a long time" and I looked at him with my cold dead eyes when I said "long time" just to let him know I was no timid rabbit.

"I like you rabbit" was all he said, and we finished eating our lunch.

After that Brian and most of the other patients called me rabbit. It wasn't a terrible nickname since I hated my own name. I liked being called rabbit. It reminded me of the innocent creature I wished I still was.

Because of my new friendship I felt safe enough to leave my room and watch television in the day room. We were watching some cheesy detective show when Brian saw something that was similar to the reason he was locked up. He proceeded to tell me his tale. He said he broke into a liquor store in the middle of the night through a hole he cut in the ceiling. After jumping down he quickly realized the doors were chained shut at night. He couldn't get out through the door and failed several attempts to get back out through the hole. When he realized, he was going to jail; He began to drink heavily from the store's inventory. When the police did finally show up Brian was plenty drunk and ready to fight his way out. He beat three of Milwaukee's boys in blue pretty bad before he was subdued. The Milwaukee County justice system sent him here because unlike jail there is no finite number of days to sit before, they have to release you. It's the perfect place to make people disappear forever. The system could keep him here forever and no one could legally question it. I didn't know if anything he said was true and I didn't care. I liked having a friend inside this nightmare and Brian was a good friend to have.

Brian's friendship was invaluable. This huge (330lb plus) woman got mad because I looked at her wrong or something. Anyway, something set off the crazy in her and she was charging like a wild rhino fully prepared to stomp me into the earth when Brian put himself in-between us and was able to keep her from me long enough for one of the staff to hit the panic button. There were panic buttons throughout the institution. Anytime something got out of control the staff hit the panic button and Valhalla released the dogs of war. I had seen the button get pressed twice in the short time I was here. Both times alarms sounded and the biggest badass motherfuckers they had working here showed up in full riot gear ready to beat any resistance back into submission. On this occasion the woman and Brian both gave up without a fight and were taken to the quiet rooms. I was grateful Brian stuck his neck out for me. I told him so when he was released back into general population.

Brian was an interesting person who loved to talk. I didn't talk much, so we got along very well. I didn't feel any inner need to share my story mostly because I didn't want to acknowledge it ever happened. Brian however rambled on and on about the Bible and the power it had to save. He often reminded me that Jesus loved us all and died for our sins. Brian would go on in great length about what this line in the Bible meant or what Jesus wanted us to do with our lives. I didn't understand most of what he said or care for that matter. I was just happy to not be alone in this hell.

Now that I wasn't afraid to speak, I met some of the other lost souls. There was Brian. My roommate Jim, an angry, little, skinny, red haired guy named Tim, and a girl in her twenties named Renee. These were the only patient's names I can remember out the two dozen or so of us that were in the Gemini program. Most of the patients were so wacked out they rarely spoke. Some I only saw during meals and others must have been completely bed ridden. I never saw who was in the rooms at the end of the hall, but I knew there were people down there. Meals were delivered to the rooms at the far end of the hall and sometimes empty trays came back out. I was pretty drugged up on the ever-changing, never-ending supply of pills. Some of the things I saw may not have been real. I could be quite certain but never really sure of anything. I was surrounded by strangeness all the time.

Since I was an escape risk and was no longer allowed outside, the only time I was able to leave the ward was for an indoor exercise period. Once a week all the patients who had earned exercise privileges went to an underground gymnasium to play volleyball. We all lined up to be counted, have our pockets checked, and finally led downstairs into a large tunnel. I'd already been to a few different places using the tunnel system but I was always amazed by how many rooms were here, deep underground, hidden from the public. This place was huge and held an army of skeletons in the closets.

I couldn't help but wonder how far the tunnels went. One week on our way to the gym my curiosity took over. In one of my compulsive mood swings, I decided to explore the tunnel. I took off running down the tunnel. Unlike the time outside, no one chased after me. I thought it was strange no one followed as I ran down the tunnel that went on into the distance for quite some length before I came to a corner. I ran around the corner and right into a steel wall with two large steel doors. The doorway was big enough to drive a truck through. I never tried to open the doors; I thought only an idiot would try to go through there. The wall and gigantic doors looked like a blast shield from a sci-fi movie. I thought I could almost make out the atomic symbol buried beneath the dust. Whatever was on the other side was undoubtedly worse than were I was, so I walked back around the corner. By this time, the group was about to reach the gym. I could see that the rest of the group still walking with their escorts. I walked back down the hall about twenty yards where the group was now waiting for me by the gym door.

The guard said, "Don't worry the gyms not going anywhere!"

Most of the group started laughing and taunting me with things like "You can't escape from the tunnels!" and "you'd need steel claws to dig out of here rabbit" After the joking stopped, while we were waiting for the guard to unlock the cabinet to retrieve a ball, one of the older ladies whispered in my ear.

"The tortured souls walk these chambers."

"What tortured souls?" I replied with genuine concern.

This woman was always scared and talking to herself anytime we were down in the tunnels, but she was not the only one who was delusional. I believed I was a tortured soul. I thought she might know how I could redeem my soul and get out of here. I pressed her for answers, but she only prattled on about bizarre experiments. She claims they did weird things to people down here for many years and continue to do all kinds of inhuman "research" in the tunnels. Again, I pressed her for details. Electric shock, lobotomy, and other horrors to gruesome to imagine she says. I was still skeptical, but she insisted if I just look closer, I will see the undeniable evidence. I was unable to continue the conversation because it was time to play volleyball.

Volleyball in the nuthouse was nothing like a real game. Only six or seven of us had the mental ability to hit a ball. Those of us who could play were split up into teams with the other half a dozen zombies mixed in. I had to wait through several dozen serves with the ball being either ignored or hitting one of the zombie statues. Most of my teammates had no interest in playing and probably didn't know where they were. When the ball did finally come to me, I'd just slam or bump it as hard as possible out of frustration. There was no point in keeping score and the only winners were the ones who stayed behind and didn't play. After two hours of that nonsense, it was a long walk back through the tunnels to the ward.

On the way back that night I thought about what the old women said earlier. She had me wondering about the strange experiments going on down here. I walked slower and I noticed more details on the doors and rooms. I envisioned some kind of human zoo with mutants and freaks locked behind the many doors.

I was on a lot of strange drugs and in a very delusional state. I can't be sure how much my memory was real and how much was pure hallucination. As I looked deep into the shadows, I saw the tortured souls, the old women spoke of. They pointed to the rooms with labels like "Electro convulsive therapy", "Transient brain anoxia" and "Neuroleptics". Some areas had radioactive symbols and warnings about "Radio magnetic microwaves" and others had what seemed to be airtight cells with some kind of air tanks running into them. There where biohazard and radioactive warnings crudely painted over. I recognized the symbols from heavy metal album covers. Whatever diabolical experiments they did here, they clearly kept them hidden from the public deep underground. The thought of the bizarre goings on here only fed my fears and belief that I was trapped in hell. My mind began to build different layers of hell. In my own paranoia I once again saw myself among the tortured souls and living dead in the reflections from the glass windows as I passed. I was terrified by the thought of what depths my suffering would reach before I was forgiven. I never misbehaved or ran off again. I did not want to find myself the newest patient in the lower levels of hell.

Beside my irrational fears about sinking further into hell I gave up hope on any escape attempt because I did not believe escape was possible. Without a valid patient privilege card to get outside I didn't think anyone could get past all the guarded steel doors with their big magnetic locks; and yet my innocent minded roommate Jim managed to do just that. A minister came to the ward to give last rights to one of the patients. When they buzzed the minister in, Jim asked him to hold the door and walked right out. I don't know why the guards were so distracted that day, but they didn't notice Jim was missing until three hours later when we lined up for dinner. After a not so intensive search, they found Jim down by the lake.

He had made it out and was just sitting on a bench watching the sun dance across the lake. I joked "He couldn't make up his mind whether to escape or not and had been sitting there thinking about it when they caught him". I guess the staff must have thought that as well because Jim was never searched or punished, they just led him back inside. He was mumbling something about the birds and happy squirrels gathering nuts for the winter when he came in our room.

The guards and staff all thought he never left the grounds and just sat down by the lake. But when he asked me for my help with something the day after they brought him back, I speculated he had left the grounds or met with someone. I began to wonder if he made up his "condition" in order to avoid jail. I could only speculate, after all I didn't know why he was in here. Jim never came to me for help with anything before so at first, I was leery of what kind of stupid crap I was being pulled into. When I asked what he needed help with he wouldn't say he just pulled the plastic cap off the top of the one of the beds legs and begs me to look down inside the metal bedframe. Just to shut him up I looked and to my amazement I saw a baggy with some joints and matchsticks stuck down in the metal tubing of his bed frame. I could tell he was agitated that he had to let me in on his secret but after he couldn't figure out how to retrieve it, he felt he had no choice. Apparently, he was sure they would search the room, so he really wedged it down in there. We didn't have anything small enough or long enough to push it out. It took some thinking and trial and error but by the next night I had rolled newspaper tightly into a long stick and pushed the bag free. He thanked me by smoking one joint with me. We huddled on the floor in the dark and blew our hits into a dirty laundry bag. It had been so many years since I did any street drugs, I almost forgot how good it felt to be baked. The combo of the weed and whatever prescription drugs I was on had a wicked hallucinogenic effect. That night I dreamed in infrared.

When I awoke the next morning Jim wasn't in the room, which was odd because he usually slept right up to breakfast. Old habits die hard, and I couldn't stop thinking about the weed. As soon as he came back into the room I asked, "Where did you stash the weed"?

He said "It's cool I put it in a safe place. Just be cool I don't want to get caught. We will smoke some more after lights out when the risk getting caught is the lowest."

For once Jim actually made sense, so I agreed "Cool, it makes sense to wait until later"

After lights out the staff would make hourly rounds while you slept. The anticipation of getting stoned again was overwhelming. I waited all day counting the minutes. That night back in our room, right after the staff made their first hourly check on us, I told Jim to "Bust out. Let's get stoned!"

Jim whispered, "I flushed it all."

"What the fu . . . you did what?" I said in utter disbelief.

Jim goes right back into his crazy "character" saying "yeah, I flushed it. I didn't want to get into trouble, do you think I should go and get it?"

I could see through his bullshit now and replied sarcastically "Sure go get it from the toilet you flushed it down." It was a really big deal to me; the drugs I was forced to take were crappy and riddled with side effects. I missed the drugs that made me feel good and I was extremely disappointed to be teased with the promise of getting high only to have the rug ripped out from under me. I had enough of Jim's crap.

I read him the riot act "Be crazy don't be crazy! I really don't care! Don't bother me with your stupid shit ever again. It's really fucking annoying!" Jim never bothered me with anything again.

This place was so fucking boring that when Brian told me about and exercise room, they took him to three times a week I instantly wanted in. After little begging, and plenty of good behavior, I was allowed to go to the exercise room. The exercise room was down a different tunnel and on the way there I wondered "what didn't they have down here? How far did these tunnels go?" It was mandatory that patients were always escorted by at least two guards. Most of the time we were escorted by Bob and another big muscle head guy. Sometimes Bob's workout buddy couldn't make it and Tracy, a nurse from our ward would fill in. It was Bob's idea to start the exercise program. Bob was an ex-military guy that found work here because they needed big forceful types to keep the crazies in line. Bob was the night guard on my ward and worked the panic squad.

He was the kind of guy that pushed his way through life. Anytime he reached a barrier he just bullied his way through it. The only mindset he understood was "Might makes right."

Bob and the other panic squad members wanted to get paid to work out. There was already a very nice exercise room right here on the grounds. The administrator refused to pay them to lift weights. Bob wouldn't take no for an answer, so he used intimidation to push through his plan. They eventually came to a happy medium; if Bob wanted to get paid to work out then he would have to supervise patients exercising. Bob agreed to the terms but only signed up one patient to participate in the program. Bob worked the night shift on our ward, so he knew Brian was always timid, polite and reading Bible stuff. Bob didn't see Brian as a threat, so he chose Brian to be the lone patient in the exercise program. When I wanted to join the group, I wasn't considered a threat, so Bob agreed to let me in. I was in need of some exercise; I weighed 115-pounds soaking wet. Brian and Bob showed me how to use all the weight machines while Tracy or the other guard would sit by the door next to the panic button. The time I spent down there was a nice addition to my endless routine, but the days continued to slowly grind away. Each day was just carbon copy of the one before with the small difference of me growing stronger.

I felt comfortable settled into my new routine. The days blurred in and out until one night everything changed. I had terrible stomach cramps from either the substandard crap they called food or my newest poison pills. Either way I had to use the toilet something fierce. The rules stated you had to stand at your doorway until given permission to leave your room and use the toilet. I waited and waited, but even after waving my arms around I couldn't get anyone in the control rooms' attention, so I quick ran across the hall to the bathroom. While I sat silently on the toilet, I could hear what sounded like muffled screams. The sounds I heard weren't that unusual around here. I should have ignored them and just gone back to my room when I finished, but I didn't. I crept down the hallway and eventually up to the control room. I peeked inside; there was an empty chair where Bob should have been. I crawled around the empty control room and peeked around the corner. I could see the TV, in the common area, was on but no one was watching it. I heard the muffled cries again and they definitely weren't coming from the TV. After trying to open the locked control room door I crept closer toward the mysterious sound.

The cries were coming from one of the "quiet" rooms on the girl's side. Something just kept calling me closer, until I found myself pushing the slightly ajar door open to see what was going on inside. Bob was stark naked. He had Renee strapped in the restraints, face down, with a pillowcase over her head. Renee was crying while she struggled to breathe as Bob pulled hard at the pillowcase as he raped her. Before I could say "What the fuck", Bob noticed me standing there and stopped what he was doing. He started walking towards me when I panicked and ran back to my room.

Bob turned back to grab his clothes which bought me just enough time to remember the simple principle of the wedge. Now I'm no "Mr. Science" but I did know if you put a wedge in a door it won't open. I pulled the sheet off the bed and jammed it the best I could into one corner of the doors' sill, between the door and the frame. I stepped back and jump slammed against the door with all my might to force it shut. All I could do then was hope it worked. It was the only way I could think of to block the door, all the furniture was bolted down. I was terrified of what Bob would do if he caught me so like a frightened child I hid under the bed. In the meantime, Bob put his clothes on and covered some of his tracks before he came to my door. I was sure he figured he had all the time in the world to

177

silence me. After all, it's not like I could leave. He was in for quite a surprise when he pushed on my door, and it wouldn't open. The harder he pushed on the door the tighter the wedge became, and he was unable to open the door. He wanted to deal with me before the other staff member came back. After several failed attempts to open the door, he became frustrated. He was caught pounding on my door and yelling obscenities when his coworker returned. Bob had to think of a lie to cover his ass fast. Bob told her I was running loose on the ward, may have raped a female patient, and now had somehow barricaded myself in my room. She immediately called for reinforcements. I truly believe Bob would have killed me if it wasn't for an angel blocking the door. Within minutes four other night guards arrived. They all believed Bob's lie and were looking for vengeance when they came for me.

Not knowing how I had blocked the door two of the frantic guards showed up outside the window. They were shining flashlights in and clanking on the outside of the window as they attempted to remove the outer locks, to climb inside and get me. Lucky for me the outdoor locks hadn't been used in forty years and they won't budge, since they were all rusted shut.

Unlucky for me, my roommate was awakened by the clatter of commotion and began freaking out. "What's going on did you tell them about the weed?" Jim asked me in full panic.

"No, I didn't tell them anything. They're coming to kill me!!" I replied from under the bed.

In an awfully short amount of time a dreadfully large number of the staff had assembled outside the window and in the hallway. They demanded from inside and out that I unblock the door. Outside the idiotic staff was still struggling with the locks. I stayed under the bed, but Jim got out of bed to see what was blocking the door. The bastard simply tugged at the sheet and freed the door. The room flooded with people. I was quickly grabbed, shot up with a big dose of Thorazine, and strapped down. The room began to descend rapidly, and I felt my world sinking into the black.

Deep in the misty haze of a midnight dream. I awoke in the forest. It was like no forest on earth, Deadly with its silence, Sorrowful in its desolation. The new moon hid its face in shame. Just a sleepy glimmer of the light struggled through the dense trees to reveal this foreboding landscape. I walked in darkness, yet I could sense the cold wood around me. My footsteps were laid with an eerie precision, like a well-rehearsed death procession. I walked on through the black. It was as if my soul had abandoned me as I walked without sound. My thoughts were being focused as I was enchanted along this path I was destined to follow.

Then it happened. I felt her presence. I knew this feeling too well. She has followed me a long time. She has waited desolate eons for this moment. Like an impatient child she tugs at me pulling me closer and closer. Then I stopped dead in my tracks. I stood frozen as she confronted me. We must have been in awe that the moment had finally come. We stood in deadlock for what seemed like an eternity. Then with one torrid gust she reached out and grasped my soul. I felt all the pain sorrow, hate, peace, and love in one frenzied rush of madness. Then I felt her pain. My life was a minute waste compared to the infinite times she had lived and died again and again. A lonely tear ran down my face as I acknowledged the suffering she'd endured. I knew then why she came to me. She sought me out this night so I could join her plodding senselessly through the spirit world. Living our burned-out lives over and over together. Reliving and regretting the infinite mistake but never believing in a future. Existing only in the isolated desperation of the past. She wants me to give up and give in to her. I understand but do not want to see. I must complete the revolution of the circle. I owe her my life and I must pay that debt for her debt can never be paid. She is trapped in her endless routine. Suffer and die, suffer and die, I complete the circle and look in her eyes. The look in her eyes could never have been clearer. The dream changes. It's only me, alone looking in a mirror. The mirror collapses but the image does not.

Once I regained something that resembles consciousness. Lynn came into the room and asked, "What occurred here last night why were you hiding under the bed with your door blocked?" I was seriously messed up on Thorazine and God knows what else. I did not want to believe the truth, so I hide behind delusion.

My eyes rolled around in my head as I slurred "I saw a demon in the hall, and I was scared"

She tried to reassure me with lies "You know there are no such things as demons. Do you see any demons here now?"

I scanned the room knowing there were plenty of demons walking among us, but there weren't any here now, so I said "no"

"I'm going to go get the doctor and come back and see you later." I could see the doctor just outside the door when she left. I could hear their voices blur together on the other side of the door when she closed it. I fell back into the sinking black that consumed my room and mind.

I don't know how long I was asleep or how long I was strapped down in isolation this time. I do remember how good it felt when they finally came to undo the restraints. Lynn, Doctor Vohn and two orderlies came into the room. They undid my hands and allowed me to sit up. I'm told by the doctor "Your medication may have had some ill effects. We're going to try some new medication for you to make sure no more demons are in the hallways, ok?" He smiles and he hands me a cup with some new pills. I'm still dazed and confused but I knew the drill. Without words I take the pills, smile and I was freed.

After stretching and using the bathroom I went to the day room still wondering what the hell was going on. I felt like I got off easy and I didn't understand why they didn't pin Renee's rape on me or a least ask about it? Renee was sitting alone at one of the tables in the corner. I had to know if I had slipped further into madness or if what I saw in the night really happened.

I sat across from her, still terrified and whispered "Are you ok? I'm not entirely sure what I saw the other night, but I thought I saw bob rap . . ."

Before I could finish, she put her finger on my lips to silence them. "You saw nothing. Right now, sugar the only thing you need to remember, is to forget whatever you think you saw" she said still holding her finger on my mouth while giving me her best sexy eyes.

Puzzled why she never reported the rape I removed her hand from my face and replied "I don't understand? You wanted that to happen?"

This visibly angered her. She grabbed my wrist and dug her nails into my flesh. "No, I didn't want that to fuckin happen, they've been doing that kind of shit to me for years, I spoke up once before and they beat me and ganged up on me. It's better to not resist and let them finish quickly!"

Outraged I tried to reason back "That's not right you can't just let them do that to you".

She replied with the only reason that made any sense here "I hate to burst your bubble sweetheart, but neither me, you or anybody else trapped here has any choice in what happens to them. We are all just rats in their maze. They can do anything they want to us and no one in the outside world would ever know or care. All the people here are already forgotten. Have you ever seen anyone one here get a visitor or any mail from the outside?"

I thought about it and realized how right she was "No, I've never seen a visitor or mail I guess we're all lost behind the walls of sanity"?

"Lost?" she pulled me closer, looked at me with her now despondent eyes and said "You're not lost sweetheart. To be lost someone has to be looking for you. No one is looking for any of the people in here." She got up to leave and whispered in my ear "Remember to forget" and she returned to her room. Our conversation left me feeling extremely depressed, so I retreated back to my room.

The next day in group everyone wanted to talk about the excitement in the middle of the night that I had caused. I told them I had problems with my medication which led to Jim bringing up questions about the demon in the hall out to kill me. The other nut cases called me crazy. Socially retarded idiots laughed and mocked me. I knew what I saw and wanted so badly to expose this atrocity. I looked to Renee for a sign or clue of what I should do. She had the same scared helpless look Lisa had when she came to me for help. I knew from the way she looked at me, this was her cross to bear and she did not want it out in the light, especially during group in front of the idiot convention. I swallowed the secret and said, "I saw a demon in the hallway and instead of fighting it I got scared and ran away to hide under my bed." I soaked the words with enough sarcasm to stop their juvenile teasing.

Brian immediately jumped in with twenty minutes of one his special interpretations of readings from the Bible. I was glad to hear Brian chime in and I encouraged him to continue his sermon since it took me out of the spotlight. As Brian spoke, I stared across at Renee. I could tell the weight of the secret was crushing her. She had her head down and I thought I saw a tear roll down her cheek. I wanted to speak to her again but after group she avoided me and went right to her room. I wanted to follow but I wasn't allowed on the girl's side. When she didn't come out for supper, I was hopelessly worried about her. There was nothing I could do but wait until the next day and try to catch her at breakfast.

The guilt of accidently discovering Renee's secret was eating me alive the next morning when I didn't see her at breakfast. When group was cancelled for unknown reasons and we went into lock down until lunch, it didn't occur to me that it had anything to do with Renee. When I didn't see her at lunch and returned to find the staff cleaning stuff out of Renee's room, I was forced to face the truth. There was a usually large number of staff in the control room that day. When my counselor Lynn came out, I asked her where Renee was. Since it was almost time for my daily sit down, we went into her office before she told me "Renee took her own life last night". I sat in shock wondering if Bob was cleaning up loose ends.

"It's not right" I said under my breath.

Lynn replied, "all the people here are very disturbed and Renee just couldn't fight her demons anymore" after awkwardly catching herself on her words she shows some concern for me "Would you like to talk about your fear of demons?"

I was angry and resentful. I could feel my demons rising from their slumber, awaked by the sorrow of another lost soul. I looked up directly at Lynn which I never did and declared "I'm not afraid of demons, their afraid of me!"

"Well good that sound like a healthy attitude, you keep up the positive thinking" Lynn said not realizing it was not positive thinking but rather a dark sentiment declaring I was ready to let the demons win.

We ended my session with that. I should have told her the truth, but I was afraid she would never believe me.

*Symptom of the time.*

*Victim of the rage.*

*Cannot see the blind.*

*Concealed within my cage.*

# CHAPTER 16

## Smash the mirror!

Renee trusted me to keep her secret and I would have if she were still alive. But the guilt of her death being added to my pile of wrongdoing, was building up inside me and I had to vent. I wanted to tell someone who I could trust. I knew Brian had a crush on Renee; we all did since she was the only semi-cute girl patient here. I hoped he would share my hatred towards Bob as I told him all about how I had discovered Bob raping Renee in the night. I went on to tell him how Renee had confessed to me multiple previous rapes. In tears I told Brian, I believed Renee killed herself because she thought I might expose her terrible secret. Brian turned away from me and stood silent in the corner. I could see his muscles tense up as the truth he didn't want to acknowledge forced its way in. Brian gathered his thoughts and tried to recite his favorite Bible passages. The words he once found so easy to recite became clouded. Try as he might, Brian could not complete any of the passages that previously comforted and subdued him. He would stop mid-sentence and ask me to repeat the disgusting details of Renee's rape over and over. After I refused to give him any more detail of something I barely saw and wanted to forget, he told me to keep everything once again a secret. "The good lord would punish the guilty sinners." He said.

I myself had acted as the sword of God smiting evil so I believed Brian when he told me God would take care of everything.

At dinner Brian was acting strangely happy. He was giddy like a little kid. I was depressed and withdrawn. Brian didn't want me to drag down his emotional high, he tried to cheer me up by constantly patting me on the back and saying things like "Cheer up rabbit. The day of reckoning is coming." Tim noticed Brian's' odd behavior from the other end of our table and when he looked over Brian caught his wandering eye and snapped "You are looking for your lucky charms ya fuckin little leprechaun?" This was extremely odd behavior from Brian because I never heard him swear before. I hoped our talk earlier would stir up some emotions in Brian. I was pleased in a way to see him so riled up. I needed a strong ally because just after supper we were scheduled to go for exercise, and this would be the first time I saw Bob since the night I caught him red handed.

Brian and I waited in the usual spot until Bob walked up. Bob looked a little nervous when he learned his muscular buddy couldn't make it and Tracy the nurse would be the second escort to the weight room instead. The drugs made it almost impossible to distinguish between fantasy and reality, so I was still uncertain if what I had seen was real. Bob however knew what was real and gave me the evil eye. Bob didn't want to do anything out of the ordinary in front of Tracy so we both acted like nothing happened. We went to the weight room and began working out, as we'd done dozens of times before. Brian had been docile since he arrived. He never showed any signs of violence, so it wasn't unusual that Bob trusted him enough to have him spot for him while he lifted weights. Brian had spotted Bob a thousand times before without danger but today would be different.

Fate and circumstance often conspire together to create chaos; this was one of those times. That day, at that exact wrong moment in time Tracy decided she urgently needed to use the bathroom. She never left Bob alone with us before. In fact, they were required to work in pairs so if something happen to one the other could call for help or simply hit the panic button. But on this day Bob gave her the green light to break protocol and leave the room. I guess she felt it was safe with the bathroom being right next door or maybe she had to go so bad she didn't care. Either way, she got up, unlocked the door, and went to use the bathroom. I don't know if Brian planned what was about to happen or the right moment just presented itself. Either way, as the door clicked shut, Brian went into action. Brian was spotting Bob and as Bob went to lower the massive barbell, Brian forced the bar down with all his might. The bar came down with a distinctive snap when it collided with Bob's throat. It happened so quickly I didn't realize what happen until Brian was grabbing Bob's unconscious twitching body and putting it in the chair by the door. I stopped what I was doing and was about to stand when Brian looked at me with pure hate and demanded I continue lifting weights! "Just act natural or I'll fuckin kill you too rabbit!" The rage on his face and the tone in his otherwise soft demeanor had changed, I could see his demons rising, and I wasn't going to cross him so I just kept working out. I was not so naïve. I had looked enough times into the eyes of evil to see it coming. I had wanted Brian to be mad enough at Bob to protect me from him, but I never wanted more bloodshed. I feared I may have created an unstoppable monster.

I remember thinking my best friend and I were about to break out of this godless hell hole. Brian put Bob's body in the chair by the door hoping Tracy would not notice anything was wrong when she returned. When she left, she took the keys and until she returned, we were locked in the exercise room. Tracy returned, saw Bobs' feet and fell for the deception. The window in the door wasn't big enough to see the person's upper body. I figured when Tracy opened the door we would grab her keys and find a way to escape through the tunnels. The seconds seemed to move in slow motion as I watched the door handle gradually turn and open. Tracy was oblivious to the danger when she crossed the threshold. When the door clicked closed again all hell broke out once again.

Before Tracy had time to notice Bob's unconscious body in the chair, Brian jumped up from the bench and punched her in the face. He hit her with such force I thought I saw her feet come off the ground. Brian was lightning fast and by the time she landed on the floor he was on her. I sat helplessly by, partly in shock but mostly in fear. I did not like physical confrontation. It made me nauseous because I'd spent years suppressing my demons and history taught me violence never led to a happy ending. I desperately wanted this to be one of my hallucinations. I closed my eyes and repeated "This isn't happening, this isn't happening" again and again in my head but my own thoughts could not drown out Tracy's cries for help. When I opened my eyes, Brian had Tracy pinned to the floor and was tearing her clothes off.

I would like to say I overcame my fears, found some inner strength and rose up. But in truth it is more like I was so scared I crawled deep inside and disappeared until another person took over. I remembered being the victim all too well; I could not let Tracy be the next victim. I got up and jumped on Brian's' back. I got him in a headlock and squeezed with all my might, but my tiny frame was no match against the raging behemoth. Brian got to his feet and slammed backward trying to crush me into the wall, but he tripped over the weight bench instead. We slammed on to the floor. With all his weight pinning to me to the floor he punched at my face, missing once, and hitting the solid floor instead, this only made the beast madder. Brian scrambled back to his feet grabbed me from the floor and held me by my throat, at arm's length and just before he hit me, I saw Tracy. She managed to get up and was about to hit the panic button. SMASH! Brian's fist collided with my face repeatedly while I swung out blindly hitting only empty air. Trying to fight back was futile as I felt my brain rattle around inside my dense skull. Brian was about to let my bloody body go and return to raping Tracy when the door burst open. The last thing I remember; were my hands and arms breaking as I tried to shield myself from a barrage of clubs being swung down upon me. Then the familiar sinking black consumed me.

## Part missing

Dreams of a final duel with death must have filled my damaged mind as my soul floated in limbo and my body lay unconscious in a coma for more than three weeks. When Tracy hit the panic button the panic squad came running. Since they did not know what happened they did the only thing they were trained for, beating the crap out of anyone wearing patient clothes. I was already half dead from Brian's beating before the panic squad clubs even hit me so it only took a couple of good whacks in my old head wound to finally put me down. I could only imagine Brian had put up one hell of a good fight before they brought him down. Bob died from a crushed larynx and broken neck. Ironically Brian didn't even kill Bob out of some biblical vengeance, unbeknown to me Brian was a serial rapist and the story about robbing the liqueur store and beating up police was all bullshit. He served over six years quiet as a mouse with his Bible pacifying him until I told him about Bob raping Renee. The emotions I stirred up must have brought some hidden dark shadows in him back to life. The old familiar feelings must have eaten away at his barely adequate defenses the entire day until the opportunity of having Tracy trapped alone presented itself.

After that day Tracy quit her job at the institution, but she didn't forget me or what I had done for her. She revealed to administration, that to her knowledge I had no part in any of the violence other than trying to stop Brian from raping her and if not for me she would probably be dead. They launched an investigation which is a fancy way of saying "buy enough time for folks to forget about it". What did they need to "investigate"? They had Tracy's testimony, and she was the only creditable witness. After the "investigation" concluded the staff decided to remove Brian from the Gemini program. The program was meant to find cures for the most extreme mentally diseased and criminally insane. Brian reverting to his perverted ways was a clear failure. All the experimental drugs in the world could not keep Brian from being who he was. Medication may have kept his dark shadows hidden but it could never eradicate them. Brian was transferred to permanent solitary confinement. I was taken to the medical ward of the institution where after chasing ghosts in the dark for weeks I awoke.

# CHAPTER 17

# Remember to forget

This was the second time I awoke in a hospital unsure of where or whom I was. Just like before, stark white lights blinded my sore eyes. I struggled to see past the bed. Tubes feeding things into me came into focus. It was like falling into the twilight zone. I was thinking if this was some kind of time warp de-ja-vu, I was not telling the cops shit this time. I didn't feel any pain, but I couldn't move. I started to wriggle from my confines thinking I was strapped down when I realized I had casts on my arms. The beating the panic squad gave me rushed through my mind. Before I could panic or escape a nurse came into the room and said, "Please try not to move you have several broken bones and I need you to stay still." I was puzzled and disoriented but mostly glad that I hadn't slipped back in time. I didn't want to relive this nightmare over and over. The nurse smiled at me while she injected a soothing liquid dream into me. I embraced the great nothing and faded away.

I awoke feeling more confused than ever. I opened my eyes to find Lynn sitting in the chair next to my bed. When she saw I was awake she stopped reading my chart and asked how I was feeling.

"I'm not really feeling anything" I replied.

Her sad face changed to a smile when she put her hand on mine and said "I'd like you to know we are all very sorry for what happened to you. Tracy wanted to thank you in person but that's not possible, so she asked me to thank you".

I can't remember anything except endless white walls and empty halls. "Thank me, for what?" I asked.

The smile left Lynn's face and sadness returned to her eyes. With uncertainty in her voice, she asked "Do you know where you are?"

"Of course, I'm in the hospital. As you can see, I'm banged up pretty bad."

"Yes, you're in the hospital, but do you know why you're in the hospital?" she pushed for answers trying to assess the amount of brain damage I'd suffered.

I had to think about the question which made my head hurt, so with a stupid grin I said, "I don't know but I think I hurt my cranium".

"Well, you just rest and get better. I'll come back and see you soon" was all she said. After looking over my chart again she left.

I was slurping away at some green Jell-O when Lynn returned with a doctor who I'd never met before. The doctor looked over my chart then removed the bandage on my head and inspected the wounds underneath. After putting the bandage back on, he looked at my chart again. Then he had me follow his finger with my eyes and said "You have a bad fracture on your skull. Can you tell me who you are?"

That was a pretty heavy question to ponder and after thinking about it the only thing that came to mind was a white rabbit running free trying to catch the wind, so I told him "I'm the white rabbit."

"A rabbit you say" The doctor laughed through his nose. After Lynn gave him a stern look to remind him of his position he asked, "Do you know how you got here?"

I wasn't thinking in the immediate terms when I closed my eyes to think about it. All my memories were shattered and jumbled back together the wrong way. The harder I tried to think of the answer to the most complex question in my life the louder the screaming voices of the dead became. All my wretched memories formed into one twisted demon beating me down. Defeated by the question I broke down in tears and let an almost silent "no" slip from my lips. My reaction to his questions gave birth to compassion. The doctor looked at me with pity and reassured me that I'll be ok in time.

Lynn had the concerned mother smile on when she went outside the room to confer with the doctor. I overheard the doctor say "He may be blacking out the traumatic experience or he may have some brain damage from the multiple fractures on his skull, some of which are considerable and the fact that he is even conscious is almost a miracle. We wait it out and see how it goes but quite frankly if you value your job, I wouldn't push it. It's better for him and the hospital that he never remembers what happened. The best thing for everyone is to put this unfortunate event behind us." I didn't know what he was talking about but as I regained my memory, I was sure to keep certain details to myself. I pretended to blank out anything from my time here in fear of whatever memory was the one they didn't want me to remember. It was just better to remember to forget.

I was kept in a semiprivate room for the remainder of my time in Winnebago. Besides Lynn the only contact I had with people was with the small staff of doctors and nurses who rarely spoke to me unless they had to. I had nothing left but the pieces of my memories. I was burning in the lake of fire once again, but this time Lynn was my angel. I had been afraid to reach out to her in fear I would pull her into oblivion. After hearing Tracy's praise for me Lynn saw me differently. She broke free from the melancholy indifference that long years on the job created. After participating in one too many horrors Lynn had hoped that by saving me, she might be granted some kind of absolution.

The first few sessions I ignored her. When she still persisted on trying to pry something decent free from my fake exterior, I was vulgar and rude to her. But Lynn's newfound faith in me couldn't be shaken. One day she arrived with a pile of wrinkled and soiled papers. I recognized them as my own but didn't want to admit any weakness, so I asked the rhetorical question "What do ya got there?"

She explained how she found the scraps of madness in my room. She thought maybe if she recited some of the words to me, they might recall my demons, so she could attempt to exorcise them. Lynn was my counselor for years and I'd never really shared much of anything other than cryptic nonsense with her. She needed a breakthrough to validate her life's work. Lynn put her hand on mine and looked me in the eyes to beg me to go back down a path I didn't want to tread "You have to go back to the past and deal with it before I can get you out of here." I didn't know why she cared about me but the feeling of being truly loved and cared for came through in everything she said. Since I couldn't hold anything up to read it she selected one of the scraps and read it aloud to me.

# Cursed are the angels.

When my angels betrayed me
And turned to fly away.
They left me here pretending.
I could find my way.
Pulled under by
my cursed destiny
Lost and found.
In my false security

The demons watched my longings.
And still ignored my pleas.
Perched and always waiting.
To satisfy my needs
I stood ready to fight them
Knowing I couldn't win.
Against their smiling faces
Or the evil in their grin

The angels took me away.
Though I can't remember when
Did they return to save me?
Or to bind me to my sin
Still, they flew me higher.
Then I'd ever seen
Confusion led to wonder.
Had I fallen in a dream?

I found my scattered feelings.
Far across sullen seas
While the angel's tattered faces
Lingered in the breeze.
Demons taunted me further.
In their never-ending chase
Inner screams were clouded out.
And left in this place.


The angel whispered sweetly.
Wake from your dream.
Tears escaped to let.
Me know what they mean.
Released from the angel's grasp.
I let out hollow screams.
I fell through the world.
Realizing there are no dreams.


Drowning In a lake of fire
I peered up without eyes.
Seeing angels for what they are
They have torn away the disguise.
Demons and angels
Are one inside my tortured brain.
Loving me eternally
Torturing me just the same

After she finished reading, she asked if I remembered writing it. The words I imprisoned on the page were not meant to be released. Lynn did not understand the power the paper held when she broke the forbidden seal. The demons from my past escaped the page and I was forced to relive the misery of my former life as an intense rush of awareness overcame me.

I broke down in tears and made one last plea for denial "I don't want to remember, the past is only filled with death, I can't and won't face the truth of who I am!"

"If you don't deal with the ghosts from your past, they will haunt you forever" she said trying to comfort me.

Lynn speaks of metaphorical ghosts not realizing the ones that haunted me were quite real. Like a child playing with matches Lynn had no idea of the danger she was inviting.

Lisa's ghost appeared above my bed and screamed "you said you'd protect me and never leave me!"

I see only Lisa and beg "Please forgive me!"

Lynn interpreted my pleas as the breakthrough she had been waiting for.

I did not want the ghosts of my past to leave me. They were the only friends I had ever known. I wanted Lisa to say she had never died, but she couldn't so I was happy to have her haunt me forever. I needed to figure out who I was. Life was something I could not remember and feeling dead was something I couldn't forget. Lately I had been on so many different pills with so many different ways to feel "right", I didn't know which way was the "correct" way to feel. I was taken off all experimental drugs while I was unconscious and the only drugs left, I could feel or not feel were the painkillers and their unconditional loving false sense of well-being. As the days went by all the drugs began to leave my system and I gained a clarity that I had not known in a very long time. I was moved off the medical ward to a new ward. I was kept locked inside a private room with an adjoining bathroom. I was never allowed to leave my room. All my meals were brought to me. Staff members came in and out of my room with smiles but rarely words. The lonely days turned to weeks and eventually my casts came off.

I had endless hours of day to kill and nothing to do. Lynn was the one person that still saw something worth redeeming in me. I had nothing but the gifts she gave me. She gave me a Bible and an Alcoholics Anonymous 12 step book. I tried reading the Bible, but I found it longwinded and I didn't understand the text. The AA book was about the same. I could not relate to any of the people in either book. The only thing I had left to occupy my time was my pile of papers. The scraps of madness Lynn salvaged from my old life, along with a new small notebook and pen. I used the time to transfer all my poems written on scraps of torn and dirty paper into the small green notebook. Lynn visited me on an almost daily basis and because I still had a lot of troubles talking about what happened to me, she suggested I write down what happened so I can begin to heal inside. Everything I wrote while I was in the asylum was particularly guarded and insanely cryptic in nature. I took on the persona of the mysterious lab rat X when I wrote the following manifesto.

### Sinking black

*Walls sinking black into my solitude. Time slipping back, the future is lost. Earth falling deep on a tired mind. Dark absorbing sleep pulling me farther down.*

*Lying in the dirt. Looking towards the light. Echoes of the hurt repeating in my ears. Letting go of now. Reality collapsing. The heavy conscience crushing closer. The walls sinking black into my tomb. Time slipping back to when I was alive.*

*White walls and empty halls. Distant calls of a better place haunting the silent spaces of my mind. Life sublime. So unkind. Rotting away the core of my existence. So distant. Follow in the chant. Take my place in their line. So insane, not to blame for the troubles that crash in my scene. Be so mean. I'm not seen. In the daily circles of discontent. The pain is sent through my cell. Is this hell? I can't tell.*

*Slam the doors, locked in bars. The cage stands supreme. Cut and saw. The bars do not give way. Cry and weep the tears do not flow. Why oh why? Plot the escape. But the heart will not play along. The heart destroys the plan. Can't break free! Caught and lost forever. Waiting and wondering, what if and however would it have been? Swirling and spinning the world around me. Locked away and standing still. Forever the air suffocating. The walls enclose. The black prevails again in this silent cage. Shake and rattle the bars, but still no answers. Rage and anger give way to submission and exhaustion. Sleep, sleep, sleep. Never again wanting or knowing of the pain. The world an empty black room. The cage stands silent.*

*Box in the corner is filled with my dreams. It sits alone. It's locked and never opened. Never free. Never breathing the sweet spring air. Never seeing the light of day or the glimmers of moonlight. Pulling it back in the box. Locking it tight. Don't look back. Turn your back. The pain resides. The box lies undisturbed. Silent it waits. The corner gives it no comfort. The walls turn away. In the corner of my mind, it waits locked and alone.*

*Platforms in the sky, the dream is alive. Hold it up. Support the framework. It stands so high so it's hard to hold it up. Strength giving out the platform will fall! Run for cover the dream is lost. The crash destroys the framework. All is lost. Ruins, ruins. Digging up out of the ashes the waste lies far and wide. Where to start? Without the dream the hope is lost in the wreckage. Digging, searching, building the dream again. The dream stands tall again. Only to fall and fall again.*

*Blurred visions cloud my thoughts. The storm can't be stopped. Raining downpour leaves me with a flooded sense of being. Fighting for air in a dismal world of icy black. I'm going under! Water filled lungs. I breathe a gasp of relief.*

*Where, when, and why. Question the questions and never learn why. Conform, learn content. Do not resent. The pain is still being sent. Just leave it at the door. I will just send more. Stack it up, block the door push it aside. It builds. The yard is full. Make a path. "The pain isn't there." I fool myself. Befriend denial. Paint the face with clear emotions. Not swaying black nor showing hate. Saving dignity. Hiding from reality. The pain grows. The city is full.*

*Hiding in my corner. The pain is gone. I see nothing. I'm isolated. I'm forgotten yet the pain grows. I will not acknowledge the pain. The pain awakens. The mob is free. The damage will be done! The spinning vortex sucks me in. The pain will win!*

*In the vision. I see only the vortex swirling below. I can feel it drain my soul. Salvation lost in sanctuary.*

*somewhere above and beyond this plain. Floating endlessly through the void. Never knowing where my salvation could be found. The emptiness of the void growing inside of me as the vortex shadows me. The emptiness is so familiar and so enticing I let it take me. I give in and let my soul escape to the center of this swirling madness. The vortex implodes and I awake finding myself still feeling the shadows of the vortex.*

*The sorrow inside is pulling me deeper and deeper into its depths. I feel it drain the meaning of my existence away. It asks me questions that I don't want to acknowledge the answers to. It wanders behind my every thought. I feel it most as the world begins another cycle of madness. Forever spinning and twisting the sanity from me. The sorrow knows me all too well. A sorrow taught by black lies and promises of yesterday and never. I can't escape these depths. The way out is maybe far worse than where I am. I'm in the place of promises lost and forgotten ways. Dark and cold. I live in the way of the sorrow. Please let me live I ask but still I cannot escape.*

*Now is the time of round and round. Clean and clean. The dirt never seen. Smashing and breaking my brain. The mounting routine. Why I ask my soul if I have one. I live a life with no purpose a life without meaning except to clean the endless mess left behind. Them in their world and me in mine*

*The breakdown. The endless hammers pound their way in. I've been found. Pulled from the corner there's no escape. Trapped now in my own sanctuary fear is my only friend. Even fear gives no protection. Double-crossed and alone. The punishment made. The agony slow and ruthless. Eating, tearing, ripping, smashing, crushing, nothing left I hide in the corner.*

*Exploding fast. Hatred takes over. Instantly all is engulfed in flames. The structure collapses. The fire rages. All is taken. All is forgotten. Only the fires of hate burning remain. All that is known burns. Burning higher and higher. The blaze is everything. No cure. No solutions. It only stops when it burns out. Leaving only cinders of what once was remaining. Ripped down. Little pieces that can't be restored. But still a new machine is built from the junk. One that can't perform the function.*

*I find myself asking what is it that can make me feel as I did so long ago. What am I looking for? Where do my answers lie? I fear that I have already set foot down the path of no return. Forever scheming and never knowing. To escape this is to tear my heart out and never be able to feel again. Today is only filled with endless circles spinning away the days.*

*Each one an almost exact blur of the one before. A Slave sentenced to live a life of death. A death that hides behind the faces of the company I kept. Lurking in the corners and hiding in the darkness of my own delusions that I can erase the pain and silence the questions. I cannot and must not answer the questions. The answer is pain.*

*So here I am locked away and kept insane. For now, I am lost in the haze of my own repeating nightmare. Reality is lost. I stand silent. I am the cage! I am the spinning vortex. The words swirl past unnoticed. I'm lost inside myself. A maze of incomprehension. The time is forever. Fall behind and fade away.*

*The world looks down upon me in this pit because I have been marked for slow slaughter for the evils I have committed. The sanitarium is where the sane are pushed over the edge of deliriousness into the realm of insanity. Who in this shithole even cares if I live or die? When I turn my back the verbal razors cut me to shreds.*

*Life is only the imprisonment of a free spirit that urges me to perish so that I can search through other dimensions until I find serenity. I envision microwave dreams spilling the blood of free will. The restrains are in reality vipers that suck the life-giving independent thoughts from me. So that I can be transformed into a brainless mutant. Only to serve a God that does not show any signs of forgiveness. I don't wonder why the walls try to crush me in my sleep or why the bed I'm forced to sleep in bites at my flesh in the dark.*

After Lynn read my twisted manifesto, she began to realize under all the layers of distrust and insanity there was just a scared kid that got tossed into a blood thirsty ruthless machine. I wasn't a cold-blooded killer and Lynn was maybe the only person to see that. Tracy, whose life I had possibly saved would never face me again in person, but I'd like to believe she knew a little about my compassionate nature. I don't blame Tracy for never turning to look back, I didn't like facing the things that reminded me of the sickness I lived through either. Lynn however, forced me face the sickness in me. Lynn worked with me for many months and slowly over time I got "better". I believed a lot of strange things in my lifetime, the types of things I'm sure most people would consider insane. I believed I was the living dead, when I was just strung out on drugs. I believed that heaven and hell were all around us and I was currently on a personal journey through the deeper layers of hell. I believed God had a vendetta against me for not saving Lisa. I believed God himself trapped me in hellish places to punish me. Lynn helped me deal with most of my insanity, but she could never fully rid me of the ghosts that continued to haunt me. I never mentioned my lingering ghosts to Lynn or anyone inside the asylum because I feared they'd have some terrible pill to erase them. I didn't want my lost love erased. I had kept my dearest ghosts secret for way too many years, and I wasn't about to reveal them now when they might hurt my chances of release.

I had a hard time believing I could ever be free or have any kind of life on the outside, but with Lynn's help my day of judgment before the hospital administration did in fact come. After I told Lynn about the things, I saw on the ward she started a crusade to end the madness of the Gemini program. She planned to use my case as a battering ram to break down the doors of hypocrisy. As I have stated before insane asylums are not like jail there are no finite time limits to serve. They only let you leave when you are determined a non-threat to society or yourself. It's a dangerous oubliette the government created to make people disappear without criminal charges, but as society progressed the same loophole now allowed many dangerous people to crawl back up from the sewer. The tricky part of the loophole is you have to know it's there and then you have to know enough law to make it open. Thanks to Lynn I found my way to it. I wasn't free just yet, but I stood at the threshold.

Before my case for release could even be considered I had to take an extensive battery of tests. I find it preposterous to believe anyone could be found sane or insane from such ludicrous tests. The first test was over five hundred questions long. All of the questions have the same multiple-choice answers to pick from; yes, no, maybe, or unsure. The questions are repeated but reworded throughout so just in case you answered "no" to the question that read "I would like to work as a florist" on page one you would be able to change your mind on page two when asked "working with flowers is something I enjoy." I don't know who came up with the test, but I remember florists, forest rangers, and bakers mentioned a lot in it; so if you are in one of these professions you might want to seek professional help. The next test was the classic ink blot thing. I don't know what you are supposed to see in smeared mess. They all look like kindergarten art projects to me. Another test involved rearranging blocks until they matched a certain pattern. This nonsense went on for days and after that I had to wait until the release board met.

The day finally came when I found myself sitting in a very hard chair trying to act comfortable as the members of the Release board sat before me in judgment. I sat as still as I could and listened as the council heard from Doctor Vohn. I hardly ever saw Doctor Vohn. He would talk to me for fifteen minutes maybe once every six months. Saying hello to me counted as a session to him. Doctor Vohn was an arrogant prick that never cared about the human beings he was prescribing all the drugs to. We were just lab rats forced to take his poison. The list of fucked up, untested drugs, they put into me alone was scary long. I deeply worried about the doctor who barely knew me now sitting in judgment of me. I don't blame him for any of the hardships I endured because after all I had "crazy" clearly stamped on my forehead when I was brought in, and he just threw me in the bin with the rest of the "crazies." I do resent the fact that if he had taken any time to look closer, he might have noticed I was miss-labeled.

I tried not to glare at Doctor Vohn as he proceeded to share, with the council, his findings from all the oddball tests I took. Doctor Vohn knew I did not like the sound of my own name, so he began by saying it loudly while he glared back at me. I cringed a little but did not let it bother me on such an important day as his speech continued "is an individual with a highly avoidant personality, markedly asocial tendencies, and anxiety. There appears to be a significant amount of affective dysphoria including an undercurrent of tension, sadness, and anger, vacillating between desire for affection, fear, and numbness of feelings. The patient exhibits great hostility for authority and expresses statements of paranoia towards not only authority figures but also most others in his life. The patient evidences chronic, periodically severe pathology evident in schizoid behaviors including social detachment, eccentricities in behavior as well as an anxious wariness and an emotional flatness. There are also strong indications of passive-aggressive tendencies with signs of being frequently irritable, displaying erratic moodiness and being easily frustrated. He exhibits petulant and fault-finding behaviors and reports feeling misunderstood, unappreciated, and demeaned by others. The patient is characteristically pessimistic, disgruntled, and disillusioned. He tends to use unpredictable behavior to provoke edgy discomfort in others! This is an individual who has a checkered history of drug use, murder, disruptions, and "predicaments" and one can expect an apparent inability to learn from previous difficulties. There is a tendency to precipitate self-defeating cycles, digressions, and setbacks as well failure to achieve any niche in life that is consonant with natural aptitudes. While currently he shows no specific psychotic behaviors, he does present an image of social detachment, preferring a life of isolation with minimal personal attachments and obligations" . . .

One of the other men spoke up "where's this going?"

Doctor Vohn paused briefly before ignoring the question and continued "the patient is guarded, suspicious of others and secretive in behavior. He exhibits periods of intense endogenous mood swings where . . ."

Again, the doctor is interrupted "Doctor Vohn does the patient present a risk to himself or society?"

Doctor Vohn fumbled at his papers in attempt to make a better case but in truth he was bitter that the Gemini program produced little results and ten deaths. Doctor Vohn knew I was just the first domino in a long line of improprieties and when I fell everything is his world would, one by one in turn come crashing down. He was failing to keep the chain reaction from occurring and the sweat rolling off him showed it.

Recently there had been allot of intense internal pressure to make me, the Gemini program, and the embarrassments of the staff just go away. My case had raised several shady questions that some wanted answered and others wanted buried. Lynn had powerful allies and one of them was hounding the very nervous doctor "Doctor Vohn is the patient a danger or not?"

Doctor Vohn was flustered and reaching at straws when he hoped a pathetic guilt by association ploy might persuade the board, I was dangerous. He reminded the council I was involved in the weight room "incident". The foolish doctor thought that bringing skeletons out of the closet would be to his advantage but in truth the council wanted to bury and forget the skeletons.

Lynn picked up on the council's impatience and used this as an opportunity to interject. "I would like to remind the council that if not for his brave actions that day in the weight room there would have been a very different outcome. I have a sworn statement here from Tracy the nurse involved in the incident."

I wanted to cry as Lynn read Tracy's affidavit. Tracy's words of kindness for me were the nicest things anyone has ever said about me. After Lynn finished reading, she added "I have personally counseled him on a near daily basis for years and in my opinion, he has been misdiagnosed and does not represent a threat to himself or others."

I was removed from the room while they argued inside. I felt like I was on the gallows steps walking toward a noose, praying to God to save me before I feel the snap of the rope. I don't know if it was Lynn's conviction, Tracy's' words, the tears I was holding back, or the councils desperate attempt to erase the shortsighted failures of the program but no matter what the reason I was spared from the hangman's rope. Lynn returned from the chamber and told me the good news. For the first time in years, I enjoyed the simple comforts of a hug at Lynn's expense.

I was returned to my room. It would take days to make my release arrangements and during those days the almighty clock that ruled my world spoke to me. The minutes stretched out as I tried to comprehend what it meant to be free. The clock taunted me with constant reminders of how much thinking it had done for me. "I tell you when to wake up, when to eat, when to shit, and when to sleep. When I'm gone and this place is gone, you'll realize you have nothing and are nothing. You belong here with the rest of the throw aways."

I had been living inside for so long I was terrified by the thought of living outside. I had daydreamed a million times about living beyond the walls but now the true facts were coming down hard. Perhaps the clock was right. I had no idea how to find a place to live, how to get a job, how to open a bank account, how to drive, or how to do any of the things normal adults did. I was a seriously messed up homeless/streetwise teenager when I went into the "system" and I was still just a child when I was released.

# CHAPTER 18

# Letting go

The last day I spent in the asylum was pretty much the same as the countless others that came before it. After I ate breakfast, I gathered up all the things that belonged to the institution and placed them in a neat pile on my bed, my bedding, clothes, etc. Then I gathered up all the things that belonged to me. I was quick to realize I owned next to nothing. My pile had the two books Lynn gave me and the little notebook that I had transcribed all the twisted poems of death into. I didn't even think about the clothes I was wearing until I was standing awkwardly naked in the room most patients only see once. I was told to remove the hospitals' clothes and was given a box of clothes to put on. I hadn't seen the vicious world in years, and I admit I was quite worried about facing it naked. Most patients are given back the "street" clothes they were wearing when they were admitted but not me. I didn't own the clothes I was wearing when I was admitted. The orange jumpsuit I had on when I came here went back to the sheriff's department and last clothes that I owned were seized as evidence, so my box was empty. I couldn't be release naked so the property clerk rummaged through some of the boxes marked "deceased" until she found something that looked like it might fit. I was given some dead persons old clothes, (which didn't really fit and smelled like urine)

After I was "dressed" the clerk had me sign a form to collect my only piece of personal property. I was given a letter addressed from a lawyer in Green Bay. I didn't have time to open it right then because I was hastily escorted to a room where Lynn was waiting with a man I'd never met.

Lynn explained "This is Gary he is a social worker. I've arranged for you to go with him to what's called a half-way house. It's a place where people like you can become readjusted to society".

I'm not sure what she meant by people like me. I was leery about going with Gary. The last time I headed down a path with someone I did not know the path led straight off a cliff.

After saying goodbye and thank you to Lynn, she graced me with another hug and tearful eyes. As Gary drove to the half-way house, I sat in silent awe noticing the subtle changes time made over many years that seemed immediate to me. The half-way house looked like any other house from the outside. When we went inside and Gary was showing me around, I was thinking "This place is worse than the institution I was just in". The paint was chipped and faded. The carpets were worn thin from anxious pacing. The whole place looked and smelled horrible. I was already missing the sterile smells I'd become accustomed to. Gary could clearly see the clothes I was wearing didn't fit and he probably smelled the pee because the first thing he showed me was boxes of free clothes from St. Vinnie's in the back hall. I quickly grabbed a few things that looked like they might fit. I was impatient to get out of the nasty clothes I was given at the institution. I wanted to shed away any reminder of that time in hell. I stepped into the bathroom to change and was nauseated by what I found. I had not seen a bathroom this gross since I was back at the battery shop strung out on drugs. The bathroom was the worst room here, it was truly sickening. The bowl was stained badly and the rug around it felt squishy. The smell made me gag. At least in the nuthouse the toilets are clean! I was happy to be free but I knew right then I had to get the hell out of this place as soon as possible.

There were eight other men besides me living in the house at that time. I was the youngest one there. Five of them were recovering alcoholics well into their forties, or least they looked it. Three housemates were guys on parole from the local prison. They were all creepy looking dudes, but the worst was the child molester guy. He was paroled from the prison too and the other two jailbirds were quick to point his crimes out to me. Other than the smell, it was very similar to the life I had become used to back at Winnebago. They had the same basic daily routine: eat, sleep, look for work, and wait to die. After I was given the tour, the daily schedule, and made my introductions, I was finally shown to my new room. It wasn't much to look at but on the bright side, I was the only one in it and it didn't have bars on the windows.

The first thing I did after my tour was drag all the boxes of free clothes to my room. I was selecting my new wardrobe from the swap meet clothes when I remembered the letter. I searched through the boxes for the nasty pants I had stuffed it into earlier. I was very relieved to find the letter. I hadn't given it much thought though out the day. I was super overwhelmed to be freed at long last. My emotional high was quickly grounded as I read the letter.

It was from my grandfather, well a lawyer who represented him anyway. It seemed while I was locked away my grandfather had passed away. The first page of the letter mentioned the funeral details and my grandfather's final resting place. On the second page there were details of my grandfather's last will and testament. My name is listed as the beneficiary on a saving bond purchased in my name the day I was born. The amount of the bond is disclosed at its purchase price not what it's worth after interest.

It's not enough to retire but it's enough to get out of the shit I was stuck in. The letter stated that I should contact the law office listed to sign some paperwork to claim my bond. There was nothing personal or heartfelt about the letter, but it still made me break down. It had been a very long time since the idea of family existed in my mind. I was crushed to be reintroduced to an idea that would only die a sentence later. I was equally perplexed by life's sudden generosity.

I had the best night's sleep. All my fears of surviving on the outside were erased by my sudden windfall and the "real" mattress that I wasn't strapped to, felt so good. The next day I asked around to see who had a car and it turned out a couple of my housemates did. I picked the least threating guy and offered him fifty dollars to drive me around for a day. He wanted the money up front, so I had to lie to conceal the fortune I was collecting. I told him my stepdad was a fancy lawyer who promised to loan me some money to get on my feet again. I don't like to lie but I do admit I am convincing. First, we went to the lawyer's office. I produced the letter and waited for an hour before someone met with me. After a short meeting filled with stories of how he knew my grandfather and condolences, I signed some papers, and the bond was mine. I went straight to a bank to cash it in.

I made my chauffeur once again wait in the car. After cashing the bond, I went into the bank's bathroom. I put everything but one hundred dollars in my sock. I was no fool. I didn't want to advertise wealth to my hungry roommates. I did however treat my driver to an expensive lunch. After the best meal I had in years I decided I wanted to pay my respects to the only member of my family that didn't forget I existed. I got no complaints from my driver when I asked to go to the cemetery in Green Bay where my grandfather was entombed. While my new chauffeur wandered the grounds, I went inside the mausoleum and after a little searching, I found the granite slab with the family name inscribed on it.

It was a very surreal moment to see my name inscribed among the dead in the house of bones. My father gave me the same first, middle and last name of my grandfather in hopes of getting back into the old man's wealthy heart. I'd come a long way from the belief that I was the living dead. But now sitting in the halls of granite I could feel all the old familiar demons come to light. They reassured me that I did die that cold day with Lisa, and I did serve my time in hell. The only question left in my mind was, "Why was I brought back from the dead once more". I was instantly reminded by my demons of the buried treasure. I reminded my demons this was a holy place as I drove them back into the shadows. I didn't want to remember the past, and I certainly didn't want others to know about my past. I ran my fingers across the letters spelling out my name and convinced myself that the person with his name cast in stone was dead. I left all my shame, my lost innocence, my past, my name, my secrets, and hopefully my demons sealed in the tomb. It was time to let go of my past life. I walked out of there reborn. Confident my demons were trapped, and my ghosts were suppressed I could begin my life anew.

The half-way house lifestyle really sucked so I was highly motivated to get the hell out of there. I was lucky enough to have a little money and allot of rabbit in my blood. I wanted to see America. I wanted to run free and fast with the wind again. I was ready to call anywhere my new home. I studied hard and in a short time I got my driver's license. Two days after I got my license Gary was driving me back from a job interview when I fell in love again. I spotted a

1972 AMC Javelin sitting in front of a church. I begged Gary to pull over and while I was peeking in the windows a gentleman farmer approached and announced he was the owner. He went on to explain the car had been in storage in the barn until recently when he hit hard times and needed to sell her. When he said he was holding out for one thousand dollars. I instantly offered him nine hundred cash. The farmer and my ride; Gary where both taken back, they laughed at the prospect of me having money but when I produced hundreds from my sock the farmer hurried back to the house for the title.

Gary had devious ideas in mind when he questioned me about my sudden wealth. Now that I had a rocket off planet control, I wasn't answering to anyone. I completely snubbed Gary and paid the farmer. Gary tried to stop me from driving away by putting his hands on me, which was the worst thing he could have done. I hated people touching me. I punched him in the face, and I drove away as fast as I could.

The Javelin was never the mainstream muscle car, but the old girl still had plenty of pep left in the big 360 block. She speeded away, rescuing me from danger to become my new best friend and home. I raced Gary back to the halfway house, grabbed my clothes and left that shithole never looking back. The few short weeks I'd spent on the outside had opened my eyes to what people often refer to as the "real world" and it sucked. The best hope guys like me had at some kind of happiness was a forty-hour work week and an endless supply of beer. Most people who try to reach up wind up on the bottom trying to scrape by. I wasn't sold on that version of the American dream. I hated Wisconsin winters, and it was about to get very cold and very dark. I wanted the everlasting blue sky and the warm sunshine I remembered from southern California.

I'd spent years tormented, thinking about the blood money I buried. For years I believed it was cursed with the blood of my dead friends but the demons I could not escape from convinced me that my current prospects were so dismal that to ignore a golden opportunity would be downright foolish. "Could it still be there after all this time?" That was the one question I asked myself 50 times a day?

Now the time had come to seek out the answer. I was starving for adventure and eager to hit the open road. I stopped at the DMV for plates then a gas station to fill up and buy a map. Just like that I drove off into the great unknown.

*"Made of dust"*

*Wood will rot. Steel will rust.*

*In-between there still be dust.*

*A simple thought you can't mistrust.*

# CHAPTER 19

# The road to madness

There are a lot of ways to leave Wisconsin; I chose highway 151 southeast out of Wisconsin because it went right through the small town, I grew up in. When I got there, I took some time to drive around town and reminisce. Those timeless places that never seemed to change reminded me of a time when I was still young and innocent riding my bike around town. The places that had changed or were not there anymore told me I was not a kid anymore. This town no longer had any meaning to me. I stopped at a local diner in hopes of maybe seeing someone I may have once known, but the faces were all strange. While chewing my lunch I felt a little forgotten and lost. I envy the people that chatted away with their lifelong neighbors and friends while I sat alone. I left the romantic daydreams of the "what if" life I could have had in the rearview mirror and once again headed south. The last thing I remembered about Wisconsin was the capital building in Madison. The highway I was traveling on goes right through Madison. At one point the road goes right up to and around the capital. Because of my late lunch it was past sunset when I drove through Madison. The capital building lights up like a Christmas tree at night. I remember thinking about all my distrust and hatred towards authority figures. I flipped the building off as if some unknown men inside were conspiring against me. After Madison there were a lot of miles to the state line in the dark. I liked to drive at night because there is a lot less traffic and if you're lucky the stars will guide your way.

The night came and went. I stopped for gas but not for sleep. I was far too obsessed with my goal to sleep. I drove on with the sun chasing me in the early morning hours. Somewhere outside of Omaha Nebraska I spotted a hitch hiker. I know most people have some apprehension that all hitch hikers are homicidal maniacs, and you should never pick them up. I didn't have those apprehensions because I was the homicidal mental patient. I was also naive and bored. All the years I was locked away had felt like time stood still. But it hadn't and this new unfamiliar world was a little scary to me. Being alone in a world I knew nothing about reminded me of my first days as a runaway. Back then, I felt comforted to have Danny as my guide through the unknown. I wanted another guide to the underworld. I was hungry for knowledge and adventure. Any smart person will tell you adventure, and risks go hand in hand. I pulled to the side of the road and looked the guy over in the rearview as he was walking up to the car. I figured if he were covered in blood or carrying an axe I could still get away.

The hitcher was a short chubby man in need of a shave. He was wearing dirty clothes and carrying a plastic bag. He totally reminded me of Danny and my time on the street, so I felt a fair amount of pity for him. By the time he reached the car I had assessed him as a non-threat, so I let him in. I tolerated his smell by rolling the windows down. He introduced himself as Wayne. He was very grateful and thanked me for the ride before asking where I was going.

I told him "To the west coast."

"You got family or something out there?" He asked.

This is where any normal person would be thinking of red flags, but I was not raised by TV hysteria so after a sad pause I told him "I don't have any family anywhere."

He said, "Why are you going to the coast then?" as he reached into his pocket. He produces a pack of bent up cigarettes and offered me one.

I took the smoke, lit it, and said "I just want to see the beach again. I lived out west in a past life and wanted to see if it was the same as I remembered."

"The past is never the same place." Wayne warns and after a brief pause continued "I just came from my brother's house. I had not seen him for 7 years because of a feud over a couple hundred bucks. When I went back to ask for his forgiveness and help, he told me to drop dead. I have an uncle in Fort Collins. I'm going there now. I hope when I get there, he won't shut me out as well. I've done a lot of bad things in the past that hurt my family. I wished a thousand times I could go back and change the past, but I can't. You can never go back. You can only go forward and hope the people in life you have hurt will forgive you."

"What makes you think I hurt someone?" I respond thinking you just met me.

"People with no family and nowhere to go are always running from something, and that something is always a pain that can't be forgot but maybe forgiven" he rambles like a wise man, but I just see a fool vagabond.

"Whatever dude" is all the further participation in that conversation I'm willing to give.

I felt pity for the stranger only because I knew what it was like to be human garbage so I told him "I will take you as far as I can, but I don't have much money left for gas so if you have got any cash for gas that would be awesome." I was not low on cash at all but after I told him I'm all alone in the world I didn't want him to think I had anything of value. And to look in my car that was true. I only had a bag of clothes in the trunk. The only things in the car were a twelve pack of soda, a half-eaten bag of chips, and a sharp knife I bought at a gas station which I always kept close.

He tells me "Don't worry if you need gas or food, I will take care of it when we get to Lincoln." Lincoln wasn't that far away so I gave him a soda and let him devour the remainder of my chips. I even bummed him a couple of cigarettes when he ran out, figuring he was going to pony up some cash when we got to Lincoln.

When we arrived in Lincoln, Wayne led me off the highway and into town. "It's been a while since I was at this one" he mumbled as he gave directions "A right up here, no wait left, yeah left"

I followed his directions but persisted "Where are we going? I thought you said when we got to Lincoln you would pay for gas and food?"

"Don't worry kid, I am!" He persisted. We drove a few more blocks before he finally said, "Pull in here."

I was getting a little irritated with the run around when I pulled into the parking lot ready to end our journey together. I looked around and saw the Salvation Army sign. I had no idea how the

Salvation Army store was going to help so I snapped at Wayne "The Salvation Army? What are we going to do? buy used fucking clothes?"

Thankfully Wayne in his old age is tolerant of my youthful ignorance. In a calm demeanor he says "Yes were at the Salvation Army, but they don't just sell old clothes and junk. They're a Christian organization that helps people in need." While sitting in the parking lot he told me that he had been crisscrossing the country for years. On one of his trips, he found himself stranded and a Good Samaritan told him about the charity available from the Salvation Army.

He'd been begging at their doorstep ever since. He said all you had to do was tell them you were stranded without gas trying to get home and they will give you gas vouchers to get you home, or at least to the next city. Wayne goes on to say some of the bigger facilities had beds, showers and offered meals to the homeless. I'm nervous about begging for stuff so I told Wayne "I think it's best if I just wait in the car for now." I had some cash, but the price of gas was quickly eating away my stash. I didn't need anyone's charity while at the same time company help pass the time.

After a few minutes I finished weighing my options and was ready to go. I fired up the engine and was pulling out when Wayne ran out of the building waving his arms about like an air traffic controller. I continued on my way, only to stop a block away at the stop sign. I would have left him there if he hadn't run that whole block to catch me.

Wayne gets in the car out of breath and hands me a voucher for ten dollars' worth of gas. The address on the voucher is a station near the freeway. After catching his breath, Wayne says "Sorry I took so long but we were too late for supper, so they gave me five dollars' worth of McDonald vouchers. Don't worry you can have all of them." It was obviously Wayne didn't want to lose his ride when he gave up all his charity crap. I was surprised anyone could get charity so easily.

I was sure he was bull-shiting me earlier and was ready to ditch him, but now that he made good on his promise, I decided to lie to make him feel better "I wasn't going to ditch ya buddy I just needed some smokes and I planned to come back. You can have the McDonalds bucks, I'm not hungry." Wayne breathes easier and smiled with relief. He tells me there are a lot of charity places around. He said it was easy to find one in almost any town. They were mostly in the bigger cities, and some weren't as nice as this one. I used the vouchers for gas while Wayne ate some McDonalds. I didn't get food because I didn't want Wayne to think I had money, besides food didn't matter to me just then. I could live for days on soda alone and the only thing I needed to keep going was the thought of what was at the end of my journey.

Nebraska is one big, long empty. It's just fields as far as the eye can see and the road seemed to go on forever. Each mile was indistinguishable from the one before or after. Wayne fills the time by telling me his life story. He tells me of serving his country in Vietnam and returning home to have hippies spit on him and call him a "baby killer". He became ashamed to wear his uniform and tried his best to fit back into society. He said it was like he came back home to the wrong planet. Everything about life that he remembered from before the war was forgotten and different when he returned. He felt, with good reason, persecuted and hated for not fitting in. I felt nothing but pity for him. I could relate to his tale. I too felt like a stranger in a strange land with nowhere to call home. His stories fade in out between horrific killing in the jungle to his own personal battles in life. He wanted to marry his high school sweetheart but was drafted instead. She only wrote him a few times while he was away and when he returned home, she was pregnant with another man's baby. He had planned to take over his father's farm, but his parents gave the farm to his younger brother instead, fearing he would never come home alive. His words somehow seemed louder when he said "Never go back home kid. You never find the things you've left behind and if you do there not the same way you've left them."

Strange he would say that I thought to myself. He knew nothing of my journey, but his words were worth considering. I didn't put a lot of faith into the warnings from a burned-out wretch of a homeless man. He had very few words of wisdom; in fact, a lot of the stuff he said didn't make any sense to me at all. My childish mind knew nothing of infidelity or any of the other things that went along with adult relationships, but Wayne continued to vent with stories of his ex-wife's' betrayal. I tried to zone him out by turning up the radio, but he just talked louder. I started to think of ways to rid myself of this burden when I saw the sign for Fort Collins just ahead. I was relieved by the thought of delivering him with a clear conscience.

We were on the off ramp for Fort Collins when Wayne changed his topic of conversation back to the present "I know where there is a bar where military widows hang out."

I had no idea where he was going with that so I asked "Why would you want to hang out with people whose spouses are dead? That is kind of morbid Wayne."

Wayne looked at me like I was speaking a foreign language "No not dead. Widow means their husbands are away in the military and they hang out at this bar looking for men to fuck."

It sounded worse when he spelled it out. I did need a place to leave Wayne, so I told him "That sounds great! Let's totally go there!" enthusiastically, but inside I was thinking "gross" still picturing widows fresh from the funeral, dressed in black drinking at a bar. It felt good to be able to deliver Wayne to where he wanted to be. Wayne was a nice guy that took a lot of unfair knocks in life. I did not want to be the guy that ditched him. He had learned to make the best of what little he had, and I respected that, so I drove him where he wanted to go.

I followed Wayne's' directions to the "widow" bar he was so hard up to get to. Curiosity and the need to stretch my legs and use a bathroom led me inside. There were women in there all right. They were not wearing funeral dresses or wailing out for dead spouses, but to my young brain the inside of the bar resembles a wake. The dimly lit bar did not hide the shame on the patrons faces. While using the restroom I started thinking of a nice way to tell Wayne I was leaving. I could not stand the familiar smell of bottom feeders. Thankfully, as soon as I returned to the bar I was asked for an I.D. I was over the legal drinking age, but I took advantage of an easy out. I tell the bartender its ok I'm leaving.

Wayne interjects "I already got you a beer buddy, you're not of age?"

Trying my best to look bummed out I said "Sorry afraid not. It's cool though, I still have a long way to go. You drink it for me buddy." I made a gun motion and shot him with my hand.

He looked happy and at home when he said "Thanks again friend, if not for you I would have had one hell of a walk" then with a big smile on his face he grabbed my hand with both of his to show his appreciation. It made me feel good to help someone find a better place and he in return had helped me. I started to believe that maybe there was hope for myself and humanity after all. I was exiting the bar when I overheard Wayne say to the other barflies "Let's drink to the kindness of strangers. That crazy fucker gave me a ride all the way from Omaha! He's ok in my book!" It was bittersweet to hear their drinks clank together. I missed the camaraderie of friendship, and it was sad to be alone again but at the same time I felt a tiny fraction better about myself. I had patched together an illusion of how people lived and died while I was separated from society. As I was exposed to "reality" my delusions began to crumble.

With the death of my preconceived notions, I began to grow into a more sensible state of mind. For the next hundred miles I tried to remember the seat next to me was empty, but the smell Wayne left in my car would not let me forget him.

As I drove south from Fort Collins the view of the Rocky Mountains began to slowly creep closer on the horizon. It was an amazing sight to behold. I felt humbled and small in comparison to the stone giants that grew from mere pebbles on the horizon. The sun began to slide behind the massive wall of stone as I reached Denver. Once in Denver I was thinking about what Wayne told me about the Salvation Army being in the big metro areas. This was definitely a big city, so I looked it up in a phone book. I tried in vain to find the Salvation Army thing that the phone book and Wayne both said was there. Perhaps misdirected by God or the Devil I wound up hopelessly lost in a "bad" part of town. I decided the best thing to do was get back to the interstate and stay in Denver for the night. I was exhausted so I rented the first cheap room I saw advertised on a billboard.

Once inside the room I felt confined. Considering where I came from this was pretty nice. I had two beds, a color TV, and my own bathroom but after running free for days the walls around me made it a little hard to breathe. I was so exhausted that I did not have the time to enjoy the room. I felt like I had been driving for days but in reality, it was a little more than twenty-eight hours. I did not bring anything in the room. I did not undress. I did not turn the TV on. I did not even pull the blankets back. I smoked a cigarette, laid on the bed, thought about how close I was getting to my goal and how far I'd run from my nightmare. My head hit the pillow and I fell fast and hard into a dream.

In the dream I could see Lisa. She seemed to be waiting for me. She ran towards me with arms wide open. But as I ran towards her, she seemed to get further away. I ran faster trying to catch her but the space between us only seemed to grow. I dropped to my knees in desperation to find myself in my own grave. The dirt from my past began to bury me at the bottom of the hole. I didn't understand what was happening and begin to panic and claw at the earth being shoveled upon me. Half buried and immobile I look up to see Lisa was throwing the dirt on me and crying. I cried out in the dream "I'm not dead yet!" only to find myself awake in the "real" world. My clothes were soaked with sweat and fear. It was only 3:30 in the morning but I could no longer face the idea of sleep and another dream. I grabbed my crappy bag of used clothes from the car, took a very brief shower and hit the road like the hotel was haunted because for me it was.

Outside the hotel in the crisp dawn air, I felt almost invisible. There didn't seem to be any sign of life this time of day except for me and the sun. As I drove up into the mountain it began to snow. My knuckles were stark white as they gripped the wheel. I wasn't an experienced driver and the sight of the drop off on the side of the road that led to certain death stressed my nerves. When large semi-trucks passed me going seventy miles an hour it felt like I was being pushed off the road. I couldn't read a map and keep a constant eye on the road so somewhere in the mountain I decided to get off the interstate.

I waited hours at a rest stop for the storm to pass but the snow showed no sign of surrender. I was getting buried and cold. I had to make a bold decision. I wanted a route off the interstate and away from the steel road hogs trying to kill me. I followed the road less traveled hoping it would not be so treacherous.

The white mess consumed everything but two tread marks on the road which I followed blindly. I got so twisted and turned around I could no longer read any of the road signs because they all had snow stuck to them and I could not risk taking my eyes from the road to read the map. I was lost and did not know if I would survive the night! The tracks I was following were disappearing like the sun. Just about the time I abandoned all hope, I rounded a bend in the darkness and saw Jesus. Jesus was standing there larger than life on one of the opposing hill tops. He seemed to be 50 feet tall at least. I wasn't going crazy again or having a religious experience. There was a giant statue of Jesus lit up with his arm outstretched on top of one of the smaller mountains. I took this as more than coincidental. I had to get closer, so I followed any road that seemed to lead to it. I believe God led me here as my car never got stuck and I never took a wrong turn on the way to it. I found a place just below the statue to park and hiked up a long path through the cold snow to discover Jesus was only about thirty feet tall. He seemed bigger from the road. When I reached the top, I discovered at the base of the massive statue there was a room. I entered and while flicking my lighter I made out a shine of some kind. There were old candles throughout the room and a mural with a Bible passage and mural painted on the wall. In an effort to warm my frozen bones I tried to lite the candles that looked like they had some life left in them. The sacred wax doesn't want me here and quickly burns out. I went back outside. At his feet I sat in the cold snow looking up at the giant Jesus and wondered which way to go. Not just on the road but in my life. Some of the things Wayne said to me were starting to eat away at me. All the talk of not going back home and his tale of life kicking him at every turn had me wondering if I was on that right path. Was it my fate to let all the shit I had endured just fester inside until it destroyed me? Looking up at the big guy wasn't much help. He pointed back the way I came. It did not really matter which way he pointed. I wanted tangible answers not subtle hints.

I asked God for a reason to turn back, but I heard nothing but the wind reply. The blowing snow urged me to leave. "All right then I will just keep going on the path I'm on, thanks for your help" I spoke aloud with genuine respect for what felt like a holy place.

I walked back down the long path and by the time I reached my car the snow started to let up. I could almost make out the moon hiding behind a wall of clouds. I followed my own tracks back to the main road and continued down the road in the opposite direction without looking at my map. "This road must go somewhere, and I was going to find out where." I thought to myself. The where turned out to be Colorado Springs! I was trying to go straight through the mountains to the west but had ended up going south. I decided to make the best of it. Instead of going back up and through the snow-covered mountains I would just keep going south into New Mexico and head west through Arizona.

I was heading south when I saw another hitchhiker walking on the side of the road. Having company made the long miles go by quicker. The sun was no longer something I hated but it was roasting the long desolate road and the stranger on it. I felt a small amount of compassion for the guy, so I once again pulled over. This time I saw a rough looking Mexican guy wearing blue jeans and a blue denim shirt. Just like Wayne he smiled with relief as he approached the car.

He asked how far south I was going, and I told him "Straight into hell my friend."

He laughed and got in. He introduced himself as Octavio, then said "Don't you know it's dangerous to pick up hitchhikers?"

I told him I was not afraid, and I did not have anything worth taking.

He looked at me with some seriousness "What about your life?"

I gave him my best crazy eyes and replied, "I've already died many times and I'm no longer afraid of death because Hell just keeps kicking me back out!"

He shook his head and laughed remarking "Your loco ese."

After talking awhile, he told me he had been on the road for hours before I came along. No one would even slow down, let alone let him in. He was prepared to walk the whole long journey back home. He thanked me again and asked where I was really headed. I told him I was going to California for a reunion with my long-lost girlfriend. This naturally brought the conversation to why he was on the road that day.

Without trying to scare or impress me, he just stated the truth. He simply said he just got out of prison and was on his way home. His family was too poor to own a car. All the "friends" he had before he went to prison had long ago forgotten him, so without anyone to pick him up he was stuck walking. Since we were enjoying such honesty, out of pure curiosity I said, "That's a bummer . . . so what's prison like?"

"What's prison like! It sucks! What do you fucking think it's like? I ought to kick your ass and throw you from the car for asking me that!" He made fists and punching motions while acting upset with me.

I thought I hit a nerve and did not want to upset Octavio, so I tried to defuse the situation "It just a question I'm sorry . . ."

Octavio interrupts by busting out in laughter. In between chuckles he manages to say "I was just fuckin with you man. You should have seen the look on your face."

After he calmed back down, he asked me in a serious tone if I really wanted to know about prison. I explained I had heard a lot of stories and just wanted to know which were true and which ones were bullshit. We had a few hours of driving ahead. Octavio did not have anything else in his life to talk about, so he agreed to tell me all about prison. He does not spare me any of the gritty details. The terrible things Octavio described were one thousand times worse than anything I had imagined. He told me about men being raped and having their teeth knocked out to give better blowjobs, but the most disturbing stories to me were the ones of sheer violence. At one point he shared a story of chaotic blood shedding during a riot; after illuminating 101 ways to kill a man Octavio's twisted tale accumulated with the hard ass criminals burning the prison narc's faces off with a blow torch. He claims they spent days torturing and killing one another before the guards retook the prison by killing prisoners indiscriminately.

I felt comfortable now that Octavio had shared his life so openly with me. I in turn shared the fact that I was labeled crazy and had also been locked away until just recently. I told him how I knew exactly how it felt to be released back into the world I no longer knew and that is why I was traveling so far to reunite with someone that still knew me. Then he shared something that stuck with me. He said "All the bullshit they feed you. It's all crap they want you to believe! It's all in your head man. The whole fucking world is a prison, and one small room can be freedom. It's all in your head. You have got to believe the world is what you want it to be and it will be."

"That is almost profound" I said enjoying the company of my new friend.

The road can't go on forever and eventually we arrived in Raton New Mexico where Octavio's family lived. I tried to make a joke by saying "Nice name for a town; Rotten." I did not get any response. The joke was lost in translation or more likely he was just preoccupied with the anticipation of seeing his family again. When we arrived at his home, we were immediately greeted in Spanish by an old woman and several other people as they came flooding out of the dilapidated house. Octavio said something to the women in Spanish and she raced over to hug and kiss me. Then the old woman led me into the house by my hand while speaking a mile a minute in Spanish. I was a little taken back and confused when I asked Octavio what was going on? "My mother says you must stay and eat with us for bringing her son back home." I was not on any schedule, and it had been some time since anyone treated me like family, so I followed along inside. Octavio led me to a room where an old man and some young kids were watching soccer on a small black and white TV. He told me "Just sit tight, I have got some things to take care of and I will be back when suppers ready." The program they were watching was in Spanish and no one in the house but Octavio and I spoke English. While Octavio was gone, I just sat and smiled as the old man spoke nonstop in a language I did not understand.

After a long and awkward wait the meal was apparently ready. Octavio reappeared and told me to come and sit at the table. We were joined by the rest of the family. Octavio Introduced his mother, father, cousins and two nephews. Then he said "This is the only guy on the road dumb enough to give me a ride" in Spanish to the group. They all looked to me and laughed. Joking aside they were grateful for my generosity.

Octavio's mother was constantly looking at me and saying "nuestra masculino" and before we are allowed to eat his mother put her hand on mine and spoke a small prayer while looking up.

The meal consisted of homemade tortillas, a bowl of some kind of cooked beans and another bowl with some red sauce. I watched what the others did and followed in suit. I placed some beans then the sauce on a tortilla folded it and bit in. The mystery sauce was blazing hot. It made my face sweat and turn red. I motioned for water by making a tipping glass gesture. They all laughed and made jokes in Spanish. Octavio hushed the crowd and gave me a warm "Milwaukee's best" beer to wash it down. I'm not a fan of warm beer or Milwaukee but that beer tasted so sweet and succulent. I drank it and another while finishing my supper. I didn't like the flammable food but I didn't want to insult them so I ate everything on my plate with heavy gulps of beer to chase away the flames. It was clear they had very little and to share was a huge gesture of kindness. I noticed when I finished my first beer the little ones were more than eager to take the empty can from me. I joked to Octavio "They really like cans huh?"

He tells me "They don't love cans. There's a five-cent deposit in New Mexico. They collect the cans for money for candy and what not."

I wanted to return kindness with kindness, so I told Octavio "In that case the back of my car is full of empty cans and garbage. Tell them if they clean out all the old fast-food bags and junk from my car, they can have all the empty cans they find." Octavio told the little kids, and they raced off, excited.

I sat on the front porch with Octavio while the kids cleaned out my car. The sun was beginning to set when Octavio produced a joint. We smoked it while watching the spectacular colors dance across the horizon. Octavio offered me a place to stay for the night, but the road was calling me, and I wanted to get as far as I could in the cool dark night. I felt like I was part of their family when I left. The whole family gathered in the yard to see me go. I thanked Octavio for his family's hospitality.

He thanked me for not being afraid to help someone in need and while he hugged me, he whispered "Just remember it's all in your head." He patted me on the back and let me go. His mother immediately latched on to me. She was hugging me tight and saying something in Spanish. I looked to Octavio for help. He said "She prays for your safe journey home. She believes God sent you to help me and she wants God to now look over you on your way home to your family." I had to shake the little ones hugging my legs free before I could climb back into my car and hit the road again. As I drove away from the small town, I thought about the prayers Octavio's' mother made for me on my journey home. I appreciated her sentiment, but I felt her prayers were in vain since I had no home and no family waiting for me. I was heading into the unknown chasing ghosts and buried treasure. Once again, the rearview mirror in my time machine changed the present into the past as I soared through the darkness.

The road through New Mexico into Arizona is a desolate waste land with very few stops for gas. Somewhere between Santa fee and Gallup I was running dangerously low on gas in the middle of nowhere. I passed a road sign that deceived me into thinking there was a gas station next to the exit, so I drove off the main highway. The off ramp led to nothing but sand and another sign teasing me with the possibility of gas. I followed the road mile after mile chasing distant lights in the dark until I found myself too far from the interstate to turn back. I was past the point of no return. I didn't notice while driving in the dark but at some point, the blacktop road had disappeared, and a dirt road took over in its place. My car was sputtering and running on fumes when I finally rolled into the gas station. I wasn't surprised to find the small town deserted and dark. My metal steed gave out a last gasp and came to a rolling stop.

I emerged from my time capsule to a land time had forgotten. The gas pump looked like it was from the nineteen forties and the place was all closed and dark. I smoked a cigarette and stretched knowing my only option was to sleep in my car until the gas station opened. I was struggling to push my car out of the way when a truck rattled out of the darkness. A thin frail old man rolled down the window to ask why I was here. I told him "I drove off the main highway looking for gas, but the station is closed so I'm just going to wait it out till they open."

He stopped his motor, emerged from the truck and pulled a gas can out from the back of his truck. He looked around my vehicle for a place to deposit the fuel but couldn't find one. He scratched his head perplexed by the advances in technology made twenty years ago. I was amused by his ignorance and showed him the hidden portal beneath the rear license plate. I tried to stop him from pouring the gas into my car by telling him it was ok I'd just wait it out until the station opened but he just kept pouring until the can was empty. I pulled my money out to show him that I could pay for fuel but try as I might to give him some money for the fuel but he would not take it. He just pulled the empty can from my machine and pointed me back to highway. Just before he drove off he said "You don't want to be here when the sun comes up. Get on your way kid." Before he disappeared into the night, I noticed a bumper sticker on the back of his truck that read "You don't have to look for Jesus. He's in all of us." It felt eerie driving away, like I was an unwanted stranger stumbling back through time and the old man had saved me from some terrible fate. I often went long periods of time with little or no food because I was too obsessed with my objective. The delusional thought patterns that went along with my reckless behavior were no strangers to me. My shattered psyche could be quite certain of what was happening but never really sure.

I returned to the highway and drove on through the night in search of more fuel. It was well past sunup when my front tire had enough and would take no more; it blew out. I was extremely fortunate or perhaps blessed to have it happened near the exit for a truck stop. I was fighting with the steering wheel trying to keep my car on the road when the other front tire went out. I rolled slowly up the ramp with what was left of my front tires flopping and slapping against the road. My baby slowly limped into the truck stop's lot. When I got out surveying the damage, I saw both tires were fucked. If I had known anything about cars or tires, I would have taken care of that before I left. But I was clueless when I bought the car and never checked or replaced anything. I should have been grateful my steel beast delivered me to the truck stop instead of leaving me stranded in the middle of the desert, but I was young and easily frustrated. I sat against the car with my head hung low cursing her out when a local mechanic came over.

The mechanic stated the obvious "Got some tire troubles huh?"

"Yep?" I responded halfhearted and despondent.

He sized me up and figured I did not have any money by the way I looked which was fine by me. He had compassion in his eyes when he asked me the one question in life that I could never answer "How did you find yourself here?"

I may have played on his sympathy a little when I lied "I'm trying to make it back home to California because my mom's on her death bed and I don't think I even have enough money for gas let alone tires can you help me out?" Some people give a lot of emotional value on going home and this man was one of them.

The man looked me in the eye, thought for a moment, and after eating my lies said "I haven't seen my mom in over two years because she lives too far away. Let me see what I can do kid." I followed him into the garage and after a little digging he pulled two matching used tires from a pile and said "I'll set you up with these for twenty bucks, they've got plenty of tread left on em. These should get you to California."

The kind stranger put the tires on while I grabbed some lunch and looked over the map. The map makes the remainder of the journey look like a pinch in space and time. I was so close I could not wait to climb back into my rocket and burn that pinch away.

I finished my lunch and went to collect my car. The mechanic was lowering my baby from the lift when he said "Kid you've got to take care of the old muscle cars like this. There aren't many left! When I checked your oil, it was dangerously low, so I topped off your fluids, but you have got to check this stuff every time you stop for gas." He showed me the basics of car care out of respect for the vintage muscle cars dying out. I thanked him again and filled the tank. I left knowing deceit was still a powerful weapon in my arsenal. I wanted to believe there was still hope for humanity but as I came closer to my personal goal, I was reminded of the self-serving goals man always reverted to; me included.

# CHAPTER 20

## The Painted Desert

A few hundred miles of pure nothing burned away before I found myself driving up into the hills and cliffs of Arizona. I was just south of Flagstaff when I spotted another hitch hiker. Since the others were entertaining and even helpful, I thought why not. I pulled over to let what from a distance appeared to be a woman with long blonde braided hair into my car. The hitchhiker was not a woman after all. Instead, it turned out to be an old hippie dude. He was wearing a rather large backpack, shorts and a tie die tee shirt. His long beard was tied into braids to match his hair. Before he got in, he wanted to know where I was headed so I told him "All the way to Cali" then he asked me if I was going to Phoenix? I hadn't looked at the map lately so I really didn't know "is it on the way to Cali?" I replied. He told me I would have to go through phoenix to get to California. "Then I guess I'm going to Phoenix" I replied.

"Cool can I ride with you to Phoenix?"

"That's why I pulled over, so sure why not I wouldn't mind some company." He tried to get his large pack behind the seat without success, so he had to untie his sleeping bag and some of the other things from his backpack to finally squeeze it all in the cramped backseat. He had a strong smell of incense mixed with some kind of hippie cologne or something. When I pushed in the cigarette lighter, he asked if I smoked. I was starting to think this guy was a few crayons short of a full box. "Yeah, that's why I pushed the lighter?"

"No, I mean smoke other stuff?" He tried to clarify himself.

I knew exactly what he meant "Oh yeah. I used to smoke weed." He wanted to know why I did not still smoke. I told him "Mostly because I haven't been able to find any in years."

"That's too bad man. I've got some do you mind if I smoke it in the car?" I didn't mind so I told him to fire it up. With that said he produced a joint from his pocket and lit it. "By the way my name is Jerry."

I only took a few puffs because I could tell by the flavor this weed was potent and I did not have the same high tolerance I had 20 years before. I was a little nervous behind the wheel as the drugs took effect. Jerry was happy to smoke most of it on his own anyway. After the joint was gone Jerry talked nonstop for endless miles. My new friend goes on and on about Government conspiracies, CIA cover-ups, drug wars, the Middle East, and how it all leads up to the end of the world as we knew it, Armageddon. The shit storm was coming. The writing on the wall clearly spelled out doom, or at least that's what Jerry believed.

I lived most of my life in a very small bubble and therefore had always perceived the world as a very small place. My journey across the country enlightened me about the true size of things while Jerry opened my eyes to the fact that the whole world was one big fucked up mess. Jerry only saw problems with no solutions. After a considerable amount of patience, I was finally able to interject

Jerry's rant "Maybe the world just needs more people who care enough to save it?"

Jerry then began to tell me tales of marching in Chicago in the sixties. He went to Chicago because a guy named Abby Hoffman and others had started the "Yippee movement" urging people to stand together for what they believed in. Jerry said he ended up getting his head knocked in by the police. Apparently, the government didn't like people standing up against them and ordered the police to stop the demonstrating by any means necessary. This led to police beating men, women, old, and young alike in the streets during a peaceful demonstration on a cold night in November. I could relate to his tale I knew exactly how it felt when the "mans" clubs came crashing down.

"So, standing up to the system didn't work out for you then? What can any of us do when facing an unstoppable machine?" I asked still looking for a glimmer of hope in Jerry's bleak outlook.

The glimmer appeared in his mind, and he remarked "Just live each day one at a time and try to make the best of what you're dealt and enjoy life while you can." The happy thought was quickly washed under by the never-ending stories spewing from his mouth. We smoked some more weed while I drove onward and he talked, and talked, and talked.

I was getting more than a little annoyed with Jerry. He was the kind of guy you would ask what time is was and he would tell you in great detail how to build a watch or how time was invented to oppress man. This guy had no "off" button and even worse he repeated himself. I had already heard all of his stories three times when we finally stopped at a rest stop just north of Phoenix. We got out to stretch and use the bathroom. He grabbed his pack and said

"I'm still going to Phoenix with you. I just need to freshen up and change before we get there."

"Cool no problem, dude. Take your time I'll wait for you." I went inside used the facilities and returned to the car. I didn't plan on ditching him but after waiting for more than half an hour I got impatient. Sure, I told him I'd wait, but I didn't owe him anything and he was getting on my nerves with his constant nonstop jibber jabber. "He'll be fine" I convinced myself, he was hitch hiking when I found him, and he did have his pack. I waited a few more minutes and thought "fuck it! I'm out of here!" I was done picking up strangers. I needed to focus. As I got closer to my goal the thoughts of Lisa and the money began to overtake all my other thoughts. I had to get there to put my demons to rest. The time for patience was over. I left Jerry in the dust and continued my quest.

As I drove down the mountain into Phoenix, I knew how the city got its name. Right before my eyes a massive concrete monster rose from the ashes of the burning hot desert. This gigantic monster of a town went on as far as the eye could see in all directions. By the time I made it halfway through town my car decided she needed a break from the constant driving. The radiator overheated in the one-hundred-and-ten-degree heat. I was forced to let her cool down at a gas station before I could feed her more water and push ahead. By the time my car cooled down I myself had run out of steam. I just wanted to find a cheap motel on the outskirts of town and check in for a badly needed rest. When I finally reached the edge of the never-ending city the sun was beginning to set and taunted me to follow her. The cool night winds played tricks on me. They were constantly begging me to just go a little further before I stopped. Like a fool I listened and kept going further and further until I had passed through Casa Grande and my last chance for a hotel.

241

The sun disappeared beyond the horizon and any sign of civilization was long gone. Nothing remained but the road and the pitch-black night. The radio lost touch with the world as the music faded into jumbled static. I turned off the radio and listened to the hum of my tires on the road. The cool desert winds felt so good after the long day of overwhelming heat. The line on the road hypnotized me into a much-needed sleep. The car veered off the road and into the great nothing. The bumping and shaking of the uneven, soft sand shattered my dreams. I awoke and slammed on the brakes. The great thing about crashing in the desert is there is not much to hit. The bad thing about going off the road in the middle of nowhere was that you never knew how long it would be before someone else discovered you. On this stretch of road, it could be hours or even days before I saw another car. I exited the car and with the headlights still beaming off into the nothing, I could see only sand. In the dark I could not tell how far back the road was, but the car seemed fine. I decided this was probably as good of a place as any to get some rest. It was so dark and silent. I shut off the engine, lit a cigarette, sat down in the sand, and enjoyed the stillness of the night. I had never heard anything so quiet.

After my cigarette I opened the trunk and grabbed one of my bags of clothes to use as a pillow. I had not slept in a car since I called Danny's rusted out crap pile my home. I felt like I had gone around one of my pointless circles winding back up were I started. Lost and forgotten by the world with only a car to call home. I got back in the car on the passenger side because it had more room. When I went to move the seat to its best reclined position, but it would not budge. The seat was jammed on something. I got out; removing what I assumed was garbage blocking the seat, to discover it wasn't garbage at all. Jerry's sleeping bag was wedged under the seat. At that moment I felt bad. I thought Jerry had all his belongings when I left him at the rest stop, but I guess I was wrong. Even though I felt bad there was not anything I could do about it. What was I going to do? Drive back a few hundred miles to a massive city and just ask around "Anybody seen Jerry the Yippee hippie? I've got his ten-dollar sleeping bag?" Maybe God wanted me to have his sleeping bag. I did after all need it right now. I remembered the prayer Octavio's mom said for me. "That Mexican lady must have had some big pull with Jesus." I thought.

With some struggle I pulled the bedroll out from under the seat. His pack had really smashed it down in there. I unrolled it and got in. I could feel a paper bag of something tucked down inside of it. I pulled it out and turned on the dome light. I was not really sure what I was looking at. It was certainly some kind of plant, but I knew it was not weed. Upon further inspection it looked like cut up mushrooms. I heard Brian talk about people eating mushrooms for a buzz. Jerry was clearly a drug user so what else could they be? Now I felt super bad for Jerry. When I ditched him, I did not know his drugs were still onboard. There was still nothing I could do about it, other than feel bad. I did not like feeling depressed and I was hard-up for a buzz. I thought if I ate some of the mushrooms it would be like beer or weed and make it easier for me to sleep. I ate a big mouthful because I did not know how much was too little or too much. I just figured you must need to eat a lot because he had a lot in the bag. Boy, was I wrong!

The mushrooms did not make me feel sleepy at all. In fact, I felt hot, itchy, and sick to my stomach. I could not stand the small tight enclosure of the sleeping bag. I had to get up and out of the car. I fell to my knees and threw up in the sand as my mind began to race. I lit a cigarette trying to get the taste of vomit out of my mouth. As I gazed at the flame something about it was different. The traces of light that followed the red-hot cherry at the end of my smoke lingered in the air. I was spellbound by the lights and new colors I saw in my mind. I cannot explain why but, in my drug induced state, I wondered off into the black. "I need to sit down. I need to sit down. I need to sit down." My own thoughts began to repeat and echo inside my head.

I sat down into the moving sand and fell through it into hell. I was lost in the dark, so I cried out "Someone please help me!" I was answered by Chris's voice "Why should I help you?" I looked up to see his flesh was gravely burned and melted. Chris glared at me with hate, out of what was left of his eyes "I thought you were my friend, but you killed me!"

"I'm sorry" is all I could say. My apology only angered him further.

Chris screamed at me "You're fuckin sorry! You blew up the whole fuckin world and everyone, but you, burned to death in the aftermath. You fuckin killed us all!"

Chris was joined by a headless Danny, a pale white Ken, and a not quite "whole" Chemist. They all began to scream at me "Our souls are dammed and you're sorry?" The demons produced clubs from behind their backs and began to violently beat me. I curled into a ball for protection as a blinding light was cast upon the scene driving my tormentors away.

When the beating stopped, I found myself in the weight room of Winnebago. Brian was there. He pulled me from the floor just like before, but this time, before he hits me, he says "You made me do it rabbit. It's all your fault rabbit!" SMASH! His fist hits my face, and the scene plays out just like it did before. The panic squad entered the room, and the clubs came crashing down. I was lifted out of my body and out of the room. As I floated above the room, I could see

Brian fighting for his life with the guards until they had to put him down forever.

I was pulled through the dark until I found myself in Renee's room. I was in her bed afraid of the dark when the door opened. It's Bob with his head on sideways because of his broken neck. I was yanked from the bed. I pleaded with Bob as he dragged me down the ever-expanding hall. As his body went forward, he looked back at me with his head and just kept saying it was my fault he was dead. I am taken to the quiet room and strapped down. After the rape was over bob took the pillowcase off me and left. I was left strapped down naked in the quiet room. I looked around to see Renee had been standing in the doorway watching. Renee twisted and contorted across the room to me and whispered in my ear "You did nothing. It's all your fault I'm dead!" She laughed as she exploded spraying me with blood just before a doctor came into my room.

It was Doctor Vohn, but he spoke with Jerry's voice "Oh dear you haven't taken enough medication." He shovels pills into a giant funnel that led to my mouth. I was choking on the pills when I broke free from the bed to puke out black syrup. The syrup filled the room, and everything went black. The scene around me was painted back in. I was now on my hands and knees in the dirt. I looked up to see the back door of the battery shop. The door opens and Ken emerges dragging Lisa outside. Ken does not notice me as he leaves Lisa in the dirt and goes back inside.

I ran to her side hoping I could still change the past and save her. She was conscious and looked me in the eyes when she spoke "Why do you keep coming back here?"

I was panicked and scared for her. I told her "I came to save you! Hurry we must get away from here and run away together right now."

I smiled and looked to her for approval, but tears of desperation fell from her eyes as she said once again "Why do you keep coming here? You know how this ends, yet you keep coming back here dragging me with you. Why do you keep bringing me here? You want the money inside? Take it and leave!" She screamed and pushed me away.

I could not stand to see this come to the same conclusion, so I pleaded with her "No!! Lisa why are you saying that? Please come with me!"

She looks back at me with the pain of death now showing "You know I can't leave this place!" Once again, I try to beg her to leave but she interrupts "What do you want from me! Why do you keep bringing me back to this place! Whatever you think you might find here is gone. I'm dead! I can't run away with you!" In disbelief I continued to plead with her. Like a broken record she skips and jumps back to the same line again and again, demanding answers in a stern tone "Why have you brought me here?" I broke down and tried to explain, but it was no use, the building exploded, and everything was incinerated.

The sun was burning my rotten flesh away with its unrelenting heat when out of my half-dead eye I saw Octavio. He was gently slapping my face while he spoke "Hey ese! Hey, you can't die in the desert. The vultures will git you man. Come on, get up you stupid Punta. Get up.! It's all in your head ese! Get up fucker!" Octavio poked and prodded me, but I could not move so he pulled me to my feet and helped me back to the car. He placed me in the driver seat, closed the door, and said "You got a good heart little dude. The world needs people like you! Just remember it's all in your head. It's all in your head. It's all in your head." Octavio's words rang out over and over in my head until the mushrooms wore off and I awoke in the driver's seat. I was stark naked, covered in sweat and sand.

I pulled what was left of my sanity together and found some clothes. I rolled the mushrooms back into the sleeping bag and put everything in the trunk. I was so thirsty and had nothing to drink. I rummaged around in the garbage for bottles still containing bits of backwash. I then threw all the garbage out of the car. I wanted a clean start. I had taken a lot of different prescription drugs, so I was used to all kind of weird effects on the psyche. That night however I was not sure if I was totally insane, or the mushrooms were the most intense drug I'd ever taken. It was not difficult to get back to the road. I simply had to go slow in reverse to get the car out of the sand. Once I was back on the pavement, I let the tires rip in exhilaration.

# CHAPTER 21

## Homecoming

As I passed through Yuma and headed into Cali, I realized I was on the same route I had been on so many years before. This was the same road out of hell I had traveled before. I was daydreaming of ascending once more from hells fiery depths to find my reward. When I made it to the hills of California my muscle car had no problem climbing the rolling hills that had given us so much agony years before. I came around a bend and descended into the valley. "I made it. I'm finally back!" I thought to myself as I saw the city, I once called home. Thousands of miles and many years had passed by but none of that mattered now that I was back in the place where it all began so long ago!

*At this point in my book, I have to take a step or two back. Not in time but from my story. It's a bittersweet feeling sitting in the "here and now" present writing this book and wondering how I should end it. I have literally spent years turning my scraps of madness into this book. I often wrestled with what to include and what to leave out. I do not exactly feel proud telling my tale but it's something I felt compelled to do. The scraps of paper that had served to hold my dark thoughts prisoner had opened their doors and freed the demons trapped inside. The only way for me to escape my paper prison was to finally face the demons and release their ghosts. One thing I have learned in life is many truths are mistaken for fiction and vice versa. I offer you and myself different versions of truth to allow the psyche to believe whatever it is comfortable with. After I finish this, I plan to burn the scraps of madness hopefully ending my obsession with understanding them and just let them go.*

## THE HOLLYWOOD HAPPY ENDING . . .

"Life is a strange illusion" I thought as I drove around the city I once knew. I went back to all the places I could remember, the school, the park, the circle church, and my old apartment complex. It was still daylight when I arrived, so I took a reminiscing tour of the city and got something to eat. At night fall I went back to the circle church. I crept behind the shrubs where we used to party and dug in the dirt. It didn't take long to locate the treasure I buried so many years ago. I pulled the package from the dirt and shouted out in excitement. Even though I held all the money in my hands I still couldn't believe it was still here! My time in hell was not in vain. I was rewarded for my suffering. I slipped away, never looking back. The world was at my mercy. I had a shitload of money and a big bag of mushrooms.

"Where to next? Vegas Maybe?" I thought as a drove away from the setting sun.

## THE CRUEL LIFE ENDING . . .

I drove around the city retracing my past life hoping to find a city changed for the better, but I was a fool to think I alone could kill meth. I realized "I am only one" and as only one, I made no impact on the drug trade. Nothing had changed; In fact, life on the streets had only gotten worse. The city was crawling with drugs and filth. The streets were rancid with decay and sickness. You could buy crack right out in the open on a dozen corners. Young bodies were bought and sold in broad daylight. It made me sick. Everything I had done to try and stop evil meant nothing. The virus spread on and on with or without my intervention. When I finally made it to the circle church I was almost out of money and gas. I was thinking "Thank God this is almost over, and I will soon retrieve my money and find some sanctuary away from this shit." My heart stopped dead when I saw the church had a new extension built on to one of the sides. It did not look the same at all. "Time moved on and fucked me in the process!" I thought but continued to circle. As I circled the building, I was relieved to see the other side was untouched and looked the same as I remembered. I could not remember which side our special party place was on.

I could not tell from driving around it which side was which. I had not been here for thirteen years, and my memory was a little blurry. I had to go back to the apartment complex I once lived in and try to retrace the old circle from there. I found the apartments I once lived in. The vacant lot was gone, but the shithole I once lived in looked the same, except someone had painted all the buildings an ugly brown. I drove from there back to the church. The extension was on the opposite side. Our special place was safe after all, but it was still daylight. I did not want anyone seeing me digging around in the bush, so I had to wait until dark.

While waiting for the sun to set I went to a local hardware store and bought some small digging tools with my last dollars. When night finally came, I was bursting with anticipation. I crept behind the shrubs while the church was having choir practice. In the dim moonlight I gently dug at the earth where I had buried my salvation thirteen years ago. About eight inches into the dirt, I found it. A piece of what looked like paper was tangled in my small rake. "This has to be it!" I thought as I dropped my hand tools and cleared some of the dirt away with my hands. There it was all right. I had broken the bag the money was in or so I thought. I reached into the small hole and tried to grab the money. I lifted the paper bills out only to have them crumble in my hands. The worms had eaten away at the money for thirteen years. The thin paper bag the money was in offered no protection from the cruel earth. The money was cursed by the blood of my friends. I had been a fool to chase it. Everything I had done to get here was in vain. The great pointless circle was complete. I had gone a long way around to find myself back at the beginning. DE JA VU! I was fucked once again. I had no family, no friends and I found myself broken and homeless, living out of a car!

## THE COMPLETE CIRCLE ENDING

I drove around the city to the places I knew would still be there. I went to my old school and to me it looked almost the same. I thought back to the time when I was still innocent and believed the blue sky shined love down on everyone. I strayed into the moment briefly, and then shook it from my head. Then I went back to my old apartment. It was not hard to find. I remembered everything like it was yesterday. I drove my old route from school to the apartment I once called home. It had not changed much except they painted it brown. I parked the car to get a closer look. I walked past memories lingering in the laundry room to the back of the complex where Lisa once lived. I looked for the hole in the fence, but it only existed in my mind now. The vacant lot was replaced with new apartments. I was peeking around to see if Lisa's mom still lived here when a young girl came up and asked if I was lost? I looked down into her still innocent eyes and smiled "No, I'm not lost." For the first time in my life I wasn't lost, I knew exactly why I came here and what I needed to do. I went back to my car and drove past the site where the battery shop once was. The old lot was now some new industrial complex. It didn't look at all like the graveyard I pictured in my mind a thousand times. After that I went back to our special place, the circle church. My heart stopped when I saw they'd built an extension right over our special place. I thought about all the things people told me about going home. Maybe they were right. Whatever I was looking for was not here anymore. Maybe it never was. I went into the church and prayed for my broken soul.

As I sat on the hard and cold pew in God's house everything bad that ever happened to me in life ran through my mind. Many times, in life I wanted to blame God for all my misfortunes. In fact, I exorcized him from my life; simultaneously I blamed him for abandoning me. Just like a thousand demons before me I started out a misguided

253

timid rabbit that chose to go down the hole. I chose to find out what the darkness hides. I spent far too many years at the bottom of that hole. I had a virtual eternity to think about what I found in the darkness. I found Lucifer's greatest secret . . . He was a scared child, alone in the infinite dark. I knew all too well how the most innocent creature could become the vilest when trapped in the dark. I also knew no matter how deep or dark a hole you fall into there is all ways a way back out. My trip across America was just what my soul needed. I was on to the scent of life. I could not see the way out, but I could smell it! It was then that I realized why my demons held me. They were still lost in the dark and they needed me to lead them back into the light so they could become rabbits again.

After driving around, a dead city filled with junkies I returned to the place where my story ends. I drove up into the hills to the cross that lit up the night sky. I knelt before the cross that I had metaphorically hung Lisa on so many years ago. I cried out to her in the earth "I'm sorry Lisa. Please forgive me. This was never about the money! The only reason I came here, was for you! I don't know what to do! I don't know if I'm crazy or just broken inside! I need you to save me. I'm lost without you. Please Lisa, I beg you please help me!"

I cried alone in the dark until Lisa came to me one last time. She was angry and demanded "Why do you keep calling me back!"

With my head hung low I told her "You were the only one that ever loved me. I miss you. I need to hear you say, 'you love me!'"

Her tone changed and she embraced me. As she held me in her arms she said "I do love you. I will always love you. I'm sorry but you must let me go. I'm dead!"

The tears choked my voice "I can never let you go. I can't live without you!"

She put her hands on my face and forced me to look into her pale blue eyes "You don't have a choice. You can't bring me back to life and the past is gone. I'm gone, but there are so many others that still need your help."

I did not want to believe her "my help? Who will I help? I have nothing left to give!"

Lisa's face began to fade as she whispered "Start with you. It's not your fault I am dead. You must let me go now." She kissed me one last time and left me crying beneath the cross.

After that night I did not care about the money anymore. To me it was cursed with the blood of my friends and tears I cried for my first true love. The money held too many bad memories and too much death for me to dig up. I left it to rot in the earth. I didn't want the nightmare to drag me back into hell so I drove as far away from there as I could get. My tears led all of my demons back to the surface. The demons that held me were rabbits once again, running free at last.

I chased the wind for years before I ran out of breath. I eventually fell in love again and faded into a small town. I felt content fading into society and pretending my childhood was happy and normal like everyone else's until the day I opened the box once again unleashing the scraps of madness. All the years I spent locked away I never shared this story with anyone until now. My counselor Lynn knew I was a drug addict, but I never shared any of the details of Lisa's death with her. I did not want anyone to know that in my youth I was a cold-blooded killer. I can never wash the blood off my hands, but maybe if I warn others of the dangers of Crystal-Death, God will forgive some of my sins. That's why I finally decided to write this book so that others might turn away before it's too late. Because once you start the circle, you're trapped in the swirling madness. There's only two ways out of the circle that I know of, either you're pulled out or you die spinning down the drain.

THE END

Empty spaces and lost traces

Of what I used to be

Empty spaces and forgotten places.

That I'll never see

Empty spaces and lost traces

Of what I used to see

Empty spaces and hopeless cases

The person I'll always be

The future chases a past wasted.

And a person I'll always be

A mind embraces memories wasted.

And my mind will always see.

Wore out places and pleasure tasted.

And things that will never be

The day displaces dreams wasted.

And a tomorrow I'll never see.

# ABOUT THE AUTHOR

    I put my blood sweat and tears into my debut novel Demons & Rabbits. I Thank you for reading it. I wrote Demons & Rabbits to offer the reader not only a sobering and graphic look at substance abuse, addiction, and the countless horrors that come with it, but also the dangers run-aways face every day. The book has a strong connection to my personal life. As the author of this book, I'm not ready to give up my anonymity. I wrote this because it was something I felt compelled to do. It is a gritty tale I'm not proud to tell. I do not want to be judged or labeled. I have had enough labels thrust upon me in life: abused, runaway, homeless, junkie, killer, prisoner, psychotic, depressed, cutter, suicidal, rehabilitated and so on. For once in my life, it is my turn to choose which label to wear. The one thing I've never been called is "ok". In fact, I'm the opposite of "ok". I am KO!